Collector's Library

THE MELANCHOLY HUSSAR

and other stories

THE MELANCHOLY HUSSAR

and other stories

Thomas Hardy

with an Afterword by
PETER HARNESS

Collector's Library

The stories selected for this volume were
first published between 1888 and 1912
This edition published in 2005 by
Collector's Library
an imprint of CRW Publishing Limited
69 Gloucester Crescent, London NW1 7EG

ISBN 1 904919 50 2

2 4 6 8 10 9 7 5 3 1

Typeset in Great Britain by Antony Gray
Printed and bound in China by Imago

Contents

The Son's Veto

ONE

To the eye of a man viewing it from behind, the nut-brown hair was a wonder and a mystery. Under the black beaver hat, surmounted by its tuft of black feathers, the long locks, braided and twisted and coiled like the rushes of a basket, composed a rare, if somewhat barbaric, example of ingenious art. One could understand such weavings and coilings being wrought to last intact for a year, or even a calendar month; but that they should be all demolished regularly at bedtime, after a single day of permanence, seemed a reckless waste of successful fabrication.

And she had done it all herself, poor thing. She had no maid, and it was almost the only accomplishment she could boast of. Hence the unstinted pains.

She was a young invalid lady – not so very much of an invalid – sitting in a wheeled chair, which had been pulled up in the front part of a green enclosure, close to a bandstand where a concert was going on, during a warm June afternoon. It had place in one of the minor parks or private gardens that are to be found in the suburbs of London, and was the effort of a local association to raise money for some charity. There are worlds within worlds in the great city, and though nobody outside the immediate district had ever heard of the charity, or the band, or the garden, the enclosure was filled with an interested audience sufficiently informed on all these.

7

As the strains proceeded many of the listeners observed the chaired lady, whose back-hair, by reason of her prominent position, so challenged inspection. Her face was not easily discernible, but the aforesaid cunning tress-weavings, the white ear and poll, and the curve of a cheek which was neither flaccid nor sallow, were signals that led to the expectation of good beauty in front. Such expectations are not infrequently disappointed as soon as the disclosure comes; and in the present case, when the lady, by a turn of the head, at length revealed herself, she was not so handsome as the people behind her had supposed, and even hoped – they did not know why.

For one thing (alas! the commonness of this complaint), she was less young than they had fancied her to be. Yet attractive her face unquestionably was; and not at all sickly. The revelation of its details came each time she turned to talk to a boy of twelve or thirteen who stood beside her, and the shape of whose hat and jacket implied that he belonged to a well-known public school. The immediate bystanders could hear that he called her Mother.

When the end of the recital was reached, and the audience withdrew, many chose to find their way out by passing at her elbow. Almost all turned their heads to take a full and near look at the interesting woman, who remained stationary in the chair till the way should be clear enough for her to be wheeled out without obstruction. As if she expected their glances, and did not mind gratifying their curiosity, she met the eyes of several of her observers by lifting her own, showing these to be soft, brown, and affectionate orbs, a little plaintive in their regard.

She was conducted out of the gardens, and passed

along the pavement till she disappeared from view, the schoolboy walking beside her. To inquiries made by some persons who watched her away, the answer came that she was the second wife of the incumbent of a neighbouring parish, and that she was lame. She was generally believed to be a woman with a story – an innocent one, but a story of some sort or other.

In conversing with her on their way home the boy who walked at her elbow said that he hoped his father had not missed them.

'He have been so comfortable these last few hours that I am sure he cannot have missed us,' she replied.

'*Has*, dear mother – not *have*!' exclaimed the public-schoolboy, with an impatient fastidiousness that was almost harsh. 'Surely you know that by this time!'

His mother hastily adopted the correction, and did not resent his making it, or retaliate, as she might well have done, by bidding him to wipe that crumby mouth of his, whose condition had been caused by surreptitious attempts to eat a piece of cake without taking it out of the pocket wherein it lay concealed. After this the pretty woman and the boy went onward in silence.

That question of grammar bore upon her history, and she fell into reverie of a somewhat sad kind, to all appearance. It might have been assumed that she was wondering if she had done wisely in shaping her life as she had shaped it, to bring out such a result as this.

In a remote nook in North Wessex, forty miles from London, near the thriving county-town of Aldbrickham, there stood a pretty village with its church and parsonage, which she knew well enough, but her son had never seen. It was her native village, Gaymead, and the first event bearing upon her present situation had occurred at that place when she was only a girl of nineteen.

How well she remembered it, that first act in her little tragi-comedy, the death of her reverend husband's first wife. It happened on a spring evening, and she who now and for many years had filled that first wife's place was then parlourmaid in the parson's house.

When everything had been done that could be done, and the death was announced, she had gone out in the dusk to visit her parents, who were living in the same village, to tell them the sad news. As she opened the white swing-gate and looked towards the trees which rose westward, shutting out the pale light of the evening sky, she discerned, without much surprise, the figure of a man standing in the hedge, though she roguishly exclaimed as a matter of form, 'Oh, Sam, how you frightened me!'

He was a young gardener of her acquaintance. She told him the particulars of the late event, and they stood silent, these two young people, in that elevated, calmly philosophic mind which is engendered when a tragedy has happened close at hand, and has not happened to the philosophers themselves. But it had its bearing upon their relations.

'And will you stay on now at the vicarage, just the same?' asked he.

She had hardly thought of that. 'Oh yes – I suppose!' she said. 'Everything will be just as usual, I imagine.'

He walked beside her towards her mother's. Presently his arm stole round her waist. She gently removed it; but he placed it there again, and she yielded the point. 'You see, dear Sophy, you don't know that you'll stay on; you may want a home; and I shall be ready to offer one someday, though I may not be ready just yet.'

'Why, Sam, how can you be so fast! I've never even said I liked 'ee; and it is all your own doing, coming after me!'

'Still, it is nonsense to say I am not to have a try at you, like the rest.' He stooped to kiss her a farewell, for they had reached her mother's door.

'No, Sam; you shan't!' she cried, putting her hand over his mouth. 'You ought to be more serious on such a night as this!' And she bade him adieu without allowing him to kiss her or to come indoors.

The vicar just left a widower was at this time a man about forty years of age, of good family, and childless. He had led a secluded existence in this college living, partly because there were no resident landowners; and his loss now intensified his habit of withdrawal from outward observation. He was seen still less than heretofore, kept himself still less in time with the rhythm and racket of the movements called progress in the world without. For many months after his wife's decease the economy of his household remained as before; the cook, the housemaid, the parlourmaid, and the man out-of-doors performed their duties or left them undone, just as Nature prompted them – the vicar knew not which. It was then represented to him that his servants seemed to have nothing to do in his small family of one. He was struck with the truth of this representation, and decided to cut down his establishment. But he was forestalled by Sophy, the parlourmaid, who said one evening that she wished to leave him.

'And why?' said the parson.

'Sam Hobson has asked me to marry him, sir.'

'Well – do you want to marry?'

'Not much. But it would be a home for me. And we have heard that one of us will have to leave.'

A day or two after she said: 'I don't want to leave just yet, sir, if you don't wish it. Sam and I have quarrelled.'

He looked up at her. He had hardly ever observed her before, though he had been frequently conscious of her soft presence in the room. What a kitten-like, flexuous, tender creature she was! She was the only one of the servants with whom he came into immediate and continuous relation. What should he do if Sophy were gone?

Sophy did not go, but one of the others did, and things went on quietly again.

When Mr Twycott, the vicar, was ill, Sophy brought up his meals to him, and she had no sooner left the room one day than he heard a noise on the stairs. She had slipped down with the tray, and so twisted her foot that she could not stand. The village surgeon was called in; the vicar got better, but Sophy was incapacitated for a long time; and she was informed that she must never again walk much or engage in any occupation which required her to stand long on her feet. As soon as she was comparatively well she spoke to him alone. Since she was forbidden to walk and bustle about, and, indeed, could not do so, it became her duty to leave. She could very well work at something sitting down, and she had an aunt a seamstress.

The parson had been very greatly moved by what she had suffered on his account, and he exclaimed, 'No, Sophy; lame or not lame, I cannot let you go. You must never leave me again!'

He came close to her, and, though she could never exactly tell how it happened, she became conscious of his lips upon her cheek. He then asked her to marry him. Sophy did not exactly love him, but she had a respect for him which almost amounted to veneration. Even if she had wished to get away from him she hardly dared refuse a personage so reverend and august in her eyes, and she assented forthwith to be his wife.

Thus it happened that one fine morning, when the doors of the church were naturally open for ventilation, and the singing birds fluttered in and alighted on the tie-beams of the roof, there was a marriage-service at the communion-rails, which hardly a soul knew of. The parson and a neighbouring curate had entered at one door, and Sophy at another, followed by two necessary persons; whereupon in a short time there emerged a newly-made husband and wife.

Mr Twycott knew perfectly well that he had committed social suicide by this step, despite Sophy's spotless character, and he had taken his measures accordingly. An exchange of livings had been arranged with an acquaintance who was incumbent of a church in the south of London, and as soon as possible the couple removed thither, abandoning their pretty country home, with trees and shrubs and glebe, for a narrow, dusty house in a long, straight street, and their fine peal of bells for the wretchedest one-tongued clangour that ever tortured mortal ears. It was all on her account. They were, however, away from everyone who had known her former position; and also under less observation from without than they would have had to put up with in any country parish.

Sophy the woman was as charming a partner as a man could possess, though Sophy the lady had her deficiencies. She showed a natural aptitude for little domestic refinements, so far as related to things and manners; but in what is called culture she was less intuitive. She had now been married more than fourteen years, and her husband had taken much trouble with her education; but she still held confused ideas on the use of 'was' and 'were', which did not beget a respect for her among the few acquaintances she made. Her great grief in this relation was that her only child, on whose education no expense had been and would be spared, was now old enough to perceive these deficiencies in his mother, and not only to see them but to feel irritated at their existence.

Thus she lived on in the city, and wasted hours in braiding her beautiful hair, till her once apple cheeks waned to pink of the very faintest. Her foot had never regained its natural strength after the accident, and she was mostly obliged to avoid walking altogether. Her husband had grown to like London for its freedom and its domestic privacy; but he was twenty years his Sophy's senior, and had latterly been seized with a serious illness. On this day, however, he had seemed to be well enough to justify her accompanying her son Randolph to the concert.

TWO

The next time we get a glimpse of her is when she appears in the mournful attire of a widow.

Mr Twycott had never rallied, and now lay in a well-packed cemetery to the south of the great city, where, if all the dead it contained had stood erect and alive, not one would have known him or recognised his name. The boy had dutifully followed him to the grave, and was now again at school.

Throughout these changes Sophy had been treated like the child she was in nature though not in years. She was left with no control over anything that had been her husband's beyond her modest personal income. In his anxiety lest her inexperience should be overreached he had safeguarded with trustees all he possibly could. The completion of the boy's course at the public school, to be followed in due time by Oxford and ordination, had been all previsioned and arranged, and she really had nothing to occupy her in the world but to eat and drink, and make a business of indolence, and go on weaving and coiling the nut-brown hair, merely keeping a home open for the son whenever he came to her during vacations.

Foreseeing his probable decease long years before her, her husband in his lifetime had purchased for her use a semi-detached villa in the same long, straight road whereon the church and parsonage faced, which was to be hers as long as she chose to live in it. Here she now resided, looking out upon the fragment of lawn in front, and through the railings at the ever-flowing traffic; or, bending forward over the windowsill on the first floor, stretching her eyes far up and down the vista of sooty trees, hazy air, and drab house-façades, along which echoed the noises common to a suburban main thoroughfare.

Somehow, her boy, with his aristocratic school-knowledge, his grammars, and his aversions, was losing those wide infantine sympathies, extending as far as to the sun and moon themselves, with which he, like other children, had been born, and which his mother, a child of nature herself, had loved in him; he was reducing their compass to a population of a few thousand wealthy and titled people, the mere veneer

15

of a thousand million or so of others who did not interest him at all. He drifted further and further away from her. Sophy's *milieu* being a suburb of minor tradesmen and under-clerks, and her almost only companions the two servants of her own house, it was not surprising that after her husband's death she soon lost the little artificial tastes she had acquired from him, and became – in her son's eyes – a mother whose mistakes and origin it was his painful lot as a gentleman to blush for. As yet he was far from being man enough – if he ever would be – to rate these sins of hers at their true infinitesimal value beside the yearning fondness that welled up and remained penned in her heart till it should be more fully accepted by him, or by some other person or thing. If he had lived at home with her he would have had all of it; but he seemed to require so very little in present circumstances, and it remained stored.

Her life became insupportably dreary; she could not take walks, and had no interest in going for drives, or, indeed, in travelling anywhere. Nearly two years passed without an event, and still she looked on that suburban road, thinking of the village in which she had been born, and whither she would have gone back – oh how gladly! – even to work in the fields.

Taking no exercise she often could not sleep, and would rise in the night or early morning to look out upon the then vacant thoroughfare, where the lamps stood like sentinels waiting for some procession to go by. An approximation to such a procession was indeed made early every morning about one o'clock, when the country vehicles passed up with loads of vegetables for Covent Garden market. She often saw them creeping along at this silent and dusky hour – wagon after wagon, bearing green bastions of cabbages nodding to their fall, yet never falling, walls of baskets enclosing masses of beans and peas, pyramids of snow-white turnips, swaying howdahs of mixed produce – creeping along behind aged night-horses, who seemed ever patiently wondering between their hollow coughs why they had always to work at that still hour when all other sentient creatures were privileged to rest. Wrapped in a cloak, it was soothing to watch and sympathise with them when depression and nervousness hindered sleep, and to see how the fresh green-stuff brightened to life as it came opposite the lamp, and how the sweating animals steamed and shone with their miles of travel.

They had an interest, almost a charm, for Sophy, these semi-rural people and vehicles moving in an urban atmosphere, leading a life quite distinct from that of the daytime toilers on the same road. One morning a man who accompanied a wagon-load of potatoes gazed rather hard at the house-fronts as he passed, and with a curious emotion she thought his form was familiar to her. She looked out for him again. His being an old-fashioned conveyance, with a yellow front, it was easily recognisable, and on the third night after she saw it a second time. The man alongside was, as she had fancied, Sam Hobson, formerly gardener at Gaymead, who would at one time have married her.

She had occasionally thought of him, and wondered if life in a cottage with him would not have been a happier lot than the life she had accepted. She had not thought of him passionately, but her now dismal situation lent an interest to his resurrection – a tender interest which it is impossible to exaggerate. She went back to bed, and began thinking. When did these market-gardeners, who travelled up to town so regularly at one or two in the morning, come back? She dimly recollected seeing their empty wagons, hardly noticeable amid the ordinary day-traffic, passing down at some hour before noon.

It was only April, but that morning, after breakfast, she had the window opened, and sat looking out, the feeble sun shining full upon her. She affected to sew, but her eyes never left the street. Between ten and eleven the desired wagon, now unladen, reappeared on its return journey. But Sam was not looking round him then, and drove on in a reverie.

'Sam!' cried she.

Turning with a start, his face lighted up. He called to him a little boy to hold the horse, alighted, and came and stood under the window.

'I can't come down easily, Sam, or I would!' she said. 'Did you know I lived here?'

'Well, Mrs Twycott, I knew you lived along here somewhere. I have often looked out for 'ee.'

He briefly explained his own presence on the scene. He had long since given up his gardening in the village near Aldbrickham, and was now manager at a market-gardener's on the south side of London, it being part of his duty to go up to Covent Garden with wagon-loads of produce two or three times a week. In answer to her curious inquiry, he admitted that he had come to this particular district because he had seen in the Aldbrickham paper, a year or two before, the announcement of the death in South London of the aforetime vicar of Gaymead, which had revived an interest in her dwelling-place that he could not extinguish, leading him to hover about the locality till his present post had been secured.

They spoke of their native village in dear old North Wessex, the spots in which they had played together as children. She tried to feel that she was a dignified personage now, that she must not be too confidential with Sam. But she could not keep it up, and the tears hanging in her eyes were indicated in her voice.

'You are not happy, Mrs Twycott, I'm afraid?' he said.

'Oh, of course not! I lost my husband only the year before last.'

'Ah! I meant in another way. You'd like to be home again?'

'This is my home – for life. The house belongs to me. But I understand.' She let it out then. 'Yes, Sam. I long for home – *our* home! I *should* like to be there, and never leave it, and die there.' But she remembered herself. 'That's only a momentary feeling. I have a son, you know, a dear boy. He's at school now.'

'Somewhere handy, I suppose? I see there's lots on 'em along this road.'

'Oh no! Not in one of these wretched holes! At a public school – one of the most distinguished in England.'

'Chok' it all! Of course! I forget, ma'am, that you've been a lady for so many years.'

'No, I am not a lady,' she said sadly. 'I never shall be. But he's a gentleman, and that – makes it – oh, how difficult for me!'

The acquaintance thus oddly reopened proceeded apace. She often looked out to get a few words with him, by night or by day. Her sorrow was that she could not accompany her one old friend on foot a little way, and talk more freely than she could do while he paused before the house. One night, at the beginning of June, when she was again on the watch after an absence of some days from the window, he entered the gate and said softly, 'Now, wouldn't some air do you good? I've only half a load this morning. Why not ride up to Covent Garden with me? There's a nice seat on the cabbages, where I've spread a sack. You can be home again in a cab before anybody is up.'

She refused at first, and then, trembling with excitement, hastily finished her dressing, and wrapped herself up in cloak and veil, afterwards sliding down-stairs by the aid of the handrail, in a way she could adopt on an emergency. When she had opened the door she found Sam on the step, and he lifted her bodily on his strong arm across the little forecourt into his vehicle. Not a soul was visible or audible in the infinite length of the straight, flat highway, with its ever-waiting lamps converging to points in each direction. The air was fresh as country air at this hour, and the stars shone, except to the north-eastward, where there was a whitish light – the dawn. Sam carefully placed her in the seat, and drove on.

They talked as they had talked in old days, Sam pulling himself up now and then, when he thought himself too familiar. More than once she said with misgiving that she wondered if she ought to have indulged in the freak. 'But I am so lonely in my house,' she added, 'and this makes me so happy!'

'You must come again, dear Mrs Twycott. There is no time o' day for taking the air like this.'

It grew lighter and lighter. The sparrows became busy in the streets, and the city waxed denser around them. When they approached the river it was day, and on the bridge they beheld the full blaze of morning sunlight in the direction of St Paul's, the river glistening towards it, and not a craft stirring.

Near Covent Garden he put her into a cab, and they parted, looking into each other's faces like the very old friends they were. She reached home without adventure, limped to the door, and let herself in with her latchkey unseen.

The air and Sam's presence had revived her: her cheeks were quite pink – almost beautiful. She had something to live for in addition to her son. A woman of pure instincts, she knew there had been nothing really wrong in the journey, but supposed it conventionally to be very wrong indeed.

Soon, however, she gave way to the temptation of going with him again, and on this occasion their conversation was distinctly tender, and Sam said he never should forget her, notwithstanding that she had served him rather badly at one time. After much hesitation he told her of a plan it was in his power to carry out, and one he should like to take in hand, since he did not care for London work: it was to set up as a master greengrocer down at Aldbrickham, the county-town of their native place. He knew of an opening – a shop kept by aged people who wished to retire.

'And why don't you do it, then, Sam?' she asked with a slight heartsinking.

'Because I'm not sure if – you'd join me. I know you wouldn't – couldn't! Such a lady as ye've been so long, you couldn't be a wife to a man like me.'

'I hardly suppose I could!' she assented, also frightened at the idea.

'If you could,' he said eagerly, 'you'd on'y have to sit in the back parlour and look through the glass partition when I was away sometimes – just to keep an eye on things. The lameness wouldn't hinder that . . . I'd keep you as genteel as ever I could, dear Sophy – if I might think of it!' he pleaded.

'Sam, I'll be frank,' she said, putting her hand on his. 'If it were only myself I would do it, and gladly, though everything I possess would be lost to me by marrying again.'

'I don't mind that! It's more independent.'

'That's good of you, dear, dear Sam. But there's something else. I have a son . . . I almost fancy when I am miserable sometimes that he is not really mine, but one I hold in trust for my late husband. He seems to belong so little to me personally, so entirely to his dead father. He is so much educated and I so little that I do not feel dignified enough to be his mother . . . Well, he would have to be told.'

'Yes. Unquestionably.' Sam saw her thought and her fear. 'Still, you can do as you like, Sophy – Mrs Twycott,' he added. 'It is not you who are the child, but he.'

'Ah, you don't know! Sam, if I could, I would marry you, someday. But you must wait a while, and let me think.'

It was enough for him, and he was blithe at their

parting. Not so she. To tell Randolph seemed impossible. She could wait till he had gone up to Oxford, when what she did would affect his life but little. But would he ever tolerate the idea? And if not, could she defy him?

She had not told him a word when the yearly cricket-match came on at Lord's between the public schools; though Sam had already gone back to Aldbrickham. Mrs Twycott felt stronger than usual: she went to the match with Randolph, and was able to leave her chair and walk about occasionally. The bright idea occurred to her that she could casually broach the subject while moving round among the spectators, when the boy's spirits were high with interest in the game, and he would weigh domestic matters as feathers in the scale beside the day's victory. They promenaded under the lurid July sun, this pair, so wide apart, yet so near, and Sophy saw the large proportion of boys like her own, in their broad white collars and dwarf hats, and all around the rows of great coaches under which was jumbled the *débris* of luxurious luncheons; bones, pie-crusts, champagne-bottles, glasses, plates, napkins, and the family silver; while on the coaches sat the proud fathers and mothers; but never a poor mother like her. If Randolph had not appertained to these, had not centred all his interests in them, had not cared exclusively for the class they belonged to, how happy would things have been! A great huzza at some small performance with the bat burst from the multitude of relatives, and Randolph jumped wildly into the air to see what had happened. Sophy fetched up the sentence that had been already shaped; but she could not get it out. The occasion was, perhaps, an inopportune one. The contrast between her story and the display of fashion to which Randolph had grown to regard himself as akin would be fatal. She awaited a better time.

It was on an evening when they were alone in their plain suburban residence, where life was not blue but brown, that she ultimately broke silence, qualifying her announcement of a probable second marriage by assuring him that it would not take place for a long time to come, when he would be living quite independently of her.

The boy thought the idea a very reasonable one, and asked if she had chosen anybody? She hesitated; and he seemed to have a misgiving. He hoped his stepfather would be a gentleman? he said.

'Not what you call a gentleman,' she answered timidly. 'He'll be much as I was before I knew your father'; and by degrees she acquainted him with the whole. The youth's face remained fixed for a moment; then he flushed, leant on the table, and burst into passionate tears.

His mother went up to him, kissed all of his face that she could get at, and patted his back as if he were still the baby he once had been, crying herself the while. When he had somewhat recovered from his paroxysm he went hastily to his own room and fastened the door.

Parleyings were attempted through the keyhole, outside which she waited and listened. It was long before he would reply, and when he did it was to say sternly at her from within: 'I am ashamed of you! It will ruin me! A miserable boor! a churl! a clown! It will degrade me in the eyes of all the gentlemen of England!'

'Say no more – perhaps I am wrong! I will struggle against it!' she cried miserably.

Before Randolph left her that summer a letter

arrived from Sam to inform her that he had been unexpectedly fortunate in obtaining the shop. He was in possession; it was the largest in the town, combining fruit with vegetables, and he thought it would form a home worthy even of her someday. Might he not run up to town to see her?

She met him by stealth, and said he must still wait for her final answer. The autumn dragged on, and when Randolph was home at Christmas for the holidays she broached the matter again. But the young gentleman was inexorable.

It was dropped for months; renewed again; abandoned under his repugnance; again attempted; and thus the gentle creature reasoned and pleaded till four or five long years had passed. Then the faithful Sam revived his suit with some peremptoriness. Sophy's son, now an undergraduate, was down from Oxford one Easter, when she again opened the subject. As soon as he was ordained, she argued, he would have a home of his own, wherein she, with her bad grammar and her ignorance, would be an encumbrance to him. Better obliterate her as much as possible.

He showed a more manly anger now, but would not agree. She on her side was more persistent, and he had doubts whether she could be trusted in his absence. But by indignation and contempt for her taste he completely maintained his ascendency; and finally taking her before a little cross and altar that he had erected in his bedroom for his private devotions, there bade her kneel, and swear that she would not wed Samuel Hobson without his consent. 'I owe this to my father!' he said.

The poor woman swore, thinking he would soften as soon as he was ordained and in full swing of clerical work. But he did not. His education had by this time sufficiently ousted his humanity to keep him quite firm; though his mother might have led an idyllic life with her faithful fruiterer and greengrocer, and nobody have been anything the worse in the world.

Her lameness became more confirmed as time went on, and she seldom or never left the house in the long southern thoroughfare, where she seemed to be pining her heart away. 'Why mayn't I say to Sam that I'll marry him? Why mayn't I?' she would murmur plaintively to herself when nobody was near.

Some four years after this date a middle-aged man was standing at the door of the largest fruiterer's shop in Aldbrickham. He was the proprietor, but today, instead of his usual business attire, he wore a neat suit of black; and his window was partly shuttered. From the railway-station a funeral procession was seen approaching: it passed his door and went out of the town towards the village of Gaymead. The man, whose eyes were wet, held his hat in his hand as the vehicles moved by; while from the mourning coach a young smooth-shaven priest in a high waistcoat looked black as a cloud at the shopkeeper standing there.

December 1891

A Tragedy of Two Ambitions

ONE

The shouts of the village-boys came in at the window, accompanied by broken laughter from loungers at the inn-door; but the brothers Halborough worked on.

They were sitting in a bedroom of the master-millwright's house, engaged in the untutored reading of Greek and Latin. It was no tale of Homeric blows and knocks, Argonautic voyaging, or Theban family woe that inflamed their imaginations and spurred them onward. They were plodding away at the Greek Testament, immersed in a chapter of the idiomatic and difficult Epistle to the Hebrews.

The dog-day sun in its decline reached the low ceiling with slanting sides, and the shadows of the great goat's-willow swayed and interchanged upon the walls like a spectral army manoeuvring. The open casement which admitted the remoter sounds now brought the voice of someone close at hand. It was their sister, a pretty girl of fourteen, who stood in the court below.

'I can see the tops of your heads! What's the use of staying up there? I like you not to go out with the street-boys; but do come and play with me!'

They treated her as an inadequate interlocutor, and put her off with some slight word. She went away disappointed. Presently there was a dull noise of heavy footsteps at the side of the house, and one of the brothers sat up. 'I fancy I hear him coming,' he murmured, his eyes on the window.

A man in the light drab clothes of an old-fashioned country tradesman approached from round the corner, reeling as he came. The elder son flushed with anger, rose from his books, and descended the stairs. The younger sat on, till, after the lapse of a few minutes, his brother re-entered the room.

'Did Rosa see him?'

'No.'

'Nor anybody?'

'No.'

'What have you done with him?'

'He's in the straw-shed. I got him in with some trouble, and he has fallen asleep. I thought this would be the explanation of his absence! No stones dressed for Miller Kench, the great wheel of the sawmills waiting for new float-boards, even the poor folk not able to get their wagons wheeled.'

'What *is* the use of poring over this!' said the younger, shutting up Donnegan's *Lexicon* with a slap. 'Oh, if we had only been able to keep mother's nine hundred pound, what we could have done!'

'How well she had estimated the sum necessary! Four hundred and fifty each, she thought. And I have no doubt that we could have done it on that, with care.'

This loss of the nine hundred pounds was the sharp thorn of their crown. It was a sum which their mother had amassed with great exertion and self-denial, by adding to a chance legacy such other small amounts as she could lay hands on from time to time; and she had intended with the hoard to indulge the dear wish of her heart – that of sending her sons, Joshua and Cornelius, to one of the Universities, having been informed that from four hundred to four hundred and fifty each might carry them through their terms with such great economy as she knew she could trust them to practise. But she had died a year or two before this time, worn out by too keen a strain towards these ends; and the money, coming unreservedly into the hands of their father, had been nearly dissipated. With its exhaustion went all opportunity and hope of a University degree for the sons.

'It drives me mad when I think of it,' said Joshua, the elder. 'And here we work and work in our own bungling way, and the utmost we can hope for is a term of years as national schoolmasters, and possible admission to a theological college, and ordination as despised licentiates.'

The anger of the elder was reflected as simple sadness in the face of the other. 'We can preach the Gospel as well without a hood on our surplices as with one,' he said with feeble consolation.

'Preach the Gospel – true,' said Joshua with a slight pursing of mouth. 'But we can't rise.'

'Let us make the best of it, and grind on.'

The other was silent, and they drearily bent over their books again.

The cause of all this gloom, the millwright Halborough, now snoring in the shed, had been a thriving master-machinist, notwithstanding his free and careless disposition, till a taste for a more than adequate quantity of strong liquor took hold of him; since when his habits had interfered with his business sadly. Already millers went elsewhere for their gear, and only one set of hands was now kept going, though there were formerly two. Already he found a difficulty in meeting his men at the week's end, and though they had been reduced in number there was barely enough work to do for those who remained.

The sun dropped lower and vanished, the shouts of the village children ceased to resound, darkness cloaked the students' bedroom, and all the scene outwardly breathed peace. None knew of the fevered youthful ambitions that throbbed in two breasts within the quiet creeper-covered walls of the millwright's house.

In a few months the brothers left the village of their birth to enter themselves as students in a training college for schoolmasters; first having placed their young sister Rosa under as efficient a tuition at a fashionable watering-place as the means at their disposal could command.

TWO

A man in semi-clerical dress was walking along the road which led from the railway-station into a provincial town. As he walked he read persistently, only looking up once now and then to see that he was keeping on the foot-track, or to avoid other passengers. At those moments, whoever had known the former students at the millwright's would have perceived that one of them, Joshua Halborough, was the peripatetic reader here.

What had been simple force in the youth's face was energised judgement in the man's. His character was gradually writing itself out in his countenance. That he was watching his own career with deeper and deeper interest, that he continually 'heard his days before him', and cared to hear little else, might have been hazarded from what was seen there. His ambitions were, in truth, passionate, yet controlled; so that the germs of many more plans than ever blossomed to maturity had place in him; and forward visions were kept purposely in twilight, to avoid distraction.

Events so far had been encouraging. Shortly after assuming the mastership of his first school he had obtained an introduction to the Bishop of a diocese far from his native county, who had looked upon him as a promising young man and taken him in hand. He was now in the second year of his residence at the theological college of the cathedral-town, and would soon be presented for ordination.

He entered the town, turned into a back street, and then into a yard, keeping his book before him till he set foot under the arch of the latter place. Round the arch was written 'National School', and the stone-work of the jambs was worn away as nothing but boys and the waves of ocean will wear it. He was soon amid the sing-song accents of the scholars.

His brother Cornelius, who was the schoolmaster here, laid down the pointer with which he was directing attention to the Capes of Europe, and came forward.

'That's his brother Jos!' whispered one of the sixth-standard boys. 'He's going to be a pa'son. He's now at college.'

'Corney is going to be one too, when he's saved enough money,' said another.

After greeting his brother, whom he had not seen for several months, the junior began to explain his system of teaching geography.

But Halborough the elder took no interest in the subject. 'How about your own studies?' he asked. 'Did you get the books I sent?'

Cornelius had received them, and he related what he was doing.

'Mind you work in the morning. What time do you get up?'

The younger replied: 'Half-past five.'

'Half-past four is not a minute too soon this time of the year. There is no time like the morning for construing. I don't know why, but when I feel even too dreary to read a novel I can translate – there is something mechanical about it I suppose. Now, Cornelius, you are rather behindhand, and have some heavy reading before you if you mean to get out of this next Christmas.'

'I am afraid I have.'

'We must soon sound the Bishop. I am sure you will get a title without difficulty when he has heard all. The sub-dean, the principal of my college, says that the best plan will be for you to come there when his lordship is present at an examination, and he'll get you a personal interview with him. Mind you make a good impression upon him. I found in my case that that was everything, and doctrine almost nothing. You'll do for a deacon, Corney, if not for a priest.'

The younger remained thoughtful. 'Have you heard from Rosa lately?' he asked. 'I had a letter this morning.'

'Yes. The little minx writes rather too often. She is homesick – though Brussels must be an attractive place enough. But she must make the most of her time over there. I thought a year would be enough for her, after that high-class school at Sandbourne, but I have decided to give her two, and make a good job of it, expensive as the establishment is.'

Their two rather harsh faces had softened directly they began to speak of their sister, whom they loved more ambitiously than they loved themselves.

'But where is the money to come from, Joshua?'

'I have already got it.' He looked round, and finding that some boys were near withdrew a few steps. 'I have borrowed it at five per cent from the farmer who used to occupy the farm next our field. You remember him.'

'But about paying him?'

'I shall pay him by degrees out of my stipend. No, Cornelius, it was no use to do the thing by halves. She promises to be a most attractive, not to say beautiful, girl. I have seen that for years; and if her face is not her fortune, her face and her brains together will be, if I observe and contrive aright. That she should be, every inch of her, an accomplished and refined woman, was indispensable for the fulfilment of her destiny, and for moving onwards and upwards with us; and she'll do it, you will see. I'd half starve myself rather than take her away from that school now.'

They looked round the school they were in. To Cornelius it was natural and familiar enough, but to Joshua, with his limited human sympathies, who had just dropped in from a superior sort of place, the sight jarred unpleasantly, as being that of something he had left behind. 'I shall be glad when you are out of this,' he said, 'and in your pulpit, and well through your first sermon.'

'You may as well say inducted into my fat living, while you are about it.'

'Ah, well – don't think lightly of the Church. There's a fine work for any man of energy in the Church, as you'll find,' he said fervidly. 'Torrents of infidelity to be stemmed, new views of old subjects to be expounded, truths in spirit to be substituted for truths in the letter . . . ' He lapsed into reverie with the vision of his career, persuading himself that it was

33

ardour for Christianity which spurred him on, and not pride of place. He had shouldered a body of doctrine, and was prepared to defend it tooth and nail, solely for the honour and glory that warriors win.

'If the Church is elastic, and stretches to the shape of the time, she'll last, I suppose,' said Cornelius. 'If not . . . Only think, I bought a copy of Paley's *Evidences*, best edition, broad margins, excellent preservation, at a bookstall the other day for – ninepence; and I thought that at this rate Christianity must be in rather a bad way.'

'No, no!' said the other almost angrily. 'It only shows that such defences are no longer necessary. Men's eyes can see the truth without extraneous assistance. Besides, we are in for Christianity, and must stick to her whether or no. I am just now going right through Pusey's *Library of the Fathers*.'

'You'll be a bishop, Joshua, before you have done!'

'Ah!' said the other bitterly, shaking his head. 'Perhaps I might have been – I might have been! But where is my D.D. or LL.D.; and how be a bishop without that kind of appendage? Archbishop Tillotson was the son of a Sowerby clothier, but he was sent to Clare College. To hail Oxford or Cambridge as *alma mater* is not for me – for us. My God, when I think of what we should have been – what fair promise has been blighted by that cursed, worthless – '

'Hush, hush! . . . But I feel it, too, as much as you. I have seen it more forcibly lately. You would have obtained your degree long before this time – possibly fellowship – and I should have been on my way to mine.'

'Don't talk of it,' said the other. 'We must do the best we can.'

They looked out of the window sadly, through the dusty panes, so high up that only the sky was visible. By degrees the haunting trouble loomed again, and Cornelius broke the silence with a whisper: 'He has called on me!'

The living pulses died on Joshua's face, which grew arid as a clinker. 'When was that?' he asked quickly.

'Last week.'

'How did he get here – so many miles?'

'Came by railway. He came to ask for money.'

'Ah!'

'He says he will call on you.'

Joshua replied resignedly. The theme of their conversation spoilt his buoyancy for that afternoon. He returned in the evening, Cornelius accompanying him to the station; but he did not read in the train which took him back to the Fountall Theological College, as he had done on the way out. That ineradicable trouble still remained as a squalid spot in the expanse of his life. He sat with the other students in the cathedral choir next day; and the recollection of the trouble obscured the purple splendour thrown by the panes upon the floor.

It was afternoon. All was as still in the Close as a cathedral-green can be between the Sunday services, and the incessant cawing of the rooks was the only sound. Joshua Halborough had finished his ascetic lunch, and had gone into the library, where he stood for a few moments looking out of the large window facing the green. He saw walking slowly across it a man in a fustian coat and a battered white hat with a much-ruffled nap, having upon his arm a tall gypsy-woman wearing long brass earrings. The man was staring quizzically at the west front of the cathedral, and

Halborough recognised in him the form and features of his father. Who the woman was he knew not. Almost as soon as Joshua became conscious of these things, the sub-dean, who was also the principal of the college, and of whom the young man stood in more awe than of the Bishop himself, emerged from the gate and entered a path across the Close. The pair met the dignitary, and to Joshua's horror his father turned and addressed the sub-dean.

What passed between them he could not tell. But as he stood in a cold sweat he saw his father place his hand familiarly on the sub-dean's shoulder; the shrinking response of the latter, and his quick withdrawal, told his feeling. The woman seemed to say nothing, but when the sub-dean had passed by they came on towards the college gate.

Halborough flew along the corridor and out at a side door, so as to intercept them before they could reach the front entrance, for which they were making. He caught them behind a clump of laurel.

'By Jerry, here's the very chap! Well, you're a fine fellow, Jos, never to send your father as much as a twist o' baccy on such an occasion, and to leave him to travel all these miles to find 'ee out!'

'First, who is this?' said Joshua Halborough with pale dignity, waving his hand towards the buxom woman with the great earrings.

'Dammy, the mis'ess! Your stepmother! Didn't you know I'd married? She helped me home from market one night, and we came to terms, and struck the bargain. Didn't we, Selinar?'

'Oi, by the great Lord an' we did!' simpered the lady.

'Well, what sort of a place is this you are living in?'

asked the millwright. 'A kind of house-of-correction, apparently?'

Joshua listened abstractedly, his features set to resignation. Sick at heart, he was going to ask them if they were in want of any necessary, any meal, when his father cut him short by saying, 'Why, we've called to ask ye to come round and take potluck with us at the Cock-and-Bottle, where we've put up for the day, on our way to see mis'ess's friends at Binegar Fair, where they'll be lying under canvas for a night or two. As for the victuals at the Cock I can't testify to 'em at all; but for the drink, they've the rarest drop of Old Tom that I've tasted for many a year.'

'Thanks; but I am a teetotaller; and I have lunched,' said Joshua, who could fully believe his father's testimony to the gin, from the odour of his breath. 'You see we have to observe regular habits here; and I couldn't be seen at the Cock-and-Bottle just now.'

'Oh dammy, then don't come, your reverence. Perhaps you won't mind standing treat for those who can be seen there?'

'Not a penny!' said the younger firmly. 'You've had enough already.'

'Thank you for nothing! By the by, who was that spindle-legged, shoe-buckled parson feller we met by now? He seemed to think we should poison him!'

Joshua remarked coldly that it was the principal of his college, guardedly enquiring, 'Did you tell him whom you were come to see?'

His father did not reply. He and his strapping gypsy wife – if she were his wife – stayed no longer, and disappeared in the direction of the High Street. Joshua Halborough went back to the library. Determined as was his nature, he wept hot tears upon the books, and was immeasurably more wretched that afternoon than the unwelcome millwright. In the evening he sat down and wrote a letter to his brother, in which, after stating what had happened, and expatiating upon this new disgrace in the gypsy wife, he propounded a plan for raising money sufficient to induce the couple to emigrate to Canada. 'It is our only chance,' he said. 'The case as it stands is maddening. For a successful painter, sculptor, musician, author, who takes society by storm, it is no drawback, it is sometimes even a romantic recommendation, to hail from outcasts and profligates. But for a clergyman of the Church of England! Cornelius, it is fatal! To succeed in the Church, people must believe in you, first of all, as a gentleman, secondly as a man of means, thirdly as a scholar, fourthly as a preacher, fifthly, perhaps, as a Christian – but always first as a gentleman, with all their heart and soul and strength. I would have faced the fact of being a small machinist's son, and have taken my chance, if he'd been in any sense respectable and decent. The essence of Christianity is humility, and by the help of God I would have brazened it out. But this terrible vagabondage and disreputable connection! If he does not accept my terms and leave the country, it will extinguish us and kill me! For how can we live, and relinquish our high aim, and bring down our dear sister Rosa to the level of a gypsy's stepdaughter?'

THREE

There was excitement in the parish of Narrobourne one day. The congregation had just come out from morning service, and the whole conversation was of the new curate, Mr Halborough, who had officiated for the first time, in the absence of the rector.

Never before had the feeling of the villagers approached a level which could be called excitement on such a matter as this. The droning which had been the rule in that quiet old place for a century seemed ended at last. They repeated the text to each other as a refrain: 'O Lord, be thou my helper!' Not within living memory till today had the subject of the sermon formed the topic of conversation from the church door to the churchyard gate, to the exclusion of personal remarks on those who had been present, and on the week's news in general.

The thrilling periods of the preacher hung about their minds all that day. The parish being steeped in indifferentism, it happened that when the youths and maidens, middle-aged and old people, who had attended church that morning, recurred as by a fascination to what Halborough had said, they did so more or less indirectly, and even with the subterfuge of a light laugh that was not real, so great was their shyness under the novelty of their sensations.

What was more curious than that these unconventional villagers should have been excited by a preacher of a new school after forty years of familiarity with the old hand who had had charge of their souls, was the effect of Halborough's address upon the occupants of the manor-house pew, including the owner of the estate. These thought they knew how to discount the mere sensational sermon, how to minimise flash oratory to its bare proportions; but they had yielded like the rest of the assembly to the charm of the newcomer.

Mr Fellmer, the landowner, was a young widower, whose mother, still in the prime of life, had returned to her old position in the family mansion since the death of her son's wife in the year after her marriage, at the birth of a fragile little girl. From the date of his loss to the present time, Fellmer had led an inactive existence in the seclusion of the parish; a lack of motive seemed to leave him listless. He had gladly reinstated his mother in the gloomy house, and his main occupation now lay in stewarding his estate, which was not large. Mrs Fellmer, who had sat beside him under Halborough this morning, was a cheerful, straightforward woman, who did her marketing and her alms-giving in person, was fond of old-fashioned flowers, and walked about the village on very wet days visiting the parishioners. These, the only two great ones of Narrobourne, were impressed by Joshua's eloquence as much as the cottagers.

Halborough had been briefly introduced to them on his arrival some days before, and, their interest being kindled, they waited a few moments till he came out of the vestry, to walk down the churchyard path with him. Mrs Fellmer spoke warmly of the sermon, of the good fortune of the parish in his advent, and hoped he had found comfortable quarters.

Halborough, faintly flushing, said that he had obtained very fair lodgings in the roomy house of a farmer, whom he named.

She feared he would find it very lonely, especially in

the evenings, and hoped they would see a good deal of him. When would he dine with them? Could he not come that day – it must be so dull for him the first Sunday evening in country lodgings?

Halborough replied that it would give him much pleasure, but that he feared he must decline. 'I am not altogether alone,' he said. 'My sister, who has just returned from Brussels, and who felt, as you do, that I should be rather dismal by myself, has accompanied me hither to stay a few days till she has put my rooms in order and set me going. She was too fatigued to come to church, and is waiting for me now at the farm.'

'Oh, but bring your sister – that will be still better! I shall be delighted to know her. How I wish I had been aware! Do tell her, please, that we had no idea of her presence.'

Halborough assured Mrs Fellmer that he would certainly bear the message; but as to her coming he was not so sure. The real truth was, however, that the matter would be decided by him, Rosa having an almost filial respect for his wishes. But he was uncertain as to the state of her wardrobe, and had determined that she should not enter the manor-house at a disadvantage that evening, when there would probably be plenty of opportunities in the future of her doing so becomingly.

He walked to the farm in long strides. This, then, was the outcome of his first morning's work as curate here. Things had gone fairly well with him. He had been ordained; he was in a comfortable parish, where he would exercise almost sole supervision, the rector being infirm. He had made a deep impression at starting, and the absence of a hood seemed to have done him no harm. Moreover, by considerable persuasion and payment, his father and the dark woman had been shipped off to Canada, where they were not likely to interfere greatly with his interests.

Rosa came out to meet him. 'Ah! you should have gone to church like a good girl,' he said.

'Yes – I wished I had afterwards. But I do so hate church as a rule that even your preaching was underestimated in my mind. It was too bad of me!'

The girl who spoke thus playfully was fair, tall, and sylph-like, in a muslin dress, and with just the coquettish *désinvolture* which an English girl brings home from abroad, and loses again after a few months of native life. Joshua was the reverse of playful; the world was too important a concern for him to indulge in light moods. He told her in decided, practical phraseology of the invitation.

'Now, Rosa, we must go – that's settled – if you've a dress that can be made fit to wear all on the hop like this. You didn't, of course, think of bringing an evening dress to such an out-of-the-way place?'

But Rosa had come from the wrong city to be caught napping in those matters. 'Yes, I did,' said she. 'One never knows what may turn up.'

'Well done! Then off we go at seven.'

The evening drew on, and at dusk they started on foot, Rosa pulling up the edge of her skirt under her cloak out of the way of the dews, so that it formed a great windbag all round her, and carrying her satin shoes under her arm. Joshua would not let her wait till she got indoors before changing them, as she proposed, but insisted on her performing that operation under a tree, so that they might enter as if they had not walked. He was nervously formal about such trifles, while Rosa took the whole proceeding – walk, dressing, dinner, and all – as a pastime. To Joshua it was a serious step in life.

A more unexpected kind of person for a curate's sister was never presented at a dinner. The surprise of Mrs Fellmer was unconcealed. She had looked forward to a Dorcas, or Martha, or Rhoda at the outside, and a shade of misgiving crossed her face. It was possible that, had the young lady accompanied her brother to church, there would have been no dining at Narrobourne House that day.

Not so with the young widower, her son. He resembled a sleeper who had awaked in a summer noon expecting to find it only dawn. He could scarcely help stretching his arms and yawning in their faces, so strong was his sense of being suddenly aroused to an unforeseen thing. When they had sat down to table he at first talked to Rosa somewhat with the air of a ruler in the land; but the woman lurking in the acquaintance soon brought him to his level, and the girl from Brussels saw him looking at her mouth, her hands, her contour, as if he could not quite comprehend how they got created: then he dropped into the more satisfactory stage which discerns no particulars.

He talked but little; she said much. The homeliness of the Fellmers, to her view, though they were regarded with such awe down here, quite disembarrassed her. The squire had become so unpractised, had dropped so far into the shade during the last year or so of his life, that he had almost forgotten what the world contained till this evening reminded him. His mother, after her first moments of doubt, appeared to think that he must be left to his own guidance, and gave her attention to Joshua.

With all his foresight and doggedness of aim, the result of that dinner exceeded Halborough's expectations. In weaving his ambitions he had viewed his sister Rosa as a slight, bright thing to be helped into notice by his abilities; but it now began to dawn upon him that the physical gifts of nature to her might do more for them both than nature's intellectual gifts to himself. While he was patiently boring the tunnel Rosa seemed about to fly over the mountain.

He wrote the next day to his brother, now occupying his own old rooms in the theological college, telling him exultingly of the unanticipated *début* of Rosa at the manor-house. The next post brought him a reply of congratulation, dashed with the counteracting intelligence that his father did not like Canada – that his gypsy wife had deserted him, which made him feel so dreary that he thought of returning home.

In his recent satisfaction at his own successes Joshua Halborough had well-nigh forgotten his chronic trouble – latterly screened by distance. But it now returned upon him; he saw more in this brief announcement than his brother seemed to see. It was the cloud no bigger than a man's hand.

FOUR

The following December, a day or two before Christmas, Mrs Fellmer and her son were walking up and down the broad gravel path which bordered the east front of the house. Till within the last half-hour the morning had been a drizzling one, and they had just emerged for a short turn before luncheon.

'You see, dear mother,' the son was saying, 'it is the

peculiarity of my position which makes her appear to me in such a desirable light. When you consider how I have been crippled at starting, how my life has been maimed; that I feel anything like publicity distasteful, that I have no political ambition, and that my chief aim and hope lie in the education of the little thing Annie has left me, you must see how desirable a wife like Miss Halborough would be, to prevent my becoming a mere vegetable.'

'If you adore her, I suppose you must have her!' replied his mother with dry indirectness. 'But you'll find that she will not be content to live on here as you do, giving her whole mind to a young child.'

'That's just where we differ. Her very disqualification, that of being a nobody, as you call it, is her recommendation in my eyes. Her lack of influential connections limits her ambition. From what I know of her, a life in this place is all that she would wish for. She would never care to go outside the park-gates if it were necessary to stay within.'

'Being in love with her, Albert, and meaning to marry her, you invent your practical reasons to make the case respectable. Well, do as you will; I have no authority over you, so why should you consult me? You mean to propose on this very occasion, no doubt. Don't you, now?'

'By no means. I am merely revolving the idea in my mind. If on further acquaintance she turns out to be as good as she has hitherto seemed – well, I shall see. Admit, now, that you like her.'

'I readily admit it. She is very captivating at first sight. But as a stepmother to your child! You seem mighty anxious, Albert, to get rid of me!'

'Not at all. And I am not so reckless as you think. I

don't make up my mind in a hurry. But the thought having occurred to me, I mention it to you at once, mother. If you dislike it, say so.'

'I don't say anything. I will try to make the best of it if you are determined. When does she come?'

'Tomorrow.'

All this time there were great preparations in train at the curate's, who was now a householder. Rosa, whose two or three weeks' stay on two occasions earlier in the year had so affected the squire, was coming again, and at the same time her younger brother Cornelius, to make up a family party. Rosa, who journeyed from the Midlands, could not arrive till late in the evening, but Cornelius was to get there in the afternoon, Joshua going out to meet him in his walk across the fields from the railway.

Everything being ready in Joshua's modest abode he started on his way, his heart buoyant and thankful, if ever it was in his life. He was of such good report himself that his brother's path into holy orders promised to be unexpectedly easy; and he longed to compare experiences with him, even though there was on hand a more exciting matter still. From his youth he had held that, in old-fashioned country places, the Church conferred social prestige up to a certain point at a cheaper price than any other profession or pursuit; and events seemed to be proving him right.

He had walked about half an hour when he saw Cornelius coming along the path; and in a few minutes the two brothers met. The experiences of Cornelius had been less immediately interesting than those of Joshua, but his personal position was satisfactory, and there was nothing to account for the singularly subdued manner that he exhibited, which at first Joshua set

46

down to the fatigue of over-study; and he proceeded to the subject of Rosa's arrival in the evening, and the probable consequences of this her third visit. 'Before next Easter she'll be his wife, my boy,' said Joshua with grave exultation.

Cornelius shook his head. 'She comes too late!' he returned.

'What do you mean?'

'Look here.' He produced the Fountall paper, and placed his finger on a paragraph, which Joshua read. It appeared under the report of Petty Sessions, and was a commonplace case of disorderly conduct, in which a man was sent to prison for seven days for breaking windows in that town.

'Well?' said Joshua.

'It happened during an evening that I was in the street; and the offender is our father.'

'Not – how – I sent him more money on his promising to stay in Canada.'

'He is home, safe enough.' Cornelius in the same gloomy tone gave the remainder of his information. He had witnessed the scene, unobserved of his father, and had heard him say that he was on his way to see his daughter, who was going to marry a rich gentleman. The only good fortune attending the untoward incident was that the millwright's name had been printed as Joshua Alborough.

'Beaten! We are to be beaten on the eve of our expected victory!' said the elder brother. 'How did he guess that Rosa was likely to marry? Good Heaven! Cornelius, you seem doomed to bring bad news always, do you not!'

'I do,' said Cornelius. 'Poor Rosa!'

It was almost in tears, so great was their heartsickness

47

and shame, that the brothers walked the remainder of the way to Joshua's dwelling. In the evening they set out to meet Rosa, bringing her to the village in a fly; and when she had come into the house, and was sitting down with them, they almost forgot their secret anxiety in contemplating her, who knew nothing about it.

Next day the Fellmers came, and the two or three days after that were a lively time. That the squire was yielding to his impulses – making up his mind – there could be no doubt. On Sunday Cornelius read the service, and Joshua preached. Mrs Fellmer was quite maternal towards Rosa, and it appeared that she had decided to welcome the inevitable with a good grace. The pretty girl was to spend yet another afternoon with the elder lady, superintending some parish treat at the house in observance of Christmas, and afterwards to stay on to dinner, her brothers to fetch her in the evening. They were also invited to dine, but they could not accept owing to an engagement.

The engagement was of a sombre sort. They were going to meet their father, who would that day be released from Fountall Gaol, and try to persuade him to keep away from Narrobourne. Every exertion was to be made to get him back to Canada, to his old home in the Midlands – anywhere, so that he would not impinge disastrously upon their courses, and blast their sister's prospects of the auspicious marriage which was just then hanging in the balance.

As soon as Rosa had been fetched away by her friends at the manor-house her brothers started on their expedition, without waiting for dinner or tea. Cornelius, to whom the millwright always addressed his letters when he wrote any, drew from his pocket and re-read as he walked the curt note which had led to this journey being undertaken; it was despatched by their father the night before, immediately upon his liberation, and stated that he was setting out for Narrobourne at the moment of writing; that having no money he would be obliged to walk all the way; that he calculated on passing through the intervening town of Ivell about six on the following day, where he should sup at the Castle Inn, and where he hoped they would meet him with a carriage-and-pair, or some other such conveyance, that he might not disgrace them by arriving like a tramp.

'That sounds as if he gave a thought to our position,' said Cornelius.

Joshua knew the satire that lurked in the paternal words, and said nothing. Silence prevailed during the greater part of their journey. The lamps were lighted in Ivell when they entered the streets, and Cornelius, who was quite unknown in this neighbourhood, and who, moreover, was not in clerical attire, decided that he should be the one to call at the Castle Inn. Here, in answer to his enquiry under the darkness of the archway, they told him that such a man as he had described left the house about a quarter of an hour earlier, after making a meal in the kitchen-settle. He was rather the worse for liquor.

'Then,' said Joshua, when Cornelius joined him outside with this intelligence, 'we must have met and passed him! And now that I think of it, we did meet someone who was unsteady in his gait, under the trees on the other side of Hendford Hill, where it was too dark to see him.'

They rapidly retraced their steps; but for a long stretch of the way home could discern nobody. When, however, they had gone about three-quarters of the distance, they became conscious of an irregular footfall in front of them, and could see a whitish figure in the gloom. They followed dubiously. The figure met another wayfarer – the single one that had been encountered upon this lonely road – and they distinctly heard him ask the way to Narrobourne. The stranger replied – what was quite true – that the nearest way was by turning in at the stile by the next bridge, and following the footpath which branched thence across the meadows.

When the brothers reached the stile they also entered the path, but did not overtake the subject of their worry till they had crossed two or three meads, and the lights from Narrobourne manor-house were visible before them through the trees. Their father was no longer walking; he was seated against the wet bank of an adjoining hedge. Observing their forms he shouted, 'I'm going to Narrobourne; who may you be?'

They went up to him, and revealed themselves, reminding him of the plan which he had himself proposed in his note, that they should meet him at Ivell.

'By Jerry, I'd forgot it!' he said. 'Well, what do you want me to do?' His tone was distinctly quarrelsome.

A long conversation followed, which became embittered at the first hint from them that he should not come to the village. The millwright drew a quart bottle from his pocket, and challenged them to drink if they meant friendly and called themselves men. Neither of the two had touched alcohol for years, but for once they thought it best to accept, so as not to needlessly provoke him.

'What's in it?' said Joshua.

'A drop of weak gin-and-water. It won't hurt 'ee. Drink from the bottle.' Joshua did so, and his father pushed up the bottom of the vessel so as to make him swallow a good deal in spite of himself. It went down into his stomach like molten lead.

'Ha, ha, that's right!' said old Halborough. 'But 'twas raw spirit – ha, ha!'

'Why should you take me in so!' said Joshua, losing his self-command, try as he would to keep calm.

'Because you took me in, my lad, in banishing me to that cursed country under pretence that it was for my good. You were a pair of hypocrites to say so. It was done to get rid of me – no more nor less. But, by Jerry, I'm a match for ye now! I'll spoil your souls for preaching. My daughter is going to be married to the squire here. I've heard the news – I saw it in a paper!'

'It is premature – '

'I know it is true; and I'm her father, and I shall give her away, or there'll be a hell of a row, I can assure 'ee! Is that where the gennleman lives?'

Joshua Halborough writhed in impotent despair. Fellmer had not yet positively declared himself, his mother was hardly won round; a scene with their father in the parish would demolish as fair a palace of hopes as was ever builded. The millwright rose. 'If that's where the squire lives I'm going to call. Just arrived from Canady with her fortune – ha, ha! I wish no harm to the gennleman, and the gennleman will wish no harm to me. But I like to take my place in the family, and stand upon my rights, and lower people's pride!'

'You've succeeded already! Where's that woman you took with you – '

'Woman! She was my wife as lawful as the Constitution – a sight more lawful than your mother was till some time after you were born!'

Joshua had for many years before heard whispers that his father had cajoled his mother in their early acquaintance, and had made somewhat tardy amends; but never from his father's lips till now. It was the last stroke, and he could not bear it. He sank back against the hedge. 'It is over!' he said. 'He ruins us all!'

The millwright moved on, waving his stick triumphantly, and the two brothers stood still. They could see his drab figure stalking along the path, and over his head the lights from the conservatory of Narrobourne House, inside which Albert Fellmer might possibly be sitting with Rosa at that moment, holding her hand, and asking her to share his home with him.

The staggering whitey-brown form, advancing to put a blot on all this, had been diminishing in the shade; and now suddenly disappeared beside a weir. There was the noise of a flounce in the water.

'He has fallen in!' said Cornelius, starting forward to run for the place at which his father had vanished.

Joshua, awaking from the stupefied reverie into which he had sunk, rushed to the other's side before he had taken ten steps. 'Stop, stop, what are you thinking of?' he whispered hoarsely, grasping Cornelius's arm.

'Pulling him out!'

'Yes, yes – so am I. But – wait a moment – '

'But Joshua!'

'Her life and happiness, you know – Cornelius – and your reputation and mine – and our chance of rising together, all three – '

He clutched his brother's arm to the bone; and as they stood breathless the splashing and floundering in the weir continued; and over it they saw the hopeful lights from the manor-house conservatory winking through the trees as their bare branches

waved to and fro. In their pause there had been time
to save him twice over.

The floundering and splashing grew weaker, and
they could hear gurgling words: 'Help – I'm drownded!
Rosie – Rosie!'

'We'll go – we *must* save him. O Joshua!'

'Yes, yes! we must!'

Still they did not move, but waited, holding each
other, each thinking the same thought. Weights of lead
seemed to be affixed to their feet, which would no
longer obey their wills. The mead became silent. Over
it they fancied they could see figures moving in the
conservatory. The air up there seemed to emit gentle
kisses.

Cornelius started forward at last, and Joshua almost
simultaneously. Two or three minutes brought them
to the brink of the stream. At first they could see
nothing in the water, though it was not so deep nor the
night so dark but that their father's light kerseymere
coat would have been visible if he had lain at the
bottom. Joshua looked this way and that.

'He has drifted into the culvert,' he said.

Below the footbridge of the weir the stream suddenly narrowed to half its width, to pass under a
barrel arch or culvert constructed for wagons to cross
into the middle of the mead in haymaking time. It
being at present the season of high water the arch was
full to the crown, against which the ripples clucked
every now and then. At this point he had just caught
sight of a pale object slipping under. In a moment it
was gone.

They went to the lower end, but nothing emerged.
For a long time they tried at both ends to effect some
communication with the interior, but to no purpose.

'We ought to have come sooner!' said the conscience-stricken Cornelius, when they were quite exhausted, and dripping wet.

'I suppose we ought,' replied Joshua heavily. He perceived his father's walking-stick on the bank; hastily picking it up he stuck it into the mud among the sedge. Then he went on.

'Shall we – say anything about this accident?' whispered Cornelius as they approached the door of Joshua's house.

'What's the use? It can do no good. We must wait until he is found.'

They went indoors and changed their clothes; after which they started for the manor-house, reaching it about ten o'clock. Besides their sister there were only three guests; an adjoining landowner and his wife, and the infirm old rector.

Rosa, although she had parted from them so recently, grasped their hands in an ecstatic, brimming, joyful manner, as if she had not seen them for years. 'You look pale,' she said.

The brothers answered that they had had a long walk, and were somewhat tired. Everybody in the room seemed charged full with some sort of interesting knowledge: the squire's neighbour and neighbour's wife looked wisely around; and Fellmer himself played the part of host with a preoccupied bearing which approached fervour. They left at eleven, not accepting the carriage offered, the distance being so short and the roads dry. The squire came rather further into the dark with them than he need have done, and wished Rosa good-night in a mysterious manner, slightly apart from the rest.

When they were walking along Joshua said, with a

desperate attempt at joviality, 'Rosa, what's going on?'

'Oh, I – ' she began between a gasp and a titter. 'He – '

'Never mind – if it disturbs you.'

She was so excited that she could not speak connectedly at first, the practised air which she had brought home with her having disappeared. Calming herself she added, 'I am not disturbed, and nothing has happened. Only he said he wanted to ask me *something*, someday; and I said never mind that now. He hasn't asked yet, and is coming to speak to you about it. He would have done so tonight, only I asked him not to be in a hurry. But he will come tomorrow, I am sure!'

FIVE

It was summertime, six months later, and mowers and haymakers were at work in the meads. The manor-house, being opposite them, frequently formed a peg for conversation during these operations; and the doings of the squire, and the squire's young wife, the curate's sister – who was at present the admired of most of them, and the interest of all – met with their due amount of criticism.

Rosa was happy, if ever woman could be said to be so. She had not learnt the fate of her father, and sometimes wondered – perhaps with a sense of relief – why he did not write to her from his supposed home in Canada. Her brother Joshua had been presented to a living in a small town, shortly after her marriage, and Cornelius had thereupon succeeded to the vacant curacy of Narrobourne.

These two had awaited in deep suspense the discovery of their father's body; and yet the discovery had not been made. Every day they expected a man or a boy to run up from the meads with the intelligence; but he had never come. Days had accumulated to weeks and months; the wedding had come and gone; Joshua had tolled and read himself in at his new parish; and never a shout of amazement over the millwright's remains.

But now, in June, when they were mowing the meads, the hatches had to be drawn and the water let out of its channels for the convenience of the mowers. It was thus that the discovery was made. A man, stooping low with his scythe, caught a view of the culvert lengthwise, and saw something entangled in the recently bared weeds of its bed. A day or two after there was an inquest; but the body was unrecognisable. Fish and flood had been busy with the millwright; he had no watch or marked article which could be identified; and a verdict of the accidental drowning of a person unknown settled the matter.

As the body was found in Narrobourne parish, there it had to be buried. Cornelius wrote to Joshua, begging him to come and read the service, or to send someone; he himself could not do it. Rather than let in a stranger Joshua came, and silently scanned the coroner's order handed him by the undertaker –

'I, Henry Giles, Coroner for the Mid-Division of Outer Wessex, do hereby order the Burial of the Body now shown to the Inquest Jury as the Body of an Adult Male Person Unknown . . . . ' etc.

Joshua Halborough got through the service in some way, and rejoined his brother Cornelius at his house. Neither accepted an invitation to lunch at their sister's; they wished to discuss parish matters together. In the afternoon she came down, though they had already called on her, and had not expected to see her again. Her bright eyes, brown hair, flowery bonnet, lemon-coloured gloves, and flush beauty, were like an irradiation into the apartment, which they in their gloom could hardly bear.

'I forgot to tell you,' she said, 'of a curious thing which happened to me a month or two before my marriage – something which I have thought may have had a connection with the accident to the poor man you have buried today. It was on that evening I was at the manor-house waiting for you to fetch me; I was in the winter-garden with Albert, and we were sitting silent together, when we fancied we heard a cry in the distant meadow. We opened the door, and while Albert ran to fetch his hat, leaving me standing there, the cry was repeated, and my excited senses made me think I heard my own name. When Albert came back all was silent, and we decided that it was only a drunken shout, and not a cry for help. We both forgot the incident, and it never has occurred to me till since the funeral today that it might have been this stranger's cry. The name of course was only fancy, or he might have had a wife or child with a name something like mine, poor man!'

When she was gone the brothers were silent till Cornelius said, 'Now mark this, Joshua. Sooner or later she'll know.'

'How?'

'From one of us. Do you think human hearts are iron-cased safes, that you suppose we can keep this secret for ever?'

'Yes, I think they are, sometimes,' said Joshua.

'No. It will out. We shall tell.'

'What, and ruin her – kill her? Disgrace her children, and pull down the whole auspicious house of Fellmer about our ears? No! May I – drown where he was drowned before I do it! Never, never. Surely you can say the same, Cornelius!'

Cornelius seemed fortified, and no more was said. For a long time after that day he did not see Joshua, and before the next year was out a son and heir was born to the Fellmers. The villagers rang the three bells every evening for a week and more, and were made merry by Mr Fellmer's ale; and when the christening came on Joshua paid Narrobourne another visit.

Among all the people who assembled on that day the brother clergymen were the least interested. Their minds were haunted by a spirit in kerseymere. In the evening they walked together in the fields.

'She's all right,' said Joshua. 'But here are you doing journey-work, Cornelius, and likely to continue at it till the end of the day, as far as I can see. I, too, with my petty living – what am I after all? . . . To tell the truth, the Church is a poor forlorn hope for people without influence, particularly when their enthusiasm begins to flag. A social regenerator has a better chance outside, where he is unhampered by dogma and tradition. As for me, I would rather have gone on mending mills, with my crust of bread and liberty.'

Almost automatically they had bent their steps along the margin of the river; they now paused. They were standing on the brink of the well-known weir. There were the hatches, there was the culvert; they could see the pebbly bed of the stream through the pellucid water. The notes of the church-bells were audible, still jangled by the enthusiastic villagers.

'Why see – it was there I hid his walking-stick!' said

Joshua, looking towards the sedge. The next moment, during a passing breeze, something flashed white on the spot to which the attention of Cornelius was drawn.

From the sedge rose a straight little silver-poplar, and it was the leaves of this sapling which caused the flicker of whiteness.

'His walking-stick has grown!' Joshua added. 'It was a rough one – cut from the hedge, I remember.'

At every puff of wind the tree turned white, till they could not bear to look at it; and they walked away.

'I see him every night,' Cornelius murmured . . . 'Ah, we read our *Hebrews* to little account, Jos! Ὑπέμεινε σταυρὸν, αἰσχύνης καταφρονήσας. To have *endured* the cross, *despising* the shame – there lay greatness! But now I often feel that I should like to put an end to trouble here in this self-same spot.'

'I have thought of it myself,' said Joshua.

'Perhaps we shall, someday,' murmured his brother.

'Perhaps,' said Joshua moodily.

With that contingency to consider in the silence of their nights and days they bent their steps homewards.

December 1888

To Please his Wife

ONE

The interior of St James's Church, in Havenpool Town, was slowly darkening under the close clouds of a winter afternoon. It was Sunday: service had just ended, the face of the parson in the pulpit was buried in his hands, and the congregation, with a cheerful sigh of release, were rising from their knees to depart.

For the moment the stillness was so complete that the surging of the sea could be heard outside the harbour-bar. Then it was broken by the footsteps of the clerk going towards the west door to open it in the usual manner for the exit of the assembly. Before, however, he had reached the doorway, the latch was lifted from without, and the dark figure of a man in a sailor's garb appeared against the light.

The clerk stepped aside, the sailor closed the door gently behind him, and advanced up the nave till he stood at the chancel-step. The parson looked up from the private little prayer which, after so many for the parish, he quite fairly took for himself, rose to his feet, and stared at the intruder.

'I beg your pardon, sir,' said the sailor, addressing the minister in a voice distinctly audible to all the congregation. 'I have come here to offer thanks for my narrow escape from shipwreck. I am given to understand that it is a proper thing to do, if you have no objection?'

The parson, after a moment's pause, said hesitatingly, 'I have no objection; certainly. It is usual to mention any such wish before service, so that the proper words may be used in the General Thanksgiving. But, if you wish, we can read from the form for use after a storm at sea.'

'Ay, sure; I ain't particular,' said the sailor.

The clerk thereupon directed the sailor to the page in the prayer-book where the collect of thanksgiving would be found, and the rector began reading it, the sailor kneeling where he stood, and repeating it after him word by word in a distinct voice. The people, who had remained agape and motionless at the proceeding, mechanically knelt down likewise; but they continued to regard the isolated form of the sailor who, in the precise middle of the chancel-step, remained fixed on his knees, facing the east, his hat beside him, his hands joined, and he quite unconscious of his appearance in their regard.

When his thanksgiving had come to an end he rose; the people rose also; and all went out of church together. As soon as the sailor emerged, so that the remaining daylight fell upon his face, old inhabitants began to recognise him as no other than Shadrach Jolliffe, a young man who had not been seen at Havenpool for several years. A son of the town, his parents had died when he was quite young, on which account he had early gone to sea, in the Newfoundland trade.

He talked with this and that townsman as he walked, informing them that, since leaving his native place years before, he had become captain and owner of a small coasting-ketch, which had providentially been saved from the gale as well as himself. Presently he drew near to two girls who were going out of the churchyard in front of him; they had been sitting in the nave at his entry, and had watched his doings with deep interest, afterwards discussing him as they moved out of church together. One was a slight and gentle creature, the other a tall, large-framed, deliberative girl. Captain Jolliffe regarded the loose curls of their hair, their backs and shoulders, down to their heels, for some time.

'Who may them two maids be?' he whispered to his neighbour.

'The little one is Emily Hanning; the tall one Joanna Phippard.'

'Ah! I recollect 'em now, to be sure.'

He advanced to their elbow, and genially stole a gaze at them.

'Emily, you don't know me?' said the sailor, turning his beaming brown eyes on her.

'I think I do, Mr Jolliffe,' said Emily shyly.

The other girl looked straight at him with her dark eyes.

'The face of Miss Joanna I don't call to mind so well,' he continued. 'But I know her beginnings and kindred.'

They walked and talked together, Jolliffe narrating particulars of his late narrow escape, till they reached the corner of Sloop Lane, in which Emily Hanning dwelt, when, with a nod and smile, she left them. Soon the sailor parted also from Joanna, and, having no especial errand or appointment, turned back towards Emily's house. She lived with her father, who called himself an accountant, the daughter, however, keeping a little stationery-shop as a supplemental provision for the gaps of his somewhat uncertain business. On entering Jolliffe found father and daughter about to begin tea.

'Oh, I didn't know it was teatime,' he said. 'Ay, I'll have a cup with much pleasure.'

He remained to tea and long afterwards, telling more tales of his seafaring life. Several neighbours called to listen, and were asked to come in. Somehow Emily Hanning lost her heart to the sailor that Sunday night, and in the course of a week or two there was a tender understanding between them.

One moonlight evening in the next month Shadrach was ascending out of the town by the long straight road eastward, to an elevated suburb where the more fashionable houses stood – if anything near this ancient port could be called fashionable – when he saw a figure before him whom, from her manner of glancing back, he took to be Emily. But, on coming up, he found she was Joanna Phippard. He gave a gallant greeting, and walked beside her.

'Go along,' she said, 'or Emily will be jealous!'

He seemed not to like the suggestion, and remained. What was said and what was done on that walk never could be clearly recollected by Shadrach; but in some way or other Joanna contrived to wean him away from her gentler and younger rival. From that week onwards, Jolliffe was seen more and more in the wake of Joanna Phippard and less in the company of Emily; and it was soon rumoured about the quay that old Jolliffe's son, who had come home from sea, was going to be married to the former young woman, to the great disappointment of the latter.

Just after this report had gone about, Joanna dressed herself for a walk one morning, and started for Emily's house in the little cross-street. Intelligence of the deep sorrow of her friend on account of the loss of Shadrach had reached her ears also, and her conscience reproached her for winning him away.

Joanna was not altogether satisfied with the sailor. She liked his attentions, and she coveted the dignity of matrimony; but she had never been deeply in love with Jolliffe. For one thing, she was ambitious, and socially his position was hardly so good as her own, and there was always the chance of an attractive woman mating considerably above her. It had long been in her mind that she would not strongly object to give him back again to Emily if her friend felt so very badly about him. To this end she had written a letter of renunciation to Shadrach, which letter she carried in her hand, intending to send it if personal observation of Emily convinced her that her friend was suffering.

Joanna entered Sloop Lane and stepped down into the stationery-shop, which was below the pavement level. Emily's father was never at home at this hour of the day, and it seemed as though Emily were not at home either, for the visitor could make nobody hear. Customers came so seldom hither that a five minutes' absence of the proprietor counted for little. Joanna waited in the little shop, where Emily had tastefully set out – as women can – articles in themselves of slight value, so as to obscure the meagreness of the stock-in-trade; till she saw a figure pausing without the window apparently absorbed in the contemplation of the six-penny books, packets of paper, and prints hung on a string. It was Captain Shadrach Jolliffe, peering in to ascertain if Emily were there alone. Moved by an impulse of reluctance to meet him in a spot which breathed of Emily, Joanna slipped through the door that communicated with the parlour at the back. She had frequently done so before, for in her friendship with Emily she had the freedom of the house without ceremony.

Jolliffe entered the shop. Through the thin blind which screened the glass partition she could see that he was disappointed at not finding Emily there. He was about to go out again, when Emily's form darkened the doorway, hastening home from some errand. At sight of Jolliffe she started back as if she would have gone out again.

'Don't run away, Emily; don't!' said he. 'What can make 'ee afraid?'

'I'm not afraid, Captain Jolliffe. Only – only I saw you all of a sudden, and – it made me jump!' Her voice showed that her heart had jumped even more than the rest of her.

'I just called as I was passing,' he said.

'For some paper?' She hastened behind the counter.

'No, no, Emily; why do you get behind there? Why not stay by me? You seem to hate me.'

'I don't hate you. How can I?'

'Then come out, so that we can talk like Christians.'

Emily obeyed with a fitful laugh, till she stood again beside him in the open part of the shop.

'There's a dear,' he said.

'You mustn't say that, Captain Jolliffe; because the words belong to somebody else.'

'Ah! I know what you mean. But, Emily, upon my life I didn't know till this morning that you cared one bit about me, or I should not have done as I have done. I have the best of feelings for Joanna, but I know that from the beginning she hasn't cared for me more than in a friendly way; and I see now the one I ought to have asked to be my wife. You know, Emily, when a man comes home from sea after a long voyage he's as blind as a bat – he can't see who's who in women. They are all alike to him, beautiful creatures, and he takes the first that comes easy, without thinking if she loves him, or if he might not soon love another better than her. From the first I inclined to you most, but you were so backward and shy that I thought you didn't want me to bother 'ee, and so I went to Joanna.'

'Don't say any more, Mr Jolliffe, don't!' said she, choking. 'You are going to marry Joanna next month, and it is wrong to – to –'

'Oh, Emily, my darling!' he cried, and clasped her little figure in his arms before she was aware.

Joanna, behind the curtain, turned pale, tried to withdraw her eyes, but could not.

'It is only you I love as a man ought to love the woman he is going to marry; and I know this from what Joanna has said, that she will willingly let me off! She wants to marry higher I know, and only said "Yes" to me out of kindness. A fine, tall girl like her isn't the sort for a plain sailor's wife: you be the best suited for that.'

He kissed her and kissed her again, her flexible form quivering in the agitation of his embrace.

'I wonder – are you sure – Joanna is going to break off with you? Oh, are you sure? Because –'

'I know she would not wish to make us miserable. She will release me.'

'Oh, I hope – I hope she will! Don't stay any longer, Captain Jolliffe!'

He lingered, however, till a customer came for a penny stick of sealing-wax, and then he withdrew.

Green envy had overspread Joanna at the scene. She looked about for a way of escape. To get out without Emily's knowledge of her visit was indispensable. She crept from the parlour into the passage, and thence to the back door of the house, where she let herself noiselessly into the street.

The sight of that caress had reversed all her resolutions. She could not let Shadrach go. Reaching home she burnt the letter, and told her mother that if Captain Jolliffe called she was too unwell to see him.

Shadrach, however, did not call: he sent her a note expressing in simple language the state of his feelings; and asked to be allowed to take advantage of the hints she had given him that her affection, too, was little more than friendly, by cancelling the engagement.

Looking out upon the harbour and the island beyond he waited and waited in his lodgings for an answer that did not come. The suspense grew to be so intolerable that after dark he went up the High Street. He could not resist calling at Joanna's to learn his fate.

Her mother said her daughter was too unwell to see him, and to his questioning admitted that it was in consequence of a letter received from himself, which had distressed her deeply.

'You know what it was about, perhaps, Mrs Phippard?' he said.

Mrs Phippard owned that she did, adding that it put them in a very painful position. Thereupon Shadrach, fearing that he had been guilty of an enormity, explained that if his letter had pained Joanna it must be owing to a misunderstanding, since he had thought it would be a relief to her. If otherwise, he would hold himself bound by his word, and she was to think of the letter as never having been written.

Next morning he received an oral message from the young woman, asking him to fetch her home from a meeting that evening. This he did, and while walking from the Town Hall to her door, with her hand in his arm, she said: 'It is all the same as before between us, isn't it, Shadrach? Your letter was sent in mistake?'

'It is all the same as before,' he answered, 'if you say it must be.'

'I wish it to be,' she murmured, with hard lineaments, as she thought of Emily.

Shadrach was a religious and scrupulous man, who respected his word as his life. Shortly afterwards the wedding took place, Jolliffe having conveyed to Emily as gently as possible the error he had fallen into when estimating Joanna's mood as one of indifference.

TWO

A month after the marriage Joanna's mother died, and the couple were obliged to turn their attention to very practical matters. Now that she was left without a parent, Joanna could not bear the notion of her husband going to sea again, but the question was, What could he do at home? They finally decided to take on a small grocer's shop in the High Street, the goodwill and stock of which were waiting to be disposed of at that time. Shadrach knew nothing of shopkeeping, and Joanna very little, but they hoped to learn.

To the management of this grocery business they now devoted all their energies, and continued to conduct it for many succeeding years, without great success. Two sons were born to them, whom their mother loved to idolatry, although she had never passionately loved her husband; and she lavished upon them all her forethought and care. But the shop did not thrive, and the large dreams she had entertained of her sons' education and career became attenuated in the face of realities. Their schooling was of the plainest, but, being by the sea, they grew alert in all such nautical arts and enterprises as were attractive to their age.

The great interest of the Jolliffes' married life, outside their own immediate household, had lain in the marriage of Emily. By one of those odd chances which lead those that lurk in unexpected corners to be discovered, while the obvious are passed by, the gentle girl had been seen and loved by a thriving merchant of the town, a widower, some years older than herself, though still in the prime of life. At first Emily had declared that she never, never could marry anyone; but Mr Lester had quietly persevered, and had at last won her reluctant assent. Two children also were the fruits of this union, and, as they grew and prospered, Emily declared that she had never supposed that she could live to be so happy.

The worthy merchant's home, one of those large, substantial brick mansions frequently jammed up in old-fashioned towns, faced directly on the High Street, nearly opposite to the grocery shop of the Jolliffes, and it now became the pain of Joanna to behold the woman whose place she had usurped out of pure covetousness, looking down from her position of comparative wealth upon the humble shop-window with its dusty sugar-loaves, heaps of raisins, and canisters of tea, over which it was her own lot to preside. The business having so dwindled, Joanna was obliged to serve in the shop herself, and it galled and mortified her that Emily Lester, sitting in her large drawing-room over the way, could witness her own dancings up and down behind the counter at the beck and call of wretched twopenny customers, whose patronage she was driven to welcome gladly: persons to whom she was compelled to be civil in the street, while Emily was bounding along with her children and her governess, and conversing with the genteelest people of the town and neighbourhood. This was what she had gained by not letting Shadrach Jolliffe, whom she had so faintly loved, carry his affection elsewhere.

Shadrach was a good and honest man, and he had been faithful to her in heart and in deed. Time had clipped the wings of his love for Emily in his devotion to the mother of his boys: he had quite lived down that impulsive earlier fancy, and Emily had become in his regard nothing more than a friend. It was the same with Emily's feelings for him. Possibly, had she found the least cause for jealousy, Joanna would almost have been better satisfied. It was in the absolute acquiescence of Emily and Shadrach in the results she herself had contrived that her discontent found nourishment.

Shadrach was not endowed with the narrow shrewdness necessary for developing a retail business in the face of many competitors. Did a customer enquire if the grocer could really recommend the wondrous substitute for eggs which a persevering bagman had forced into his stock, he would answer that 'when you did not put eggs into a pudding it was difficult to taste them there'; and when he was asked if his 'real Mocha coffee' was real Mocha, he would say grimly, 'as understood in small shops'. The way to wealth was not by this route.

One summer day, when the big brick house opposite

was reflecting the oppressive sun's heat into the shop, and nobody was present but husband and wife, Joanna looked across at Emily's door, where a wealthy visitor's carriage had drawn up. Traces of patronage had been visible in Emily's manner of late.

'Shadrach, the truth is, you are not a businessman,' his wife sadly murmured. 'You were not brought up to shopkeeping, and it is impossible for a man to make a fortune at an occupation he has jumped into, as you did into this.'

Jolliffe agreed with her, in this as in everything else. 'Not that I care a rope's end about making a fortune,' he said cheerfully. 'I am happy enough, and we can rub on somehow.'

She looked again at the great house through the screen of bottled pickles.

'Rub on – yes,' she said bitterly. 'But see how well off Emmy Lester is, who used to be so poor! Her boys will go to College, no doubt; and think of yours – obliged to go to the Parish School!'

Shadrach's thoughts had flown to Emily.

'Nobody,' he said good-humouredly, 'ever did Emily a better turn than you did, Joanna, when you warned her off me and put an end to that little simpering nonsense between us, so as to leave it in her power to say "Aye" to Lester when he came along.'

This almost maddened her.

'Don't speak of bygones!' she implored, in stern sadness. 'But think, for the boys' and my sake, if not for your own, what are we to do to get richer?'

'Well,' he said, becoming serious, 'to tell the truth, I have always felt myself unfit for this business, though I've never liked to say so. I seem to want more room for sprawling; a more open space to strike out in than here

72

among friends and neighbours. I could get rich as well as any man, if I tried my own way.'

'I wish you would! What is your way?'

'To go to sea again.'

She had been the very one to keep him at home, hating the semi-widowed existence of sailors' wives. But her ambition checked her instincts now, and she said: 'Do you think success really lies that way?'

'I am sure it lies in no other.'

'Do you want to go, Shadrach?'

'Not for the pleasure of it, I can tell 'ee. There's no such pleasure at sea, Joanna, as I can find in my back parlour here. To speak honest, I have no love for the brine. I never had much. But if it comes to a question of a fortune for you and the lads, it is another thing. That's the only way to it for one born and bred a seafarer as I.'

'Would it take long to earn?'

'Well, that depends; perhaps not.'

The next morning Shadrach pulled from a chest of drawers the nautical jacket he had worn during the first months of his return, brushed out the moths, donned it, and walked down to the quay. The port still did a fair business in the Newfoundland trade, though not so much as formerly.

It was not long after this that he invested all he possessed in purchasing a part-ownership in a brig, of which he was appointed captain. A few months were passed in coast-trading, during which interval Shadrach wore off the land-rust that had accumulated upon him in his grocery phase; and in the spring the brig sailed for Newfoundland.

Joanna lived on at home with her sons, who were now growing up into strong lads, and occupying themselves in various ways about the harbour and quay.

'Never mind, let them work a little,' their fond mother said to herself. 'Our necessities compel it now, but when Shadrach comes home they will be only seventeen and eighteen, and they shall be removed from the port, and their education thoroughly taken in hand by a tutor; and with the money they'll have they will perhaps be as near to gentlemen as Emmy Lester's precious two, with their algebra and their Latin!'

The date for Shadrach's return drew near and arrived, and he did not appear. Joanna was assured that there was no cause for anxiety, sailing-ships being so uncertain in their coming; which assurance proved to be well grounded, for late one wet evening, about a month after the calculated time, the ship was announced as at hand, and presently the slip-slop step of Shadrach as the sailor sounded in the passage, and he entered. The boys had gone out and had missed him, and Joanna was sitting alone.

As soon as the first emotion of reunion between the couple had passed, Jolliffe explained the delay as owing to a small speculative contract, which had produced good results.

'I was determined not to disappoint 'ee,' he said; 'and I think you'll own that I haven't!'

With this he pulled out an enormous canvas bag, full and rotund as the money-bag of the giant whom Jack slew, untied it, and shook the contents out into her lap as she sat in her low chair by the fire. A mass of sovereigns and guineas (there were guineas on the earth in those days) fell into her lap with a sudden thud, weighing down her gown to the floor.

'There!' said Shadrach complacently. 'I told 'ee, dear, I'd do it; and have I done it or no?'

Somehow her face, after the first excitement of possession, did not retain its glory.

'It is a lot of gold, indeed,' she said. 'And – is this *all*?'

'All? Why, dear Joanna, do you know you can count to three hundred in that heap? It is a fortune!'

'Yes – yes. A fortune – judged by sea; but judged by land – '

However, she banished considerations of the money for the nonce. Soon the boys came in, and next Sunday Shadrach returned thanks to God – this time by the more ordinary channel of the italics in the General Thanksgiving. But a few days after, when the question of investing the money arose, he remarked that she did not seem so satisfied as he had hoped.

'Well you see, Shadrach,' she answered, '*we* count by hundreds; *they* count by thousands' (nodding towards the other side of the street). 'They have set up a carriage and pair since you left.'

'Oh, have they?'

'My dear Shadrach, you don't know how the world moves. However, we'll do the best we can with it. But they are rich, and we are poor still!'

The greater part of a year was desultorily spent. She moved sadly about the house and shop, and the boys were still occupying themselves in and around the harbour.

'Joanna,' he said, one day, 'I see by your movements that it is not enough.'

'It is not enough,' said she. 'My boys will have to live by steering the ships that the Lesters own; and I was once above her!'

Jolliffe was not an argumentative man, and he only

murmured that he thought he would make another voyage. He meditated for several days, and coming home from the quay one afternoon said suddenly: 'I could do it for 'ee, dear, in one more trip, for certain, if – if – '

'Do what, Shadrach?'

'Enable 'ee to count by thousands instead of hundreds.'

'If what?'

'If I might take the boys.'

She turned pale.

'Don't say that, Shadrach,' she answered hastily.

'Why?'

'I don't like to hear it! There's danger at sea. I want them to be something genteel, and no danger to them. I couldn't let them risk their lives at sea. Oh, I couldn't ever, ever!'

'Very well, dear, it shan't be done.'

Next day, after a silence, she asked a question: 'If they were to go with you it would make a great deal of difference, I suppose, to the profit?'

' 'Twould treble what I should get from the venture single-handed. Under my eye they would be as good as two more of myself.'

Later on she said: 'Tell me more about this.'

'Well, the boys are almost as clever as master-mariners in handling a craft, upon my life! There isn't a more cranky place in the Northern Seas than about the sandbanks of this harbour, and they've practised here from their infancy. And they are so steady. I couldn't get their steadiness and their trustworthiness in half a dozen men twice their age.'

'And is it *very* dangerous at sea; now, too, there are rumours of war?' she asked uneasily.

'Oh, well, there be risks. Still . . . '

The idea grew and magnified, and the mother's heart was crushed and stifled by it. Emmy was growing *too* patronising; it could not be borne. Shadrach's wife could not help nagging him about their comparative poverty. The young men, amiable as their father, when spoken to on the subject of a voyage of enterprise, were quite willing to embark; and though they, like their father, had no great love for the sea, they became quite enthusiastic when the proposal was detailed.

Everything now hung upon their mother's assent. She withheld it long, but at last gave the word: the young men might accompany their father. Shadrach was unusually cheerful about it: Heaven had preserved him hitherto, and he had uttered his thanks. God would not forsake those who were faithful to him.

All that the Jolliffes possessed in the world was put into the enterprise. The grocery stock was pared down to the least that possibly could afford a bare sustenance to Joanna during the absence, which was to last through the usual 'New-f'nland spell'. How she would endure the weary time she hardly knew, for the boys had been with her formerly; but she nerved herself for the trial.

The ship was laden with boots and shoes, ready-made clothing, fishing-tackle, butter, cheese, cordage, sailcloth, and many other commodities; and was to bring back oil, furs, skins, fish, cranberries, and what else came to hand. But much speculative trading to other ports was to be undertaken between the voyages out and homeward, and thereby much money made.

The brig sailed on a Monday morning in spring; but Joanna did not witness its departure. She could not bear the sight that she had been the means of bringing about. Knowing this, her husband told her overnight that they were to sail sometime before noon next day; hence when, awakening at five the next morning, she heard them bustling about downstairs, she did not hasten to descend, but lay trying to nerve herself for the parting, imagining they would leave about nine, as her husband had done on his previous voyage. When she did descend she beheld words chalked upon the sloping face of the bureau; but no husband or sons. In the hastily-scrawled lines Shadrach said they had gone off thus not to pain her by a leave-taking; and the sons had chalked under his words: 'Goodbye, mother!'

She rushed to the quay, and looked down the harbour towards the blue rim of the sea, but she could only see the masts and bulging sails of the *Joanna*; no human figures. ' 'Tis I have sent them!' she said wildly, and burst into tears. In the house the chalked 'Goodbye' nearly broke her heart. But when she had re-entered the front room, and looked across at Emily's, a gleam of triumph lit her thin face at her anticipated release from the thraldom of subservience.

To do Emily Lester justice, her assumption of superiority was mainly a figment of Joanna's brain. That the circumstances of the merchant's wife were more luxurious than Joanna's, the former could not conceal; though whenever the two met, which was not very often now, Emily endeavoured to subdue the difference by every means in her power.

The first summer lapsed away; and Joanna meagrely maintained herself by the shop, which now consisted of little more than a window and a counter. Emily was, in truth, her only large customer; and Mrs Lester's kindly readiness to buy anything and everything without questioning the quality had a sting of bitterness in it, for it was the uncritical attitude of a patron, and almost of a donor. The long dreary winter moved on; the face of the bureau had been turned to the wall to protect the chalked words of farewell, for Joanna could never bring herself to rub them out; and she often glanced at them with wet eyes. Emily's handsome boys came home for the Christmas holidays; the University was talked of for them; and still Joanna subsisted as it were with held breath, like a person submerged. Only one summer more, and the 'spell' would end. Towards the close of the time Emily called on her quondam friend. She had heard that Joanna began to feel anxious; she had received no letter from husband or sons for some months. Emily's silks rustled arrogantly when, in response to Joanna's almost dumb invitation, she squeezed through the opening of the counter and into the parlour behind the shop.

'*You* are all success, and *I* am all the other way!' said Joanna.

'But why do you think so?' said Emily. 'They are to bring back a fortune, I hear.'

'Ah! will they come? The doubt is more than a woman can bear. All three in one ship – think of that! And I have not heard of them for months!'

'But the time is not up. You should not meet misfortune halfway.'

79

'Nothing will repay me for the grief of their absence!'

'Then why did you let them go? You were doing fairly well.'

'I *made* them go!' she said, turning vehemently upon Emily. 'And I'll tell you why! I could not bear that we should be only muddling on, and you so rich and thriving! Now I have told you, and you may hate me if you will!'

'I shall never hate you, Joanna.'

And she proved the truth of her words afterwards. The end of autumn came, and the brig should have been in port; but nothing like the *Joanna* appeared in the channel between the sands. It was now really time to be uneasy. Joanna Jolliffe sat by the fire, and every gust of wind caused her a cold thrill. She had always feared and detested the sea; to her it was a treacherous, restless, slimy creature, glorying in the griefs of women. 'Still,' she said, 'they *must* come!'

She recalled to her mind that Shadrach had said before starting that if they returned safe and sound, with success crowning their enterprise, he would go as he had gone after his shipwreck, and kneel with his sons in the church, and offer sincere thanks for their deliverance. She went to church regularly morning and afternoon, and sat in the most forward pew, nearest the chancel-step. Her eyes were mostly fixed on that step, where Shadrach had knelt in the bloom of his young manhood: she knew to an inch the spot which his knees had pressed twenty winters before; his outline as he had knelt, his hat on the step beside him. God was good. Surely her husband must kneel there again: a son on each side as he had said; George just here, Jim just there. By long watching the spot as she worshipped, it became as if she saw the three returned ones there kneeling; the two slim outlines of her boys, the more bulky form between them; their hands clasped, their heads shaped against the eastern wall. The fancy grew almost to an hallucination: she could never turn her worn eyes to the step without seeing them there.

Nevertheless they did not come. Heaven was merciful, but it was not yet pleased to relieve her soul. This was her purgation for the sin of making them the slaves of her ambition. But it became more than purgation soon, and her mood approached despair. Months had passed since the brig had been due, but it had not returned.

Joanna was always hearing or seeing evidences of their arrival. When on the hill behind the port, whence a view of the open Channel could be obtained, she felt sure that a little speck on the horizon, breaking the eternally level waste of waters southward, was the truck of the *Joanna*'s mainmast. Or when indoors, a shout or excitement of any kind at the corner of the Town Cellar, where the High Street joined the Quay, caused her to spring to her feet and cry: ' 'Tis they!'

But it was not. The visionary forms knelt every Sunday afternoon on the chancel-step, but not the real. Her shop had, as it were, eaten itself hollow. In the apathy which had resulted from her loneliness and grief she had ceased to take in the smallest supplies, and thus had sent away her last customer.

In this strait Emily Lester tried by every means in her power to aid the afflicted woman; but she met with constant repulses.

'I don't like you! I can't bear to see you!' Joanna would whisper hoarsely when Emily came to her and made advances.

'But I want to help and soothe you, Joanna,' Emily would say.

'You are a lady, with a rich husband and fine sons! What can you want with a bereaved crone like me!'

'Joanna, I want this: I want you to come and live in my house, and not stay alone in this dismal place any longer.'

'And suppose they come and don't find me at home? You wish to separate me and mine! No, I'll stay here. I don't like you, and I can't thank you, whatever kindness you do me!'

However, as time went on Joanna could not afford to pay the rent of the shop and house without an income. She was assured that all hope of the return of Shadrach and his sons was vain, and she reluctantly consented to accept the asylum of the Lesters' house. Here she was allotted a room of her own on the second floor, and went and came as she chose, without contact with the family. Her hair greyed and whitened, deep lines channelled her forehead, and her form grew gaunt and stooping. But she still expected the lost ones, and when she met Emily on the staircase she would say morosely: 'I know why you've got me here! They'll come, and be disappointed at not finding me at home, and perhaps go away again; and then you'll be revenged for my taking Shadrach away from 'ee!'

Emily Lester bore these reproaches from the grief-stricken soul. She was sure – all the people of Haven-pool were sure – that Shadrach and his sons had gone to the bottom. For years the vessel had been given up as lost. Nevertheless, when awakened at night by any noise, Joanna would rise from bed and glance at the shop opposite by the light from the flickering lamp, to make sure it was not they.

It was a damp and dark December night, six years after the departure of the brig *Joanna*. The wind was from the sea, and brought up a fishy mist which mopped the face like moist flannel. Joanna had prayed her usual prayer for the absent ones with more fervour and confidence than she had felt for months, and had fallen asleep about eleven. It must have been between one and two when she suddenly started up. She had certainly heard steps in the street, and the voices of Shadrach and her sons calling at the door of the grocery shop. She sprang out of bed, and, hardly knowing what clothing she dragged on herself, hastened down Emily's large and carpeted staircase, put the candle on the hall-table, unfastened the bolts and chain, and stepped into the street. The mist, blowing up the street from the Quay, hindered her seeing the shop, although it was so near; but she had crossed to it in a moment. How was it? Nobody stood there. The wretched woman walked wildly up and down with her bare feet – there was not a soul. She returned and knocked with all her might at the door which had once been her own – they might have been admitted for the night, unwilling to disturb her till the morning. It was not till several minutes had elapsed that the young man who now kept the shop looked out of an upper window, and saw the skeleton of something human standing below half-dressed.

'Has anybody come?' asked the form.

'Oh, Mrs Jolliffe, I didn't know it was you,' said the young man kindly, for he was aware how her baseless expectations moved her. 'No; nobody has come.'

June 1891

83

The Fiddler of the Reels

'Talking of Exhibitions, World's Fairs, and what not,' said the old gentleman, 'I would not go round the corner to see a dozen of them nowadays. The only exhibition that ever made, or ever will make, any impression upon my imagination was the first of the series, the parent of them all, and now a thing of old times – the Great Exhibition of 1851, in Hyde Park, London. None of the younger generation can realise the sense of novelty it produced in us who were then in our prime. A noun substantive went so far as to become an adjective in honour of the occasion. It was "exhibition" hat, "exhibition" razor-strop, "exhibition" watch; nay, even "exhibition" weather, "exhibition" spirits, sweethearts, babies, wives – for the time.

'For South Wessex, the year formed in many ways an extraordinary chronological frontier or transit-line, at which there occurred what one might call a precipice in Time. As in a geological "fault", we had presented to us a sudden bringing of ancient and modern into absolute contact, such as probably in no other single year since the Conquest was ever witnessed in this part of the country.'

These observations led us onward to talk of the different personages, gentle and simple, who lived and moved within our narrow and peaceful horizon at that time; and of three people in particular, whose queer little history was oddly touched at points by the Exhibition, more concerned with it than that of

85

anybody else who dwelt in those outlying shades of the world, Stickleford, Mellstock, and Egdon. First in prominence among these three came Wat Ollamoor – if that were his real name – whom the seniors in our party had known well.

He was a woman's man, they said, – supremely so – externally little else. To men he was not attractive; perhaps a little repulsive at times. Musician, dandy, and company-man in practice; veterinary surgeon in theory, he lodged awhile in Mellstock village, coming from nobody knew where; though some said his first appearance in this neighbourhood had been as fiddle-player in a show at Greenhill Fair.

Many a worthy villager envied him his power over unsophisticated maidenhood – a power which seemed sometimes to have a touch of the weird and wizardly in it. Personally he was not ill-favoured, though rather un-English, his complexion being a rich olive, his rank hair dark and rather clammy – made still clammier by secret ointments, which, when he came fresh to a party, caused him to smell like 'boys'-love' (southernwood) steeped in lamp-oil. On occasion he wore curls – a double row – running almost horizontally around his head. But as these were sometimes noticeably absent, it was concluded that they were not altogether of nature's making. By girls whose love for him had turned to hatred he had been nicknamed 'Mop', from this abundance of hair, which was long enough to rest upon his shoulders; as time passed the name more and more prevailed.

His fiddling possibly had the most to do with the fascination he exercised, for, to speak fairly, it could claim for itself a most peculiar and personal quality, like that in a moving preacher. There were tones in it which bred the immediate conviction that indolence and averseness to systematic application were all that lay between 'Mop' and the career of a second Paganini.

While playing he invariably closed his eyes; using no notes, and, as it were, allowing the violin to wander on at will into the most plaintive passages ever heard by rustic man. There was a certain lingual character in the supplicatory expressions he produced, which would well-nigh have drawn an ache from the heart of a gatepost. He could make any child in the parish, who was at all sensitive to music, burst into tears in a few minutes by simply fiddling one of the old dance-tunes he almost entirely affected – country jigs, reels, and 'Favourite Quick Steps' of the last century – some mutilated remains of which even now reappear as nameless phantoms in new quadrilles and gallops, where they are recognised only by the curious, or by such old-fashioned and far-between people as have been thrown with men like Wat Ollamoor in their early life.

His date was a little later than that of the old Mellstock quire-band which comprised the Dewys, Mail, and the rest – in fact, he did not rise above the horizon thereabout till those well-known musicians were disbanded as ecclesiastical functionaries. In their honest love of thoroughness they despised the new man's style. Theophilus Dewy (Reuben the tranter's younger brother) used to say there was no 'plumness' in it – no bowing, no solidity – it was all fantastical. And probably this was true. Anyhow, Mop had, very obviously, never bowed a note of church-music from his birth; he never once sat in the gallery of Mellstock church where the others had tuned their venerable psalmody so many hundreds of times; had never, in all likelihood, entered a church at all. All were devil's tunes in his repertory. 'He could no more play the Wold Hundredth to his true time than he could play the brazen serpent,' the tranter would say. (The brazen serpent was supposed in Mellstock to be a musical instrument particularly hard to blow.)

Occasionally Mop could produce the aforesaid moving effect upon the souls of grown-up persons, especially young women of fragile and responsive organisation. Such an one was Car'line Aspent. Though she was already engaged to be married before she met him, Car'line, of them all, was the most influenced by Mop Ollamoor's heart-stealing melodies, to her discomfort, nay, positive pain and ultimate injury. She was a pretty, invocating, weak-mouthed girl, whose chief defect as a companion with her sex was a tendency to peevishness now and then. At this time she was not a resident in Mellstock parish where Mop lodged, but lived some miles off at Stickleford, further down the river.

How and where she first made acquaintance with him and his fiddling is not truly known, but the story was that it either began or was developed on one spring evening, when, in passing through Lower Mellstock, she chanced to pause on the bridge near his house to rest herself, and languidly leaned over the parapet. Mop was standing on his doorstep, as was his custom, spinning the insidious thread of semi- and demi-semiquavers from the E string of his fiddle for the benefit of passers-by, and laughing as the tears rolled down the cheeks of the little children hanging around him. Car'line pretended to be engrossed with the rippling of the stream under the arches, but in reality she was listening, as he knew. Presently the aching of the heart seized her simultaneously with a wild desire to glide airily in the mazes of an infinite dance. To shake off the fascination she resolved to go on, although it would be necessary to pass him as he played. On stealthily glancing ahead at the performer, she found to her relief that his eyes were closed in abandonment to instrumentation, and she strode on boldly. But when closer her step grew timid, her tread convulsed itself more and more accordingly with the time of the melody, till she very nearly danced along. Gaining another glance at him when immediately opposite, she saw that *one* of his eyes was open, quizzing her as he smiled at her emotional state. Her gait could not divest itself of its compelled capers till she had gone a long way past the house; and Car'line was unable to shake off the strange infatuation for hours.

After that day, whenever there was to be in the neighbourhood a dance to which she could get an invitation, and where Mop Ollamoor was to be the musician, Car'line contrived to be present, though it sometimes involved a walk of several miles; for he did not play so often in Stickleford as elsewhere.

The next evidences of his influence over her were singular enough, and it would require a neurologist to fully explain them. She would be sitting quietly, any evening after dark, in the house of her father, the parish clerk, which stood in the middle of Stickleford village street, this being the highroad between Lower Mellstock and Moreford, five miles eastward. Here, without a moment's warning, and in the midst of a general conversation between her father, sister, and the young man before alluded to, who devotedly wooed her in ignorance of her infatuation, she would start from her seat in the chimney-corner as if she had received a galvanic shock, and spring convulsively towards the ceiling; then she would burst into tears, and it was not till some half-hour had passed that she grew calm as usual. Her father, knowing her hysterical tendencies, was always excessively anxious about this trait in his youngest girl, and feared the attack to be a species of epileptic fit. Not so her sister Julia. Julia had found out what was the cause. At the moment before the jumping, only an exceptionally sensitive ear situated in the chimney-nook could have caught from down the flue the beat of a man's footstep along the highway without. But it was in that footfall, for which she had been waiting, that the origin of Car'line's involuntary springing lay. The pedestrian was Mop Ollamoor, as the girl well knew; but his business that way was not to visit her; he sought another woman whom he spoke of as his Intended, and who lived at Moreford, two miles further on. On one, and only one, occasion did it happen that Car'line could not control her utterance; it was when her sister alone chanced to be present. 'Oh – Oh – Oh – !' she cried. 'He's going to *her*, and not coming to *me*!'

To do the fiddler justice he had not at first thought greatly of, or spoken much to, this girl of impressionable mould. But he had soon found out her secret, and could not resist a little by-play with her too easily hurt heart, as an interlude between his more serious lovemakings at Moreford. The two became well acquainted, though only by stealth, hardly a soul in Stickleford except her sister, and her lover Ned Hipcroft, being aware of the attachment. Her father disapproved of her coldness to

Ned; her sister, too, hoped she might get over this nervous passion for a man of whom so little was known. The ultimate result was that Car'line's manly and simple wooer Edward found his suit becoming practically hopeless. He was a respectable mechanic, in a far sounder position than Mop the nominal horse-doctor; but when, before leaving her, Ned put his flat and final question, would she marry him, then and there, now or never, it was with little expectation of obtaining more than the negative she gave him. Though her father supported him and her sister supported him, he could not play the fiddle so as to draw your soul out of your body like a spider's thread, as Mop did, till you felt as limp as withywind and yearned for something to cling to. Indeed, Hipcroft had not the slightest ear for music; could not sing two notes in tune, much less play them.

The No he had expected and got from her, in spite of a preliminary encouragement, gave Ned a new start in life. It had been uttered in such a tone of sad entreaty that he resolved to persecute her no more; she should not even be distressed by a sight of his form in the distant perspective of the street and lane. He left the place, and his natural course was to London.

The railway to South Wessex was in process of construction, but it was not as yet opened for traffic; and Hipcroft reached the capital by a six days' trudge on foot, as many a better man had done before him. He was one of the last of the artisan class who used that now extinct method of travel to the great centres of labour, so customary then from time immemorial.

In London he lived and worked regularly at his trade. More fortunate than many, his disinterested willingness recommended him from the first. During the ensuing four years he was never out of employment. He neither advanced nor receded in the modern sense; he improved as a workman, but he did not shift one jot in social position. About his love for Car'line he maintained a rigid silence. No doubt he often thought of her; but being always occupied, and having no relations at Stickleford, he held no communication with that part of the country, and showed no desire to return. In his quiet lodging in Lambeth he moved about after working-hours with the facility of a woman, doing his own cooking, attending to his stocking-heels, and shaping himself by degrees to a life-long bachelorhood. For this conduct one is bound to advance the canonical reason that time could not efface from his heart the image of little Car'line Aspent – and it may be in part true; but there was also the inference that his was a nature not greatly dependent upon the ministrations of the other sex for its comforts.

The fourth year of his residence as a mechanic in London was the year of the Hyde-Park Exhibition already mentioned, and at the construction of this huge glasshouse, then unexampled in the world's history, he worked daily. It was an era of great hope and activity among the nations and industries. Though Hipcroft was, in his small way, a central man in the movement, he plodded on with his usual outward placidity. Yet for him, too, the year was destined to have its surprises, for when the bustle of getting the building ready for the opening day was past, the ceremonies had been witnessed, and people were flocking thither from all parts of the globe, he received a letter from Car'line. Till that day the silence of four years between himself and Stickleford had never been broken.

She informed her old lover, in an uncertain pen-manship which suggested a trembling hand, of the trouble she had been put to in ascertaining his address, and then broached the subject which had prompted her to write. Four years ago, she said with the greatest delicacy of which she was capable, she had been so foolish as to refuse him. Her wilful wrong-headedness had since been a grief to her many times, and of late particularly. As for Mr Ollamoor, he had been absent almost as long as Ned – she did not know where. She would gladly marry Ned now if he were to ask her again, and be a tender little wife to him till her life's end.

A tide of warm feeling must have surged through Ned Hipcroft's frame on receipt of this news, if we may judge by the issue. Unquestionably he loved her still, even if not to the exclusion of every other happiness. This from his Car'line, she who had been dead to him these many years, alive to him again as of old, was in itself a pleasant, gratifying thing. Ned had grown so resigned to, or satisfied with, his lonely lot, that he probably would not have shown much jubilation at anything. Still, a certain ardour of preoccupation, after his first surprise, revealed how deeply her confession of faith in him had stirred him. Measured and methodical in his ways, he did not answer the letter that day, nor the next, nor the next. He was having 'a good think'. When he did answer it, there was a great deal of sound reasoning mixed in with the unmistakable tenderness of his reply; but the tenderness itself was sufficient to reveal that he was pleased with her straightforward frankness; that the anchorage she had once obtained in his heart was renewable, if it had not been continuously firm.

He told her – and as he wrote his lips twitched

humorously over the few gentle words of raillery he indited among the rest of his sentences – that it was all very well for her to come round at this time of day. Why wouldn't she have him when he wanted her? She had no doubt learned that he was not married, but suppose his affections had since been fixed on another? She ought to beg his pardon. Still, he was not the man to forget her. But considering how he had been used, and what he had suffered, she could not quite expect him to go down to Stickleford and fetch her. But if she would come to him, and say she was sorry, as was only fair; why, yes, he would marry her, knowing what a good little woman she was at the core. He added that the request for her to come to him was a less one to make than it would have been when he first left Stickleford, or even a few months ago; for the new railway into South Wessex was now open, and there had just begun to be run wonderfully contrived special trains, called excursion-trains, on account of the Great Exhibition; so that she could come up easily alone.

She said in her reply how good it was of him to treat her so generously, after her hot and cold treatment of him; that though she felt frightened at the magnitude of the journey, and was never as yet in a railway-train, having only seen one pass at a distance, she embraced his offer with all her heart; and would, indeed, own to him how sorry she was, and beg his pardon, and try to be a good wife always, and make up for lost time.

The remaining details of when and where were soon settled, Car'line informing him, for her ready identification in the crowd, that she would be wearing 'my new sprigged-laylock cotton gown', and Ned gaily responding that, having married her the morning after her arrival, he would make a day of it by taking her to the Exhibition. One early summer afternoon, accordingly, he came from his place of work, and hastened towards Waterloo Station to meet her. It was as wet and chilly as an English June day can occasionally be, but as he waited on the platform in the drizzle he glowed inwardly, and seemed to have something to live for again.

The 'excursion-train' – an absolutely new departure in the history of travel – was still a novelty on the Wessex line, and probably everywhere. Crowds of people had flocked to all the stations on the way up to witness the unwonted sight of so long a train's passage, even where they did not take advantage of the opportunity it offered. The seats for the humbler class of travellers in these early experiments in steam-locomotion were open trucks, without any protection whatever from the wind and rain; and damp weather having set in with the afternoon, the unfortunate occupants of these vehicles were, on the train drawing up at the London terminus, found to be in a pitiable condition from their long journey; blue-faced, stiff-necked, sneezing, rain-beaten, chilled to the marrow, many of the men being hatless; in fact, they resembled people who had been out all night in an open boat on a rough sea, rather than inland excursionists for pleasure. The women had in some degree protected themselves by turning up the skirts of their gowns over their heads, but as by this arrangement they were additionally exposed about the hips, they were all more or less in a sorry plight.

In the bustle and crush of alighting forms of both sexes which followed the entry of the huge concatenation into the station, Ned Hipcroft soon discerned the slim little figure his eye was in search of, in the sprigged lilac, as described. She came up to him with a frightened smile – still pretty, though so damp, weather-beaten, and shivering from long exposure to the wind.

'Oh Ned!' she sputtered, 'I – I – ' He clasped her in his arms and kissed her, whereupon she burst into a flood of tears.

'You are wet, my poor dear! I hope you'll not get cold,' he said. And surveying her and her multifarious surrounding packages, he noticed that by the hand she led a toddling child – a little girl of three or so – whose hood was as clammy and tender face as blue as those of the other travellers.

'Who is this – somebody you know?' asked Ned, curiously.

'Yes, Ned. She's mine.'

'Yours?'

'Yes – my own.'

'Your own child?'

'Yes!'

'But who's the father?'

'The young man I had after you courted me.'

'Well – as God's in – '

'Ned, I didn't name it in my letter, because, you see, it would have been so hard to explain! I thought that when we met I could tell you how she happened to be born, so much better than in writing! I hope you'll excuse it this once, dear Ned, and not scold me, now I've come so many, many miles!'

'This means Mr Mop Ollamoor, I reckon!' said Hipcroft, gazing palely at them from the distance of the yard or two to which he had withdrawn with a start.

Car'line gasped. 'But he's been gone away for years!' she supplicated. 'And I never had a young man before! And I was so onlucky to be catched the first time he took advantage o' me, though some of the girls down there go on like anything!'

Ned remained in silence, pondering.

'You'll forgive me, dear Ned?' she added, beginning to sob outright. 'I haven't taken 'ee in after all, because – because you can pack us back again, if you want to; though 'tis hundreds o' miles, and so wet, and night a-coming on, and I with no money!'

'What the devil can I do!' Hipcroft groaned.

A more pitiable picture than the pair of helpless creatures presented was never seen on a rainy day, as they stood on the great, gaunt, puddled platform, a whiff of drizzle blowing under the roof upon them now and then; the pretty attire in which they had started from Stickleford in the early morning bemuddled and sodden, weariness on their faces, and fear of him in their eyes; for the child began to look as if she thought she too had done some wrong, remaining in an appalled silence till the tears rolled down her chubby cheeks.

'What's the matter, my little maid?' said Ned mechanically.

'I do want to go home!' she let out, in tones that told of a bursting heart. 'And my totties be cold, an' I shan't have no bread an' butter no more!'

'I don't know what to say to it all!' declared Ned, his own eye moist as he turned and walked a few steps with his head down; then regarded them again point-blank. From the child escaped troubled breaths and silently welling tears.

'Want some bread and butter, do 'ee?' he said, with factitious hardness.

'Ye–e–s!'

'Well, I dare say I can get 'ee a bit. Naturally, you must want some. And you, too, for that matter, Car'line.'

'I do feel a little hungered. But I can keep it off,' she murmured.

'Folk shouldn't do that,' he said gruffly . . . 'There, come along!' He caught up the child, as he added, 'You must bide here tonight, anyhow, I s'pose! What can you do otherwise? I'll get 'ee some tea and victuals; and as for this job, I'm sure I don't know what to say! This is the way out.'

They pursued their way, without speaking, to Ned's lodgings, which were not far off. There he dried them and made them comfortable, and prepared tea; they thankfully sat down. The ready-made household of which he suddenly found himself the head imparted a cosy aspect to his room, and a paternal one to himself. Presently he turned to the child and kissed her now blooming cheeks; and, looking wistfully at Car'line, kissed her also.

'I don't see how I can send you back all them miles,' he growled, 'now you've come all the way o' purpose to join me. But you must trust me, Car'line, and show you've real faith in me. Well, do you feel better now, my little woman?'

The child nodded beamingly, her mouth being otherwise occupied.

'I did trust you, Ned, in coming; and I shall always!'

Thus, without any definite agreement to forgive her, he tacitly acquiesced in the fate that Heaven had sent him; and on the day of their marriage (which was not quite so soon as he had expected it could be, on account of the time necessary for banns) he took her to the Exhibition when they came back from church, as he had promised. While standing near a large mirror in one of the courts devoted to furniture, Car'line started, for in the glass appeared the reflection of a form exactly resembling Mop Ollamoor's – so exactly, that it seemed impossible to believe anybody but that artist in person to be the original. On passing round the objects which hemmed in Ned, her, and the child from a direct view, no Mop was to be seen. Whether he were really in London or not at that time was never known; and Car'line always stoutly denied that her readiness to go and meet Ned in town arose from any rumour that Mop had also gone thither; which denial there was no reasonable ground for doubting.

And then the year glided away, and the Exhibition folded itself up and became a thing of the past. The park trees that had been enclosed for six months were again exposed to the winds and storms, and the sod grew green anew. Ned found that Car'line resolved herself into a very good wife and companion, though she had made herself what is called cheap to him; but in that she was like another domestic article, a cheap teapot, which often brews better tea than a dear one. One autumn Hipcroft found himself with but little work to do, and a prospect of less for the winter. Both being country born and bred, they fancied they would like to live again in their natural atmosphere. It was accordingly decided between them that they should leave the pent-up London lodging, and that Ned should seek out employment near his native place, his wife and her daughter staying with Car'line's father during the search for occupation and an abode of their own.

Tinglings of pride pervaded Car'line's spasmodic little frame as she journeyed down with Ned to the place she had left two or three years before, in silence and under a cloud. To return to where she had once been despised, a smiling London wife with a distinct London accent, was a triumph which the world did not witness every day.

The train did not stop at the petty roadside station that lay nearest to Stickleford, and the trio went on to Casterbridge. Ned thought it a good opportunity to make a few preliminary enquiries for employment at workshops in the borough where he had been known; and feeling cold from her journey, and it being dry underfoot and only dusk as yet, with a moon on the point of rising, Car'line and her little girl walked on towards Stickleford, leaving Ned to follow at a quicker pace, and pick her up at a certain halfway house, widely known as an inn.

The woman and child pursued the well-remembered way comfortably enough, though they were both becoming wearied. In the course of three miles they had passed Heedless-William's Pond, the familiar land-mark by Bloom's End, and were drawing near the Quiet Woman, a lone roadside hostel on the lower verge of the Egdon Heath, since and for many years abolished. In stepping up towards it Car'line heard more voices within than had formerly been customary at such an hour, and she learned that an auction of fat stock had been held near the spot that afternoon. The child would be the better for a rest as well as herself, she thought, and she entered.

The guests and customers overflowed into the passage, and Car'line had no sooner crossed the threshold than a man whom she remembered by sight came forward with a glass and mug in his hands towards a friend leaning against the wall; but, seeing her, very gallantly offered her a drink of the liquor, which was gin-and-beer hot, pouring her out a tumblerful and saying, in a moment or two: 'Surely, 'tis little Car'line Aspent that was – down at Stickleford?'

She assented, and, though she did not exactly want this beverage, she drank it since it was offered, and her entertainer begged her to come in further and sit down. Once within the room she found that all the persons present were seated close against the walls, and there being a chair vacant she did the same. An explanation of their position occurred the next moment. In the opposite corner stood Mop, rosining his bow and looking just the same as ever. The company had cleared the middle of the room for dancing, and they were about to dance again. As she wore a veil to keep off the wind she did not think he had recognised her, or could possibly guess the identity of the child; and to her satisfied surprise she found that she could confront him quite calmly – mistress of herself in the dignity her London life had given her. Before she had quite emptied her glass the dance was called, the dancers formed in two lines, the music sounded, and the figure began.

Then matters changed for Car'line. A tremor quickened itself to life in her, and her hand so shook that she could hardly set down her glass. It was not the dance nor the dancers, but the notes of that old violin which thrilled the London wife, these having still all the witchery that she had so well known of yore, and under which she had used to lose her power of independent will. How it all came back! There was the fiddling figure against the wall; the large, oily, mop-like head of him, and beneath the mop the face with closed eyes.

After the first moments of paralysed reverie the

familiar tune in the familiar rendering made her laugh and shed tears simultaneously. Then a man at the bottom of the dance, whose partner had dropped away, stretched out his hand and beckoned to her to take the place. She did not want to dance; she entreated by signs to be left where she was, but she was entreating of the tune and its player rather than of the dancing man. The saltatory tendency which the fiddler and his cunning instrument had ever been able to start in her was seizing Car'line just as it had done in earlier years, possibly assisted by the gin-and-beer hot. Tired as she was she grasped her little girl by the hand, and plunging in at the bottom of the figure, whirled about with the rest. She found that her companions were mostly people of the neighbouring hamlets and farms – Bloom's End, Mellstock, Lewgate, and elsewhere; and by degrees she was recognised as she convulsively danced on, wishing that Mop would cease and let her heart rest from the aching he caused, and her feet also.

After long and many minutes the dance ended, when she was urged to fortify herself with more gin-and-beer; which she did, feeling very weak and overpowered with hysteric emotion. She refrained from unveiling, to keep Mop in ignorance of her presence, if possible. Several of the guests having left, Car'line hastily wiped her lips and also turned to go; but, according to the account of some who remained, at that very moment a five-handed reel was proposed, in which two or three begged her to join.

She declined on the plea of being tired and having to walk to Stickleford, when Mop began aggressively tweedling 'My Fancy-Lad', in D major, as the air to which the reel was to be footed. He must have recognised her, though she did not know it, for it was the strain of all seductive strains which she was least able to resist – the one he had played when she was leaning over the bridge at the date of their first acquaintance. Car'line stepped despairingly into the middle of the room with the other four.

Reels were resorted to hereabouts at this time by the more robust spirits, for the reduction of superfluous energy which the ordinary figure-dances were not powerful enough to exhaust. As everybody knows, or does not know, the five reelers stood in the form of a cross, the reel being performed by each line of three alternately, the persons who successively came to the middle place dancing in both directions. Car'line soon found herself in this place, the axis of the whole performance, and could not get out of it, the tune turning into the first part without giving her opportunity. And now she began to suspect that Mop did know her, and was doing this on purpose, though whenever she stole a glance at him his closed eyes betokened obliviousness to everything outside his own brain. She continued to wend her way through the figure of 8 that was formed by her course, the fiddler introducing into his notes the wild and agonising sweetness of a living voice in one too highly wrought; its pathos running high and running low in endless variation, projecting through her nerves excruciating spasms, a sort of blissful torture. The room swam, the tune was endless; and in about a quarter of an hour the only other woman in the figure dropped out exhausted, and sank panting on a bench.

The reel instantly resolved itself into a four-handed one. Car'line would have given anything to leave off; but she had, or fancied she had, no power, while Mop played such tunes; and thus another ten minutes slipped by, a haze of dust now clouding the candles, the floor being of stone, sanded. Then another dancer fell out – one of the men – and went into the passage in a frantic search for liquor. To turn the figure into a three-handed reel was the work of a second, Mop modulating at the same time into 'The Fairy Dance', as better suited to the contracted movement, and no less one of those foods of love which, as manufactured by his bow, had always intoxicated her.

In a reel for three there was no rest whatever, and four or five minutes were enough to make her remaining two partners, now thoroughly blown, stamp their last bar, and, like their predecessors, limp off into the next room to get something to drink. Car'line, half-stifled inside her veil, was left dancing alone, the apartment now being empty of everybody save herself, Mop, and their little girl.

She flung up the veil, and cast her eyes upon him, as if imploring him to withdraw himself and his acoustic magnetism from the atmosphere. Mop opened one of his own orbs, as though for the first time, fixed it peeringly upon her, and smiling dreamily, threw into his strains the reserve of expression which he could not afford to waste on a big and noisy dance. Crowds of little chromatic subtleties, capable of drawing tears from a statue, proceeded straightway from the ancient fiddle, as if it were dying of the emotion which had been pent up within it ever since its banishment from some Italian or German city where it first took shape and sound. There was that in the look of Mop's one dark eye which said: 'You cannot leave off, dear, whether you would or no!' and it bred in her a paroxysm of desperation that defied him to tire her down.

She thus continued to dance alone, defiantly as she thought, but in truth slavishly and abjectly, subject to every wave of the melody, and probed by the gimlet-like gaze of her fascinator's open eye; keeping up at the same time a feeble smile in his face, as a feint to signify it was still her own pleasure which led her on. A terrified embarrassment as to what she could say to him if she were to leave off, had its unrecognised share in keeping her going. The child, who was beginning to be distressed by the strange situation, came up and whimpered: 'Stop, mother, stop, and let's go home!' as she seized Car'line's hand.

Suddenly Car'line sank staggering to the floor; and rolling over on her face, prone she remained. Mop's fiddle thereupon emitted an elfin shriek of finality; stepping quickly down from the nine-gallon beer-cask which had formed his rostrum, he went to the little girl, who disconsolately bent over her mother.

The guests who had gone into the back-room for liquor and change of air, hearing something unusual, trooped back hitherward, where they endeavoured to revive poor, weak Car'line by blowing her with the bellows and opening the window. Ned, her husband, who had been detained in Casterbridge, as aforesaid, came along the road at this juncture, and hearing excited voices through the open casement, and to his great surprise, the mention of his wife's name, he entered amid the rest upon the scene. Car'line was now in convulsions, weeping violently, and for a long time nothing could be done with her. While he was sending for a cart to take her onward to Stickleford Hipcroft anxiously enquired how it had all happened; and then the assembly explained that a fiddler formerly known in the locality had lately visited his old haunts, and had taken upon himself without invitation to play that evening at the inn and raise a dance.

Ned demanded the fiddler's name, and they said Ollamoor.

'Ah!' exclaimed Ned, looking round him. 'Where is he, and where – where's my little girl?'

Ollamoor had disappeared, and so had the child. Hipcroft was in ordinary a quiet and tractable fellow, but a determination which was to be feared settled in his face now. 'Blast him!' he cried. 'I'll beat his skull in for'n, if I swing for it tomorrow!'

He had rushed to the poker which lay on the hearth, and hastened down the passage, the people following. Outside the house, on the other side of the highway, a mass of dark heathland rose sullenly upward to its not easily accessible interior, a ravined plateau, whereon jutted into the sky, at the distance of a couple of miles, the fir woods of Mistover backed by the Yalbury coppices – a place of Dantesque gloom at this hour, which would have afforded secure hiding for a battery of artillery, much less a man and a child.

Some other men plunged thitherward with him, and more went along the road. They were gone about twenty minutes altogether, returning without result to the inn. Ned sat down in the settle, and clasped his forehead with his hands.

'Well – what a fool the man is, and hev been all these years, if he thinks the child his, as a' do seem to!' they whispered. 'And everybody else knowing otherwise!'

'No, I don't think 'tis mine!' cried Ned hoarsely, as he looked up from his hands. 'But she *is* mine, all the same! Ha'n't I nussed her? Ha'n't I fed her and teached her? Ha'n't I played wi' her? Oh, little Carry – gone with that rogue – gone!'

'You ha'n't lost your mis'ess, anyhow,' they said to console him. 'She's throwed up the sperrits, and she is feeling better, and she's more to 'ee than a child that isn't yours.'

'She isn't! She's not so particular much to me, especially now she's lost the little maid! But Carry's the whole world to me!'

'Well, ver' like you'll find her tomorrow.'

'Ah – but shall I? Yet he *can't* hurt her – surely he can't! Well – how's Car'line now? I am ready. Is the cart here?'

She was lifted into the vehicle, and they sadly lumbered on toward Stickleford. Next day she was calmer; but the fits were still upon her; and her will seemed shattered. For the child she appeared to show singularly little anxiety, though Ned was nearly distracted by his passionate paternal love for a child not his own. It was nevertheless quite expected that the impish Mop would restore the lost one after a freak of a day or two; but time went on, and neither he nor she could be heard of, and Hipcroft murmured that perhaps he was exercising upon her some unholy musical charm, as he had done upon Car'line herself. Weeks passed, and still they could obtain no clue either to the fiddler's whereabouts or to the girl's; and how he could have induced her to go with him remained a mystery.

Then Ned, who had obtained only temporary employment in the neighbourhood, took a sudden hatred toward his native district, and a rumour reaching his ears through the police that a somewhat similar man and child had been seen at a fair near London, he playing a violin, she dancing on stilts, a new interest in the capital took possession of Hipcroft with an intensity which would scarcely allow him time to pack before returning thither. He did not, however, find the lost one, though he made it the entire business of his over-hours to stand about in by-streets in the hope of discovering her, and would start up in the night, saying, 'That rascal's torturing her to maintain him!' To which his wife would answer peevishly, 'Don't 'ee raft yourself so, Ned! You prevent my getting a bit o' rest! He won't hurt her!' and fall asleep again.

That Carry and her father had emigrated to America was the general opinion; Mop, no doubt, finding the girl a highly desirable companion when he had trained her to keep him by her earnings as a dancer. There, for that matter, they may be performing in some capacity now, though he must be an old scamp verging on three-score-and-ten, and she a woman of four-and-forty.

May 1893

The Melancholy Hussar of the
German Legion

ONE

Here stretch the downs, high and breezy and green,
absolutely unchanged since those eventful days. A
plough has never disturbed the turf, and the sod that
was uppermost then is uppermost now. Here stood
the camp; here are distinct traces of the banks thrown
up for the horses of the cavalry, and spots where the
midden-heaps lay are still to be observed. At night
when I walk across the lonely place it is impossible to
avoid hearing, amid the scourings of the wind over the
grass-bents and thistles, the old trumpet and bugle
calls, the rattle of the halters; to help seeing rows of
spectral tents and the *impedimenta* of the soldiery; from
within the canvases come guttural syllables of foreign
tongues, and broken songs of the fatherland; for they
were mainly regiments of the King's German Legion
that slept round the tent-poles hereabout at that time.

It was nearly ninety years ago. The British uniform
of the period, with its immense epaulettes, queer
cocked hat, breeches, gaiters, ponderous cartridge-
box, buckled shoes, and what not, would look strange
and barbarous now. Ideas have changed; invention
has followed invention. Soldiers were monumental
objects then. A divinity still hedged kings here and
there; and war was considered a glorious thing.

Secluded old manor-houses and hamlets lie in the ravines and hollows among these hills, where a stranger had hardly ever been seen till the king chose to take the baths yearly at the seaside watering-place a few miles to the south; as a consequence of which battalions descended in a cloud upon the open country around. Is it necessary to add that the echoes of many characteristic tales, dating from that picturesque time, still linger about here, in more or less fragmentary form to be caught by the attentive ear? Some of them I have repeated; most of them I have forgotten; one I have never repeated, and assuredly can never forget.

Phyllis told me the story with her own lips. She was then an old lady of seventy-five, and her auditor a lad of fifteen. She enjoined silence as to her share in the incident till she should be 'dead, buried, and forgotten'. Her life was prolonged twelve years after the day of her narration, and she has now been dead nearly twenty. The oblivion which, in her modesty and humility, she courted for herself, has only partially fallen on her, with the unfortunate result of inflicting an injustice upon her memory; since such fragments of her story as got abroad at the time, and have been kept alive ever since, are precisely those which are most unfavourable to her character.

It all began with the arrival of the York Hussars, one of the foreign regiments above alluded to. Before that day scarcely a soul had been seen near her father's house for weeks. When a noise like the brushing skirt of a visitor was heard on the doorstep it proved to be a scudding leaf; when a carriage seemed to be nearing the door it was her father grinding his sickle on the stone in the garden for his favourite relaxation of trimming the box-tree borders to the plots. A sound like luggage thrown down from the coach was a gun far away at sea; and what looked like a tall man by the gate at dusk was a yew bush cut into a quaint and attenuated shape. There is no such solitude in country places now as there was in those old days.

Yet all the while King George and his court were at his favourite seaside resort, not more than five miles off.

The daughter's seclusion was great, but beyond the seclusion of the girl lay the seclusion of the father. If her social condition was twilight his was darkness. Yet he enjoyed his darkness while her twilight oppressed her. Dr Grove had been a professional man whose taste for lonely meditation over metaphysical questions had diminished his practice till it no longer paid him to keep it going; after which he had relinquished it and hired at a nominal rent the small, dilapidated, half farmhouse half manor-house of this obscure inland nook, to make a sufficiency of an income which in a town would have been inadequate for their maintenance. He stayed in his garden the greater part of the day, growing more and more irritable with the lapse of time, and the increasing perception that he had wasted his life in the pursuit of illusions. He saw his friends less and less frequently. Phyllis became so shy that if she met a stranger anywhere in her short rambles she felt ashamed at his gaze, walked awkwardly, and blushed to her shoulders.

Yet Phyllis was discovered even here by an admirer, and her hand most unexpectedly asked in marriage.

The king as aforesaid was at the neighbouring town, where he had taken up his abode at Gloucester Lodge; and his presence in the town naturally brought many county people thither. Among these idlers, many of whom professed to have connections and interests with the Court, was one Humphrey Gould, a bachelor; a personage neither young nor old; neither good-looking nor positively plain. Too steady going to be 'a buck' (as fast and unmarried men were then called) he was an approximately fashionable man of a mild type. This bachelor of thirty found his way to the village on the down; beheld Phyllis, made her father's acquaintance in order to make hers; and by some means or other she sufficiently inflamed his heart to lead him in that direction almost daily: till he became engaged to marry her.

As he was of an old local family, some of whose members were held in respect in the county, Phyllis, in bringing him to her feet, had accomplished what was considered a brilliant move for one in her constrained position. How she had done it was not quite known to Phyllis herself. In those days unequal marriages were regarded rather as a violation of the laws of nature than as a mere infringement of convention, the more modern view; and hence when Phyllis of the watering-place *bourgeoisie* was chosen by such a gentlemanly fellow it was as if she were going to be taken to Heaven; though perhaps the uninformed would have seen no great difference in the respective positions of the pair, the said Gould being as poor as a crow.

This pecuniary condition was his excuse – probably a true one – for postponing their union; and as the winter drew nearer, and the king departed for the season, Mr Humphrey Gould set out for Bath, promising to return to Phyllis in a few weeks. The winter arrived, the date of his promise passed; yet Gould postponed his coming, on the ground that he could not very easily leave his father in the city of their sojourn, the elder having no other relative near him. Phyllis, though lonely in the extreme, was content. The man who had asked her in marriage was a desirable husband for her in many ways; her father highly approved of his suit: but this neglect of her was awkward if not painful for Phyllis. Love him in the true sense of the word she assured me she never did; but she had a genuine regard for him; admired a certain methodical and dogged way in which he sometimes took his pleasure; valued his knowledge of what the Court was doing, had done, or was about to do; and she was not without a feeling of pride that he had chosen her when he might have exercised a more ambitious choice.

But he did not come; and the spring developed. His letters were regular though formal; and it is not to be wondered that the uncertainty of her position, linked with the fact that there was not much passion in her thoughts of Humphrey, bred an indescribable dreariness in the heart of Phyllis Grove. The spring was soon summer, and the summer brought the king; but still no Humphrey Gould. All this while the engagement by letter was maintained intact.

At this point of time a golden radiance flashed in upon the lives of people here, and charged all youthful thought with emotional interest. This radiance was the aforesaid York Hussars.

The present generation has probably but a very dim notion of the celebrated York Hussars of ninety years ago. They were one of the regiments of the King's German Legion and (though they somewhat degenerated later on) their brilliant uniform, their splendid horses, and above all, their foreign air, and mustachios (rare appendages then) drew crowds of admirers of both sexes wherever they went. These, with other regiments, had come to encamp on the downs and pastures, because of the presence of the king in the neighbouring town.

The spot was high and airy, and the view extensive, commanding Portland – the Isle of Slingers – in front, and reaching to St Aldhelm's Head eastward, and almost to the Start on the west. Phyllis, though not precisely a girl of the village, was as interested as any of them in this military investment. Her father's home stood somewhat apart, and on the highest point of ground, to which the lane ascended, so that it was almost level with the top of the church tower in the lower part of the parish. Immediately from the outside of the garden wall the grass spread away to a great distance, and it was crossed by a path which came close to the wall. Ever since her childhood it had been Phyllis's pleasure to clamber up this fence, and sit on the top, a feat not so difficult as it may seem, the walls in this district being built of rubble, without mortar, so that there were plenty of crevices for small toes.

She was sitting up here one day, listlessly surveying the pasture without, when her attention was arrested by a solitary figure walking along the path. It was one of the renowned German Hussars, and he moved onward with his eyes on the ground, and with the manner of one who wished to escape company. His head would probably have been bent like his eyes but for his stiff neck-gear. On nearer view she perceived that his face was marked with deep sadness. Without observing her he advanced by the footpath till it brought him almost immediately under the wall.

Phyllis was much surprised to see a fine tall soldier in such a mood as this. Her theory of the military, and of the York Hussars in particular (derived entirely from hearsay, for she had never talked to a soldier in her life), was that their hearts were as gay as their accoutrements.

At this moment the Hussar lifted his eyes and noticed her on her perch, the white muslin neckerchief which covered her shoulders and neck where left bare by her low gown, and her white raiment in general, showing conspicuously in the bright sunlight of this summer day. He blushed a little at the suddenness of the encounter, and without halting a moment from his pace passed on.

All that day the foreigner's face haunted Phyllis; its aspect was so striking, so handsome, and his eyes were so blue, and sad, and abstracted. It was perhaps only natural that on some following day at the same hour she should look over that wall again, and wait till he had passed a second time. On this occasion he was reading a letter, and at the sight of her his manner was that of one who had half expected or hoped to discover her. He almost stopped, smiled, and made a courteous salute. The end of the meeting was that they exchanged a few words. She asked him what he was reading, and he readily informed her that he was reperusing letters from his mother in Germany; he did not get them often, he said, and was forced to read the old ones a great many times. This was all that passed at the present interview; but others of the same kind followed.

Phyllis used to say that his English, though not good, was quite intelligible to her, so that their acquaintance was never hindered by difficulties of speech. Whenever the subject became too delicate, subtle, or tender, for such words of English as were at his command, the eyes no doubt helped out the tongue, and – though this was later on – the lips helped out the eyes. In short this acquaintance, unguardedly made, and rash enough on her part, developed, and ripened. Like Desdemona, she pitied him, and learnt his history.

His name was Matthäus Tina, and Saarbruck his native town, where his mother was still living. His age was twenty-two, and he had already risen to the grade of corporal, though he had not long been in the army. Phyllis used to assert that no such refined or well-educated young man could have been found in the ranks of the purely English regiments, some of these foreign soldiers having rather the graceful manner and presence of our native officers than of our rank and file.

She by degrees learnt from her foreign friend a circumstance about himself and his comrades which Phyllis would least have expected of the York Hussars. So far from being as gay as its uniform the regiment was pervaded by a dreadful melancholy, a chronic homesickness, which depressed many of the men to such an extent that they could hardly attend to their drill. The worst sufferers were the younger soldiers who had not been over here long. They hated England and English life; they took no interest whatever in King George and his island kingdom, and they only wished

to be out of it and never to see it any more. Their
bodies were here, but their hearts and minds were
always far away in their dear fatherland, of which –
brave men and stoical as they were in many ways –
they would speak with tears in their eyes. One of the
worst of the sufferers from this home-woe, as he called
it in his own tongue, was Matthäus Tina, whose
dreamy musing nature felt the gloom of exile still more
intensely from the fact that he had left a lonely mother
at home with nobody to cheer her.

Though Phyllis, touched by all this, and interested in
his history, did not disdain her soldier's acquaintance,
she declined (according to her own account at least) to
permit the young man to overstep the line of mere
friendship for a long while – as long, indeed, as she
considered herself likely to become the possession of
another; though it is probable that she had lost her heart
to Matthäus before she was herself aware. The stone
wall of necessity made anything like intimacy difficult;
and he had never ventured to come, or to ask to come,
inside the garden, so that all their conversation had
been overtly conducted across this boundary.

THREE

But news reached the village from a friend of Phyllis's
father, concerning Mr Humphrey Gould, her remark-
ably cool and patient betrothed. This gentleman had
been heard to say in Bath that he considered his
overtures to Miss Phyllis Grove to have reached only
the stage of a half-understanding; and in view of his
enforced absence on his father's account, who was too
great an invalid now to attend to his affairs, he thought

it best that there should be no definite promise as yet on either side. He was not sure, indeed, that he might not cast his eyes elsewhere.

This account – though only a piece of hearsay and as such entitled to no absolute credit – tallied so well with the infrequency of his letters, and their lack of warmth, that Phyllis did not doubt its truth for one moment; and from that hour she felt herself free to bestow her heart as she should choose. Not so her father; he declared the whole story to be a fabrication. He had known Mr Gould's family from his boyhood: and if there was one proverb which expressed the matrimonial aspect of that family well it was 'Love me little love me long.' Humphrey was an honourable man who would not think of treating his engagement so lightly. 'Do you wait in patience,' he said. 'All will be right enough in time.'

From these words Phyllis at first imagined that her father was in correspondence with Mr Gould; and her heart sank within her; for in spite of her original intentions she had been relieved to hear that her engagement had come to nothing. But she presently learnt that her father had heard no more of Humphrey Gould than she herself had done: while he would not write and address her affianced directly on the subject lest it should be deemed an imputation on that bachelor's honour.

'You want an excuse for encouraging one or other of those foreign fellows to flatter you with his unmeaning attentions,' her father exclaimed, his mood having of late been a very unkind one towards her. 'I see more than I say. Don't you ever set foot outside that garden-fence without my permission. If you want to see the camp I'll take you myself some Sunday afternoon.'

Phyllis had not the smallest intention of disobeying him in her actions, but she assumed herself to be independent with respect to her feelings. She no longer checked her fancy for the Hussar, though she was far from regarding him as her lover in the serious sense in which an Englishman might have been regarded as such. The young foreign soldier was almost an ideal being to her, with none of the appurtenances of an ordinary house-dweller; one who had descended she knew not whence, and would disappear she knew not whither; the subject of a fascinating dream, no more.

They met continually now – mostly at dusk – during the brief interval between the going down of the sun and the minute at which the last trumpet-call summoned him to his tent. Perhaps her manner had become less restrained latterly: at any rate that of the Hussar was so; he had grown more tender every day, and at parting after these hurried interviews she reached down her hand from the top of the wall that he might press it. One evening he held it such a while that she exclaimed, 'The wall is white, and somebody in the field may see your shape against it.'

He lingered so long that night that it was with the greatest difficulty that he could run across the inter-vening stretch of ground and enter the camp in time. On the next occasion of his awaiting her she did not appear in her usual place at the usual hour. His disappointment was unspeakably keen: he remained staring blankly at the spot, like a man in a trance. The trumpets and tattoo sounded, and still he did not go.

She had been delayed purely by an accident. When she arrived she was anxious because of the lateness of the hour, having heard as well as he the sounds denoting the closing of the camp. She implored him to leave immediately.

'No,' he said, gloomily. 'I shall not go in yet – the moment you come – I have thought of your coming all day.'

'But you may be disgraced at being after time.'

'I don't mind that. I should have disappeared from the world some time ago if it had not been for two persons – my beloved, here; and my mother in Saarbruck. I hate the army. I care more for a minute of your company than for all the promotion in the world.'

Thus he stayed and talked to her, and told her interesting details of his native place, and incidents of his childhood, till she was in a simmer of distress at his recklessness in remaining. It was only because she insisted on bidding him good-night and leaving the wall that he returned to his quarters.

The next time that she saw him he was without the stripes that had adorned his sleeve. He had been broken to the level of private for his lateness that night: and as Phyllis considered herself to be the cause of his disgrace her sorrow was great. But the position was now reversed: it was his turn to cheer her.

'Don't grieve, *meine Liebliche!*' he said. 'I have got a remedy for whatever comes. First, even supposing I regain my stripes, would your father allow you to marry a noncommissioned officer in the York Hussars?'

She flushed. This practical step had not been in her mind in relation to such an unrealistic person as he was; and a moment's reflection was enough for it. 'My father would not – certainly would not,' she answered unflinchingly. 'It cannot be thought of! My dear friend, please do forget me: I fear I am ruining you and your prospects!'

'Not at all!' said he. 'You are giving this country of yours just sufficient interest to me to make me care to keep alive in it. If my dear land were here also, and my old parent, with you, I could be happy as I am, and would do my best as a soldier. But it is not so. And now listen. This is my plan. That you go with me to my own country, and be my wife there, and live there with my mother and me. I am not a Hanoverian, as you know, though I entered the army as such; my country is by the Saar, and is at peace with France, and if I were once in it I should be free.'

'But how to get there?' she asked. Phyllis had been rather amazed than shocked at his proposition. Her position in her father's house was growing irksome and painful in the extreme; his parental affection seemed to be quite dried up. She was not a native of the village, like all the joyous girls around her; and in some way Matthäus Tina had infected her with his own passionate longing for his country and mother and home.

'But how?' she repeated, finding that he did not answer. 'Will you buy your discharge?'

'Ah, no,' he said. 'That's impossible in these times. No. I came here against my will: why should I not escape? Now is the time, as we shall soon be striking camp, and I might see you no more. This is my scheme. I will ask you to meet me on the highway two miles off on some calm night next week that may be appointed. There will be nothing unbecoming in it, or to cause you shame; you will not fly alone with me, for I will bring with me my devoted young friend Christoph, an Alsatian, who has lately joined the regiment, and who has agreed to assist in this enterprise. We shall have come from yonder harbour, where we shall have examined the boats, and found one suited to our purpose. Christoph has already a chart of the channel, and we will then go to the harbour, and at midnight cut the boat from her moorings, and row away round the point out of sight; and by the next morning we are on the coast of France, near Cherbourg. The rest is easy, for I have saved money for the land journey, and can get a change of clothes. I will write to my mother; who will meet us on the way.'

He added details in reply to her enquiries which left no doubt in Phyllis's mind of the feasibility of the undertaking. But its magnitude almost appalled her; and it is questionable if she would ever have gone further in the wild adventure if, on entering the house that night, her father had not accosted her in the most significant terms.

'How about the York Hussars?' he said.

'They are still at the camp; but they are soon going away, I believe.'

'It is useless for you to attempt to cloak your actions in that way. You have been meeting one of those fellows: you have been seen walking with him – foreign barbarians not much better than the French themselves. I have made up my mind – don't speak a word till I have done please! – I have made up my mind that you shall stay here no longer while they are on the spot. You shall go to your aunt's.'

It was useless for her to protest that she had never taken a walk with any soldier or man under the sun except himself. Her protestations were feeble too, for though he was not literally correct in his assertion he was virtually only half in error.

The house of her father's sister was a prison to

Phyllis. She had quite recently undergone experience of its gloom; and when her father went on to direct her to pack what would be necessary for her to take her heart died within her. In after years she never attempted to excuse her conduct during this week of agitation; but the result of her self-communing was that she decided to join in the scheme of her lover and his friend, and fly to the country which he had coloured with such lovely hues in her imagination. She always said that the one feature in his proposal which overcame her hesitation was the obvious purity and straightforwardness of his intentions. He showed himself to be so virtuous and kind: he treated her with a respect to which she had never before been accustomed; and she was braced to the obvious risks of the voyage by her confidence in him.

FOUR

It was on a soft, dark evening of the following week that they engaged in the adventure. Tina was to meet her at a point in the highway at which the lane to the village branched off. Christoph was to go ahead of them to the harbour where the boat lay, row it round the Nothe – or Lookout as it was called in those days – and pick them up on the other side of the promontory, which they were to reach by crossing the harbour bridge on foot, and climbing over the Lookout hill.

As soon as her father had ascended to his room she left the house, and, bundle in hand, proceeded at a trot along the lane. At such an hour not a soul was afoot anywhere in the village, and she reached the junction of the lane with the highway unobserved. Here she took up her position in the obscurity formed by the angle of a fence, whence she could discern everyone who approached along the turnpike road, without being herself seen.

She had not remained thus waiting for her lover longer than a minute – though from the tension of her nerves the lapse of even that short time was trying – when, instead of the expected footsteps the stagecoach could be heard descending the hill. She knew that Tina would not show himself till the road was clear, and waited impatiently for the coach to pass. Nearing the corner where she was it slackened speed, and, instead of going by as usual, drew up within a few yards of her. A passenger alighted, and she heard his voice. It was Humphrey Gould's.

He had brought a friend with him, and luggage. The luggage was deposited on the grass, and the coach went on its route to the royal watering-place.

'I wonder where that young man is with the horse and trap?' said her former admirer to his companion. 'I hope we shan't have to wait here long. I told him half-past nine o'clock precisely.'

'Have you got her present safe?'

'Phyllis's? Oh yes. It is in this trunk. I hope it will please her.'

'Of course it will. What woman would not be pleased with such a handsome peace-offering?'

'Well – she deserves it. I've treated her rather badly. But she has been in my mind these last two days much more than I should care to confess to everybody. Ah well; I'll say no more about that. It cannot be that she is so bad as they make out. I am quite sure that a girl of her good wit would know better than to get entangled with any of those Hanoverian soldiers. I won't believe it of her, and there's an end on't.'

More words in the same strain were casually dropped as the two men waited; words which revealed to her, as by a sudden illumination, the enormity of her conduct. The conversation was at length cut off by the arrival of the man with the vehicle. The luggage was placed in it, and they mounted, and were driven on in the direction from which she had just come.

Phyllis was so conscience-stricken that she was at first inclined to follow them; but a moment's reflection led her to feel that it would only be bare justice to Matthäus to wait till he arrived, and explain candidly that she had changed her mind – difficult as the struggle would be when she stood face to face with him. She bitterly reproached herself for having believed reports which represented Humphrey Gould as false to his engagement, when, from what she now heard from his own lips she gathered that he had been living full of trust in her; but she knew well enough who had won her love. Without him her life seemed a dreary prospect; yet the more she looked at his proposal the more she feared to accept it – so wild as it was, so vague, so venturesome. She had promised Humphrey Gould, and it was only his assumed faith-lessness which had led her to treat that promise as nought. His solicitude in bringing her these gifts touched her; her promise must be kept, and esteem must take the place of love. She would preserve her self-respect. She would stay at home, and marry him, and suffer.

Phyllis had thus braced herself to an exceptional fortitude when, a few minutes later, the outline of Matthäus Tina appeared behind a field-gate; over which he lightly leapt as she stepped forward. There was no evading it: he pressed her to his breast.

'It is the first and last time!' she wildly thought as she stood encircled by his arms.

How Phyllis got through the terrible ordeal of that night she could never clearly recollect. She always attributed her success in carrying out her resolve to her lover's honour, for as soon as she declared to him in feeble words that she had changed her mind, and felt that she could not, dared not, fly with him, he forbore to urge her, grieved as he was at her decision. Unscrupulous pressure on his part, seeing how romantically she had become attached to him, would no doubt have turned the balance in his favour. But he did nothing to tempt her unduly or unfairly.

On her side, fearing for his safety, she begged him to remain. This, he declared, could not be. 'I cannot break faith with my friend,' said he. Had he stood alone he would have abandoned his plan. But Christoph, with the boat and compass and chart, was waiting on the shore; the tide would soon turn; his mother had been warned of his coming; go he must.

Many precious minutes were lost while he tarried, unable to tear himself away. Phyllis held to her resolve, though it cost her many a bitter pang. At last they parted, and he went down the hill. Before his footsteps had quite died away she felt a desire to behold at least his outline once more, and running noiselessly after him regained view of his diminishing figure. For one moment she was sufficiently excited to be on the point of rushing forward and linking her fate with his. But she could not. The courage which at the critical instant failed Cleopatra of Egypt could scarcely be expected of Phyllis Grove.

A dark shape similar to his own joined him in the highway: it was Christoph, his friend. She could see no more; they had hastened on in the direction of the town and harbour, four miles ahead. With a feeling akin to despair she turned and slowly pursued her way homeward. Tattoo sounded in the camp; but there was no camp for her now. It was as dead as the camp of the Assyrians after the passage of the destroying angel.

She noiselessly entered the house, seeing nobody; and went to bed. Grief, which kept her awake at first, ultimately wrapped her in a heavy sleep. The next morning her father met her at the foot of the stairs.

'Mr Gould is come!' he said triumphantly.

Humphrey was staying at the inn, and had already called to enquire for her. He had brought her a present of a very handsome looking-glass in a frame of *repoussé* silver-work, which her father held in his hand. He had promised to call again in the course of an hour, to ask Phyllis to walk with him.

Pretty mirrors were rarer in country-houses at that day than they are now, and the one before her won Phyllis's admiration. She looked into it, saw how heavy her eyes were, and endeavoured to brighten them. She was in that wretched state of mind which leads a woman to move mechanically onward in what she conceives to be her allotted path. Mr Humphrey had, in his undemonstrative way, been adhering all along to the old understanding: it was for her to do the same; and to say not a word of her own lapse. She put on her bonnet and tippet, and when he arrived at the hour named she was at the door awaiting him.

Phyllis thanked him for his beautiful gift; but the talking was soon entirely on Humphrey's side as they walked along. He told her of the latest movements of the world of fashion – a subject which she willingly discussed to the exclusion of anything more personal – and his measured language helped to still her disquieted heart and brain. Had not her own sadness been what it was she must have observed his embarrassment. At last he abruptly changed the subject.

'I am glad you are pleased with my little present,' he said. 'The truth is that I brought it to propitiate 'ee, and to get you to help me out of a mighty difficulty.'

It was inconceivable to Phyllis that this independent bachelor – whom she admired in some respects – could have a difficulty.

'Phyllis – I'll tell you my secret at once; for I have a monstrous secret to confide before I can ask your counsel. The case is, then, that I am married: yes, I have privately married a dear young *belle*, and if you knew her, and I hope you will, you would say everything in her praise. But she is not quite the one that my father would have chosen for me – you know the paternal idea as well as I – and I have kept it secret. There will be a terrible noise, no doubt; but I think that with your help I may get over it. If you would only do me this good turn – when I have told my father I mean – say that you never could have married me, you know, or something of that sort – 'pon my life it will help to smooth the way vastly. I am so anxious to win him round to my point of view, and not to cause any estrangement.'

What Phyllis replied she scarcely knew, or how she counselled him as to his unexpected situation. Yet the relief that his announcement brought her was perceptible. To have confided her trouble in return was what her aching heart longed to do; and had Humphrey been a woman she would instantly have poured out her tale. But to him she feared to confess; and there was a real reason for silence till a sufficient time had elapsed to allow her lover and his comrade to get out of harm's way.

As soon as she reached home again she sought a solitary place, and spent the time in half regretting that she had not gone away, and in dreaming over the meetings with Matthäus Tina from their beginning to their end. In his own country, amongst his own countrywomen, he would possibly soon forget her, even to her very name.

Her listlessness was such that she did not go out of the house for several days. There came a morning which broke in fog and mist, behind which the down could be discerned in greenish grey; and the outlines of the tents, and the rows of horses at the ropes. The smoke from the canteen fires drooped heavily.

The spot at the bottom of the garden where she had been accustomed to climb the wall to meet Matthäus was the only inch of English ground in which she took any interest; and in spite of the disagreeable haze prevailing she walked out there till she reached the well-known corner. Every blade of grass was weighted with little liquid globes, and slugs and snails had crept out upon the plots. She could hear the usual faint noises from the camp, and in the other direction the trot of farmers on the road to the town, for it was market-day. She observed that her frequent visits to this corner had quite trodden down the grass in the angle of the wall and left marks of garden-soil on the stepping-stones by which she had mounted to look over the top: seldom having gone there till dusk she had not considered that her traces might be visible by day. Perhaps it was these which had revealed her trysts to her father.

While she paused in melancholy regard she fancied that the customary sounds from the tents were changing their character. Indifferent as Phyllis was to camp doings now, she mounted by the steps to the old place. What she beheld at first awed and perplexed her: then she stood rigid, her fingers hooked to the wall, her eyes starting out of her head, and her face as if hardened to stone.

On the open green stretching before her all the regiments in the camp were drawn up in line, in the mid-front of which two empty coffins lay on the ground. The unwonted sounds which she had noticed came from an advancing procession; it consisted of the band of the York Hussars playing a dead march, next two soldiers of that regiment in a mourning coach, guarded on each side, and accompanied by two priests. Behind came a crowd of rustics who had been attracted by the event. The melancholy procession marched along the front of the line, returned to the centre, and halted beside the coffins, where the two condemned men were blindfolded, and each placed kneeling on his coffin; a few minutes' pause was now given, while they prayed.

A firing-party of twenty-four men stood ready with levelled carbines. The commanding officer, who had his sword drawn, waved it through some cuts of the sword-exercise till he reached the downward stroke, whereat the firing-party discharged their volley. The two victims fell, one upon his face across his coffin, the other backwards.

As the volley resounded there arose a shriek from the wall of Dr Grove's garden, and someone fell down inside; but nobody among the spectators without noticed it at the time.

The two executed hussars were Matthäus Tina and his friend Christoph. The soldiers on guard placed the bodies in the coffins almost instantly; but the Colonel of the regiment – an Englishman – rode up and exclaimed in a stern voice: 'Turn them out – as an example to the men!'

The coffins were lifted endwise, and the dead Germans flung out upon their faces on the grass. Then all the regiments wheeled in sections, and marched past the spot in slow time. When the survey was over the corpses were again coffined, and borne away.

Meanwhile Dr Grove, attracted by the noise of the volley, had rushed out into his garden, where he saw his wretched daughter lying motionless against the wall. She was taken indoors, but it was long before she recovered consciousness; and for weeks they despaired of her reason.

It transpired that the luckless deserters from the York Hussars had cut the boat from her moorings in the adjacent harbour, according to their plan, and, with two other comrades who were smarting under ill-treatment from their Colonel, had sailed in safety across the Channel. But mistaking their bearings they steered into Jersey, thinking that island the French coast. Here they were perceived to be deserters, and delivered up to the authorities. Matthäus and Christoph interceded for the other two at the court-martial, saying that it was entirely by the former's representations that these were induced to go. Their sentence was accordingly commuted to flogging, the death punishment being reserved for their leaders.

The visitor to the well-known old Georgian watering-place, who may care to ramble to the neighbouring village under the hills, and examine the register of burials, will there find two entries in these words:

Matth. Tina (Corpl.) in His Majesty's Regmt. of York Hussars and Shot for Desertion was Buried June 30th 1801, aged 22 Years. Born in the town of Sarrbruk Germany.

Christopher Bless belonging to His Majesty's Regmt. of York Hussars who was Shot for Desertion was Buried June 30th 1801, aged 22 Years. Born at Lothaargen Alsassia.

Their graves were dug at the back of the little church, near the wall. There is no memorial to mark the spot, but Phyllis pointed it out to me. While she lived she used to keep their mounds neat; but now they are overgrown with nettles, and sunk nearly flat. The older villagers, however, who know of the episode from their parents, still recollect the place where the soldiers lie. Phyllis lies near.

October 1889

The Distracted Preacher

ONE

How his Cold was Cured

Something delayed the arrival of the Wesleyan minister, and a young man came temporarily in his stead. It was on the thirteenth of January, 183—, that Mr Stockdale, the young man in question, made his humble entry into the village, unknown, and almost unseen. But when those of the inhabitants who styled themselves of his connection became acquainted with him, they were rather pleased with the substitute than otherwise, though he had scarcely as yet acquired ballast of character sufficient to steady the consciences of the hundred and forty Methodists of pure blood who, at this time, lived in Nether-Moynton, and to give in addition supplementary support to the mixed race which went to church in the morning and chapel in the evening, or when there was a tea – as many as a hundred and ten people more, all told, and including the parish clerk in the wintertime, when it was too dark for the vicar to observe who passed up the street at seven o'clock – which, to be just to him, he was never anxious to do.

It was owing to this overlapping of creeds that the celebrated population puzzle arose among the denser gentry of the district around Nether-Moynton: how could it be that a parish containing fifteen score of strong, full-grown Episcopalians, and nearly thirteen score of well-matured Dissenters, numbered barely two-and-twenty score adults in all?

The young man being personally interesting, those with whom he came in contact were content to waive for a while the graver question of his sufficiency. It is said that at this time of his life his eyes were affectionate, though without a ray of levity; that his hair was curly, and his figure tall; that he was, in short, a very lovable youth, who won upon his female hearers as soon as they saw and heard him, and caused them to say, 'Why didn't we know of this before he came, that we might have gi'ed him a warmer welcome!'

The fact was that, knowing him to be only provisionally selected, and expecting nothing remarkable in his person or doctrine, they and the rest of his flock in Nether-Moynton had felt almost as indifferent about his advent as if they had been the soundest churchgoing parishioners in the country, and he their true and appointed parson. Thus when Stockdale set foot in the place nobody had secured a lodging for him, and though his journey had given him a bad cold in the head, he was forced to attend to that business himself. On enquiry he learnt that the only possible accommodation in the village would be found at the house of one Mrs Lizzy Newberry, at the upper end of the street.

It was a youth who gave this information, and Stockdale asked him who Mrs Newberry might be.

The boy said that she was a widow-woman, who had got no husband, because he was dead. Mr Newberry, he added, had been a well-to-do man enough, as the saying was, and a farmer; but he had gone off in a decline. As regarded Mrs Newberry's serious side,

Stockdale gathered that she was one of the trimmers who went to church and chapel both.

'I'll go there,' said Stockdale, feeling that, in the absence of purely sectarian lodgings, he could do no better.

'She's a little particular, and won't hae gover'ment folks, or curates, or the pa'son's friends, or suchlike,' said the lad dubiously.

'Ah, that may be a promising sign: I'll call. Or, no; just you go up and ask first if she can find room for me. I have to see one or two persons on another matter. You will find me down at the carrier's.'

In a quarter of an hour the lad came back, and said that Mrs Newberry would have no objection to accommodate him, whereupon Stockdale called at the house. It stood within a garden-hedge, and seemed to be roomy and comfortable. He saw an elderly woman, with whom he made arrangements to come the same night, since there was no inn in the place, and he wished to house himself as soon as possible; the village being a local centre from which he was to radiate at once to the different small chapels in the neighbourhood. He forthwith sent his luggage to Mrs Newberry's from the carrier's, where he had taken shelter, and in the evening walked up to his temporary home.

As he now lived there, Stockdale felt it unnecessary to knock at the door; and entering quietly he had the pleasure of hearing footsteps scudding away like mice into the back quarters. He advanced to the parlour, as the front room was called, though its stone floor was scarcely disguised by the carpet, which only overlaid the trodden areas, leaving sandy deserts under the furniture. But the room looked snug and cheerful. The firelight shone out brightly, trembling on the bulging mouldings of the table-legs, playing with brass knobs and handles, and lurking in great strength on the under surface of the chimney-piece. A deep armchair, covered with horsehair, and studded with a countless throng of brass nails, was pulled up on one side of the fireplace. The tea-things were on the table, the teapot cover was open, and a little hand-bell had been laid at that precise point towards which a person seated in the great chair might be expected instinctively to stretch his hand.

Stockdale sat down, not objecting to his experience of the room thus far, and began his residence by tinkling the bell. A little girl crept in at the summons, and made tea for him. Her name, she said, was Marther Sarer, and she lived out there, nodding towards the road and village generally. Before Stockdale had got far with his meal, a tap sounded on the door behind him, and on his telling the enquirer to come in, a rustle of garments caused him to turn his head. He saw before him a fine and extremely well-made young woman, with dark hair, a wide, sensible, beautiful forehead, eyes that warmed him before he knew it, and a mouth that was in itself a picture to all appreciative souls.

'Can I get you anything else for tea?' she said, coming forward a step or two, an expression of liveliness on her features, and her hand waving the door by its edge.

'Nothing, thank you,' said Stockdale, thinking less of what he replied than of what might be her relation to the household.

'You are quite sure?' said the young woman, apparently aware that he had not considered his answer.

He conscientiously examined the tea-things, and found them all there. 'Quite sure, Miss Newberry,' he said.

'It is Mrs Newberry,' she said. 'Lizzy Newberry. I used to be Lizzy Simpkins.'

'Oh, I beg your pardon, Mrs Newberry.' And before he had occasion to say more, she left the room.

Stockdale remained in some doubt till Martha Sarah came to clear the table. 'Whose house is this, my little woman?' said he.

'Mrs Lizzy Newberry's, sir.'

'Then Mrs Newberry is not the old lady I saw this afternoon?'

'No. That's Mrs Newberry's mother. It was Mrs Newberry who comed in to you just by now, because she wanted to see if you was good-looking.'

Later in the evening, when Stockdale was about to begin supper, she came again. 'I have come myself, Mr Stockdale,' she said. The minister stood up in acknowledgement of the honour. 'I am afraid little Marther might not make you understand. What will you have for supper? – there's cold rabbit, and there's a ham uncut.'

Stockdale said he could get on nicely with those viands, and supper was laid. He had no more than cut a slice when tap-tap came to the door again. The minister had already learnt that this particular rhythm in taps denoted the fingers of his enkindling landlady, and the doomed young fellow buried his first mouthful under a look of receptive blandness.

'We have a chicken in the house, Mr Stockdale – I quite forgot to mention it just now. Perhaps you would like Marther Sarer to bring it up?'

Stockdale had advanced far enough in the art of

being a young man to say that he did not want the chicken, unless she brought it up herself; but when it was uttered he blushed at the daring gallantry of the speech, perhaps a shade too strong for a serious man and a minister. In three minutes the chicken appeared, but to his great surprise, only in the hands of Martha Sarah. Stockdale was disappointed, which perhaps it was intended that he should be.

He finished supper, and was not in the least anticipating Mrs Newberry again that night, when she tapped and entered as before. Stockdale's gratified look told that she had lost nothing by not appearing when expected. It happened that the cold in the head from which the young man suffered had increased with the approach of night, and before she had spoken he was seized with a violent fit of sneezing which he could not anyhow repress.

Mrs Newberry looked full of pity. 'Your cold is very bad tonight, Mr Stockdale.'

Stockdale replied that it was rather troublesome.

'And I've a good mind – ' she added archly, looking at the cheerless glass of water on the table, which the abstemious minister was going to drink.

'Yes, Mrs Newberry?'

'I've a good mind that you should have something more likely to cure it than that cold stuff.'

'Well,' said Stockdale, looking down at the glass, 'as there is no inn here, and nothing better to be got in the village, of course it will do.'

To this she replied, 'There is something better, not far off, though not in the house. I really think you must try it, or you may be ill. Yes, Mr Stockdale, you shall.' She held up her finger, seeing that he was about to speak. 'Don't ask what it is; wait, and you shall see.'

Lizzy went away, and Stockdale waited in a pleasant mood. Presently she returned with her bonnet and cloak on, saying, 'I am so sorry, but you must help me to get it. Mother has gone to bed. Will you wrap yourself up, and come this way, and please bring that cup with you.'

Stockdale, a lonely young fellow, who had for weeks felt a great craving for somebody on whom to throw away superfluous interest, and even tenderness, was not sorry to join her; and followed his guide through the back door, across the garden, to the bottom, where the boundary was a wall. This wall was low, and beyond it Stockdale discerned in the night shades several grey headstones, and the outlines of the church roof and tower.

'It is easy to get up this way,' she said, stepping upon a bank which abutted on the wall; then putting her foot on the top of the stonework, and descending by a spring inside, where the ground was much higher, as is the manner of graveyards to be. Stockdale did the same, and followed her in the dusk across the irregular ground till they came to the tower door, which, when they had entered, she softly closed behind them.

'You can keep a secret?' she said in a musical voice.

'Like an iron chest!' said he, fervently.

Then from under her cloak she produced a small lighted lantern, which the minister had not noticed that she carried at all. The light showed them to be close to the singing gallery stairs, under which lay a heap of lumber of all sorts, but consisting mostly of decayed framework, pews, panels, and pieces of flooring, that from time to time had been removed from their original fixings in the body of the edifice and replaced by new.

'Perhaps you will drag some of those boards aside?' she said, holding the lantern over her head to light him better. 'Or will you take the lantern while I move them?'

'I can manage it,' said the young man, and acting as she ordered, he uncovered, to his surprise, a row of little barrels bound with wood hoops, each barrel being about as large as the nave of a heavy wagon-wheel. When they were laid open Lizzy fixed her eyes on him, as if she wondered what he would say.

'You know what they are?' she asked, finding that he did not speak.

'Yes, barrels,' said Stockdale, simply. He was an inland man, the son of highly respectable parents, and brought up with a single eye to the ministry, and the sight suggested nothing beyond the fact that such articles were there.

'You are quite right, they are barrels,' she said, in an emphatic tone of candour that was not without a touch of irony.

Stockdale looked at her with an eye of sudden misgiving. 'Not smugglers' liquor?' he said.

'Yes,' said she. 'They are tubs of spirit that have accidentally floated over in the dark from France.'

In Nether-Moynton and its vicinity at this date people always smiled at the sort of sin called in the outside world illicit trading; and these little kegs of gin and brandy were as well known to the inhabitants as turnips. So that Stockdale's innocent ignorance, and his look of alarm when he guessed the sinister mystery, seemed to strike Lizzy first as ludicrous, and then as very awkward for the good impression that she wished to produce upon him.

'Smuggling is carried on here by some of the

people,' she said in a gentle, apologetic voice. 'It has been their practice for generations, and they think it no harm. Now, will you roll out one of the tubs?'

'What to do with it?' said the minister.

'To draw a little from it to cure your cold,' she answered. 'It is so 'nation strong that it drives away that sort of thing in a jiffy. Oh, it is all right about our taking it. I may have what I like; the owner of the tubs says so. I ought to have had some in the house, and then I shouldn't ha' been put to this trouble; but I drink none myself, and so I often forget to keep it indoors.'

'You are allowed to help yourself, I suppose, that you may not inform where their hiding-place is?'

'Well, no; not that particularly; but I may take any if I want it. So help yourself.'

'I will, to oblige you, since you have a right to it,' murmured the minister; and though he was not quite satisfied with his part in the performance, he rolled one of the 'tubs' out from the corner into the middle of the tower floor. 'How do you wish me to get it out – with a gimlet, I suppose?'

'No, I'll show you,' said his interesting companion; and she held up with her other hand a shoemaker's awl and a hammer. 'You must never do these things with a gimlet, because the wood-dust gets in; and when the buyers pour out the brandy that would tell them that the tub had been broached. An awl makes no dust, and the hole nearly closes up again. Now tap one of the hoops forward.'

Stockdale took the hammer and did so.

'Now make the hole in the part that was covered by the hoop.'

He made the hole as directed. 'It won't run out,' he said.

'Oh yes it will,' said she. 'Take the tub between your knees, and squeeze the heads; and I'll hold the cup.'

Stockdale obeyed; and the pressure taking effect upon the tub, which seemed to be thin, the spirit spirted out in a stream. When the cup was full he ceased pressing, and the flow immediately stopped. 'Now we must fill up the keg with water,' said Lizzy, 'or it will cluck like forty hens when it is handled, and show that 'tis not full.'

'But they tell you you may take it?'

'Yes, the *smugglers*, but the *buyers* must not know that the smugglers have been kind to me at their expense.'

'I see,' said Stockdale, doubtfully. 'I much question the honesty of this proceeding.'

By her direction he held the tub with the hole upwards, and while he went through the process of alternately pressing and ceasing to press, she produced a bottle of water, from which she took mouthfuls, conveying each to the keg by putting her pretty lips to the hole, where it was sucked in at each recovery of the cask from pressure. When it was again full he plugged the hole, knocked the hoop down to its place, and buried the tub in the lumber as before.

'Aren't the smugglers afraid that you will tell?' he asked as they recrossed the churchyard.

'Oh no. They are not afraid of that. I couldn't do such a thing.'

'They have put you into a very awkward corner,' said Stockdale emphatically. 'You must, of course, as an honest person, sometimes feel that it is your duty to inform – really you must.'

'Well, I have never particularly felt it as a duty; and, besides, my first husband – ' She stopped, and there was some confusion in her voice. Stockdale was so honest and unsophisticated that he did not at once discern why she paused; but at last he did perceive that the words were a slip, and that no woman would have uttered 'first husband' by accident unless she had thought pretty frequently of a second. He felt for her confusion, and allowed her time to recover and proceed. 'My husband,' she said, in a self-corrected tone, 'used to know of their doings, and so did my father, and kept the secret. I cannot inform, in fact, against anybody.'

'I see the hardness of it,' he continued, like a man who looked far into the moral of things. 'And it is very cruel that you should be tossed and tantalised between your memories and your conscience. I do hope, Mrs Newberry, that you will soon see your way out of this unpleasant position.'

'Well, I don't just now,' she murmured.

By this time they had passed over the wall and entered the house; where she brought him a glass and hot water, and left him to his own reflections. He looked after her vanishing form, asking himself whether he, as a respectable man, and a minister, and a shining light, even though as yet only of the half-penny-candle sort, were quite justified in doing this thing. A sneeze settled the question; and he found that when the fiery liquor was lowered by the addition of twice or thrice the quantity of water, it was one of the prettiest cures for a cold in the head that he had ever known, particularly at this chilly time of the year.

Stockdale sat in the deep chair about twenty minutes sipping and meditating, till he at length took warmer views of things, and longed for the morrow, when he would see Mrs Newberry again. He then felt that, though chronologically at a short distance, it would in an emotional sense be very long before tomorrow came, and walked restlessly round the room. His eye was attracted by a framed and glazed sampler in which a running ornament of fir trees and peacocks surrounded the following pretty bit of sentiment –

Rose-leaves smell when roses thrive
Here's my work while I'm alive;
Rose-leaves smell when shrunk and shed,
Here's my work when I am dead.
Lizzy Simpkins.
Fear God.
Honour the King.
Aged 11 years.

' 'Tis hers,' he said to himself. 'Heavens, how I like that name!'

Before he had done thinking that no other name from Abigail to Zenobia would have suited his young landlady so well, tap-tap came again upon the door; and the minister started as her face appeared yet another time, looking so disinterested that the most ingenious would have refrained from asserting that she had come to affect his feelings by her seductive eyes.

'Would you like a fire in your room, Mr Stockdale, on account of your cold?'

The minister, being still a little pricked in the conscience for countenancing her in watering the spirits, saw here a way to self-chastisement. 'No, I thank you,' he said firmly, 'it is not necessary. I have never been used to one in my life, and it would be giving way to luxury too far.'

'Then I won't insist,' she said, and disconcerted him by vanishing instantly. Wondering if she was vexed by

his refusal, he wished that he had chosen to have a fire,
even though it should have scorched him out of bed
and endangered his self-discipline for a dozen days.
However, he consoled himself with what was in truth
a rare consolation for a budding lover, that he was
under the same roof with Lizzy; her guest, in fact, to
take a poetical view of the term lodger; and that he
would certainly see her on the morrow.

The morrow came, and Stockdale rose early, his
cold quite gone. He had never in his life so longed for
the breakfast hour as he did that day, and punctually at
eight o'clock, after a short walk to reconnoitre the
premises, he re-entered the door of his dwelling.
Breakfast passed, and Martha Sarah attended, but
nobody came voluntarily as on the night before to
enquire if there were other wants which he had not
mentioned, and which she would attempt to gratify.
He was disappointed, and went out, hoping to see her
at dinner. Dinner-time came; he sat down to the meal,
finished it, lingered on for a whole hour, although two
new teachers were at that moment waiting at the
chapel door to speak to him by appointment. It was
useless to wait longer, and he slowly went his way
down the lane, cheered by the thought that, after all, he
would see her in the evening, and perhaps engage again
in the delightful tub-broaching in the neighbouring
church tower, which proceeding he resolved to render
more moral by steadfastly insisting that no water
should be introduced to fill up, though the tub should
cluck like all the hens in Christendom. But nothing
could disguise the fact that it was a queer business; and
his countenance fell when he thought how much more
his mind was interested in that matter than in his
serious duties.

...ompunction vanished with the decline ...t came, and his tea and supper; but no ...ewberry, and no sweet temptations. At last the ...er could bear it no longer, and said to his quaint little attendant, 'Where is Mrs Newberry today?' judiciously handing a penny as he spoke.

'She's busy,' said Martha.

'Anything serious happened?' he asked, handing another penny, and revealing yet additional pennies in the background.

'Oh no – nothing at all,' said she, with breathless confidence. 'Nothing ever happens to her. She's only biding upstairs in bed because 'tis her way sometimes.'

Being a young man of some honour, he would not question further, and assuming that Lizzy must have a bad headache, or other slight ailment, in spite of what the girl had said, he went to bed dissatisfied, not even setting eyes on old Mrs Simpkins. 'I said last night that I should see her tomorrow,' he reflected; 'but that was not to be!'

Next day he had better fortune, or worse, meeting her at the foot of the stairs in the morning, and being favoured by a visit or two from her during the day – once for the purpose of making kindly enquiries about his comfort, as on the first evening, and at another time to place a bunch of winter violets on his table, with a promise to renew them when they drooped. On these occasions there was something in her smile which showed how conscious she was of the effect she produced, though it must be said that it was rather a humorous than a designing consciousness, and savoured more of pride than of vanity.

As for Stockdale, he clearly perceived that he possessed unlimited capacity for backsliding, and wished that tutelary saints were not denied to Dissenters. He set a watch upon his tongue and eyes for the space of one hour and a half; after which he found it was useless to struggle further, and gave himself up to the situation. 'The other minister will be here in a month,' he said to himself when sitting over the fire. 'Then I shall be off, and she will distract my mind no more! . . . And then, shall I go on living by myself for ever? No; when my two years of probation are finished, I shall have a furnished house to live in, with a varnished door and a brass knocker; and I'll march straight back to her, and ask her flat, as soon as the last plate is on the dresser.'

Thus a titillating fortnight was passed by young Stockdale, during which time things proceeded much as such matters have done ever since the beginning of history: he saw the object of attachment several times one day, did not see her at all the next, met her when he least expected to do so, missed her when hints and signs as to where she should be at a given hour almost amounted to an appointment. This mild coquetry was perhaps fair enough under the circumstances of their being so closely lodged, and Stockdale put up with it as philosophically as he was able. Being in her own house she could, after vexing him or disappointing him of her presence, easily win him back by suddenly surrounding him with those little attentions which her position as his landlady put it in her power to bestow. When he had waited indoors half the day to see her, and on finding that she would not be seen had gone off in a huff to the dreariest and dampest walk he could discover, she would restore equilibrium in the evening with 'Mr Stockdale, I have fancied you must feel draught o' nights from your bedroom window, and so

I have been putting up thicker curtains this afternoon while you were out'; or 'I noticed that you sneezed twice again this morning, Mr Stockdale. Depend upon it that cold is hanging about you yet; I am sure it is – I have thought of it continually; and you must let me make a posset for you.'

Sometimes in coming home he found his sitting-room rearranged, chairs placed where the table had stood, and the table ornamented with the few fresh flowers and leaves that could be obtained at this season, so as to add a novelty to the room. At times she would be standing on a chair outside the house, trying to nail up a branch of the monthly rose which the winter wind had blown down; and of course he stepped forward to assist her, when their hands got mixed in passing the shreds and nails.

Thus they became friends again after a disagreement. She would utter on these occasions some pretty and deprecatory remark on the necessity of her troubling him anew; and he would straightway say that he would do a hundred times as much for her if she should so require.

TWO

How He Saw Two Other Men

Matters being in this advancing state, Stockdale was rather surprised one cloudy evening, while sitting in his room, at hearing her speak in low tones of expostulation to someone at the door. It was nearly dark, but the shutters were not yet closed, nor the candles lighted; and Stockdale was tempted to stretch his head towards the window. He saw outside the door a young man in clothes of a whitish colour, and upon reflection judged their wearer to be the well-built and rather handsome miller who lived below. The miller's voice was alternately low and firm, and sometimes it reached the level of positive entreaty; but what the words were Stockdale could in no way hear.

Before the colloquy had ended, the minister's attention was attracted by a second incident. Opposite Lizzy's home grew a clump of laurels, forming a thick and permanent shade. One of the laurel boughs now quivered against the light background of sky, and in a moment the head of a man peered out, and remained still. He seemed to be also much interested in the conversation at the door, and was plainly lingering there to watch and listen. Had Stockdale stood in any other relation to Lizzy than that of a lover, he might have gone out and investigated the meaning of this; but, being as yet but an unprivileged ally, he did nothing more than stand up and show himself against the firelight, whereupon the listener disappeared, and Lizzy and the miller spoke in lower tones.

Stockdale was made so uneasy by the circumstance, that as soon as the miller was gone, he said, 'Mrs Newberry, are you aware that you were watched just now, and your conversation heard?'

'When?' she said.

'When you were talking to that miller. A man was looking from the laurel tree as jealously as if he could have eaten you.'

She showed more concern than the trifling event seemed to demand, and he added, 'Perhaps you were talking of things you did not wish to be overheard?'

'I was talking only on business,' she said.

'Lizzy, be frank,' said the young man. 'If it was only on business, why should anybody wish to listen to you?'

She look curiously at him. 'What else do you think it could be, then?'

'Well – the only talk between a young woman and man that is likely to amuse an eavesdropper.'

'Ah, yes,' she said, smiling in spite of her pre-occupation. 'Well, my cousin Owlett has spoken to me about matrimony, every now and then, that's true; but he was not speaking of it then. I wish he had been speaking of it, with all my heart. It would have been much less serious for me.'

'Oh, Mrs Newberry!'

'It would. Not that I should ha' chimed in with him, of course. I wish it for other reasons. I am glad, Mr Stockdale, that you have told me of that listener. It is a timely warning, and I must see my cousin again.'

'But don't go away till I have spoken,' said the minister. 'I'll out with it at once, and make no more ado. Let it be Yes or No between us, Lizzy; please do!' And he held out his hand, in which she freely allowed her own to rest, but without speaking.

'You mean Yes by that?' he asked, after waiting awhile.

'You may be my sweetheart, if you will.'

'Why not say at once you will wait for me until I have a house and can come back to marry you?'

'Because I am thinking – thinking of something else,' she said with embarrassment. 'It all comes upon me at once, and I must settle one thing at a time.'

'At any rate, dear Lizzy, you can assure me that the miller shall not be allowed to speak to you except on business? You have never directly encouraged him?'

She parried the question by saying, 'You see, he and his party have been in the habit of leaving things on my premises sometimes, and as I have not denied him, it makes him rather forward.'

'Things – what things?'

'Tubs – they are called Things here.'

'But why don't you deny him, my dear Lizzy?'

'I cannot well.'

'You are too timid. It is unfair of him to impose so upon you, and get your good name into danger by his smuggling tricks. Promise me that the next time he wants to leave his tubs here you will let me roll them into the street?'

She shook her head. 'I would not venture to offend the neighbours so much as that,' said she, 'or do anything that would be so likely to put poor Owlett into the hands of the Customs-men.'

Stockdale sighed, and said that he thought hers a mistaken generosity when it extended to assisting those who cheated the king of his dues. 'At any rate, you will let me make him keep his distance as your lover, and tell him flatly that you are not for him?'

'Please not, at present,' she said. 'I don't wish to offend my old neighbours. It is not only Mr Owlett who is concerned.'

'This is too bad,' said Stockdale impatiently.

'On my honour, I won't encourage him as my lover,' Lizzy answered earnestly. 'A reasonable man will be satisfied with that.'

'Well, so I am,' said Stockdale, his countenance clearing.

The Mysterious Greatcoat

Stockdale now began to notice more particularly a feature in the life of his fair landlady, which he had casually observed, but scarcely ever thought of before. It was that she was markedly irregular in her hours of rising. For a week or two she would be tolerably punctual, reaching the ground-floor within a few minutes of half-past seven. Then suddenly she would not be visible till twelve at noon, perhaps for three or four days in succession; and twice he had certain proof that she did not leave her room till half-past three in the afternoon. The second time that this extreme lateness came under his notice was on a day when he had particularly wished to consult with her about his future movements; and he concluded, as he always had done, that she had a cold, headache, or other ailment, unless she had kept herself invisible to avoid meeting and talking to him, which he could hardly believe. The former supposition was disproved, however, by her innocently saying, some days later, when they were speaking on a question of health, that she had never had a moment's heaviness, headache, or illness of any kind since the previous January twelvemonth.

'I am glad to hear it,' said he. 'I thought quite otherwise.'

'What, do I look sickly?' she asked, turning up her face to show the impossibility of his gazing on it and holding such a belief for a moment.

'Not at all; I merely thought so from your being

sometimes obliged to keep your room through the best part of the day.'

'Oh, as for that – it means nothing,' she murmured, with a look which some might have called cold, and which was the worst look that he liked to see upon her. 'It is pure sleepiness, Mr Stockdale.'

'Never!'

'It is, I tell you. When I stay in my room till half-past three in the afternoon, you may always be sure that I slept soundly till three, or I shouldn't have stayed there.'

'It is dreadful,' said Stockdale, thinking of the disastrous effects of such indulgence upon the house-hold of a minister should it become a habit of everyday occurrence.

'But then,' she said, divining his good and prescient thoughts, 'it only happens when I stay awake all night. I don't go to sleep till five or six in the morning sometimes.'

'Ah, that's another matter,' said Stockdale. 'Sleep-lessness to such an alarming extent is real illness. Have you spoken to a doctor?'

'Oh no – there is no need for doing that – it is all natural to me.' And she went away without further remark.

Stockdale might have waited a long time to know the real cause of her sleeplessness, had it not happened that one dark night he was sitting in his bedroom jotting down notes for a sermon, which occupied him perfunctorily for a considerable time after the other members of the household had retired. He did not get to bed till one o'clock. Before he had fallen asleep he heard a knocking at the front door, first rather timidly performed, and then louder. Nobody answered it, and the person knocked again. As the house still remained undisturbed, Stockdale got out of bed, went to his window, which overlooked the door, and opening it, asked who was there.

A young woman's voice replied that Susan Wallis was there, and that she had come to ask if Mrs Newberry could give her some mustard to make a plaster with, as her father was taken very ill on the chest.

The minister, having neither bell nor servant, was compelled to act in person. 'I will call Mrs Newberry,' he said. Partly dressing himself, he went along the passage and tapped at Lizzy's door. She did not answer, and, thinking of her erratic habits in the matter of sleep, he thumped the door persistently, when he discovered, by its moving ajar under his knocking, that it had only been gently pushed to. As there was now a sufficient entry for the voice, he knocked no longer, but said in firm tones, 'Mrs Newberry, you are wanted.'

The room was quite silent; not a breathing, not a rustle, came from any part of it. Stockdale now sent a positive shout through the open space of the door: 'Mrs Newberry!' – still no answer, or movement of any kind within. Then he heard sounds from the opposite room, that of Lizzy's mother, as if she had been aroused by his uproar though Lizzy had not, and was dressing herself hastily. Stockdale softly closed the younger woman's door and went on to the other, which was opened by Mrs Simpkins before he could reach it. She was in her ordinary clothes, and had a light in her hand.

'What's the person calling about?' she said in alarm.

Stockdale told the girl's errand, adding seriously, 'I cannot wake Mrs Newberry.'

'It is no matter,' said her mother. 'I can let the girl have what she wants as well as my daughter.' And she came out of the room and went downstairs.

Stockdale retired towards his own apartment, saying, however, to Mrs Simpkins from the landing, as if on second thoughts, 'I suppose there is nothing the matter with Mrs Newberry, that I could not wake her?'

'Oh no,' said the old lady hastily. 'Nothing at all.'

Still the minister was not satisfied. 'Will you go in and see?' he said. 'I should be much more at ease.'

Mrs Simpkins returned up the staircase, went to her daughter's room, and came out again almost instantly. 'There is nothing at all the matter with Lizzy,' she said; and descended again to attend to the applicant, who, having seen the light, had remained quiet during this interval.

Stockdale went into his room and lay down as before. He heard Lizzy's mother open the front door, admit the girl, and then the murmured discourse of both as they went to the store-cupboard for the medicament required. The girl departed, the door was fastened, Mrs Simpkins came upstairs, and the house was again in silence. Still the minister did not fall asleep. He could not get rid of a singular suspicion, which was all the more harassing, in being, if true, the most unaccountable thing within his experience. That Lizzy Newberry was in her bedroom when he made such a clamour at the door he could not possibly convince himself, notwithstanding that he had heard her come upstairs at the usual time, go into her chamber, and shut herself up in the usual way. Yet all reason was so much against her being elsewhere, that he was constrained to go back again to the unlikely theory of a heavy sleep, though he had heard neither breath nor movement during a shouting and knocking loud enough to rouse the Seven Sleepers.

Before coming to any positive conclusion he fell asleep himself, and did not awake till day. He saw nothing of Mrs Newberry in the morning, before he went out to meet the rising sun, as he liked to do when the weather was fine; but as this was by no means unusual, he took no notice of it. At breakfast-time he knew that she was not far off by hearing her in the kitchen, and though he saw nothing of her person, that back apartment being rigorously closed against his eyes, she seemed to be talking, ordering, and bustling about among the pots and skimmers in so ordinary a manner, that there was no reason for his wasting more time in fruitless surmise.

The minister suffered from these distractions, and his extemporised sermons were not improved thereby. Already he often said Romans for Corinthians in the pulpit, and gave out hymns in strange cramped metres, that hitherto had always been skipped, because the congregation could not raise a tune to fit them. He fully resolved that as soon as his few weeks of stay approached their end he would cut the matter short, and commit himself by proposing a definite engagement, repenting at leisure if necessary.

With this end in view, he suggested to her on the evening after her mysterious sleep that they should take a walk together just before dark, the latter part of the proposition being introduced that they might return home unseen. She consented to go; and away they went over a stile, to a shrouded footpath suited for the occasion. But, in spite of attempts on both sides, they were unable to infuse much spirit into the ramble.

She looked rather paler than usual, and sometimes turned her head away.

'Lizzy,' said Stockdale reproachfully, when they had walked in silence a long distance.

'Yes,' said she.

'You yawned – much my company is to you!' He put it in that way, but he was really wondering whether her yawn could possibly have more to do with physical weariness from the night before than mental weariness of that present moment. Lizzy apologised, and owned that she was rather tired, which gave him an opening for a direct question on the point; but his modesty would not allow him to put it to her; and he uncomfortably resolved to wait.

The month of February passed with alternations of mud and frost, rain and sleet, east winds and north-westerly gales. The hollow places in the ploughed fields showed themselves as pools of water, which had settled there from the higher levels, and had not yet found time to soak away. The birds began to get lively, and a single thrush came just before sunset each evening, and sang hopefully on the large elm tree which stood nearest to Mrs Newberry's house. Cold blasts and brittle earth had given place to an oozing dampness more unpleasant in itself than frost; but it suggested coming spring, and its unpleasantness was of a bearable kind.

Stockdale had been going to bring about a practical understanding with Lizzy at least half a dozen times; but, what with the mystery of her apparent absence on the night of the neighbour's call, and her curious way of lying in bed at unaccountable times, he felt a check within him whenever he wanted to speak out. Thus they still lived on as indefinitely affianced lovers, each of whom hardly acknowledged the other's claim to the name of chosen one. Stockdale persuaded himself that his hesitation was owing to the postponement of the ordained minister's arrival, and the consequent delay in his own departure, which did away with all necessity for haste in his courtship; but perhaps it was only that his discretion was reasserting itself, and telling him that he had better get clearer ideas of Lizzy before arranging for the grand contract of his life with her. She, on her part, always seemed ready to be urged further on that question than he had hitherto attempted to go; but she was none the less independent, and to a degree which would have kept from flagging the passion of a far more mutable man.

On the evening of the 1st of March he went casually into his bedroom about dusk, and noticed lying on a chair a greatcoat, hat, and breeches. Having no recollection of leaving any clothes of his own in that spot, he went and examined them as well as he could in the twilight, and found that they did not belong to him. He paused for a moment to consider how they might have got there. He was the only man living in the house; and yet these were not his garments, unless he had made a mistake. No, they were not his. He called up Martha Sarah.

'How did these things come in my room?' he said, flinging the objectionable articles to the floor.

Martha said that Mrs Newberry had given them to her to brush, and that she had brought them up there thinking they must be Mr Stockdale's, as there was no other gentleman a-lodging there.

'Of course you did,' said Stockdale. 'Now take them down to your mis'ess, and say they are some clothes I have found here and know nothing about.'

As the door was left open he heard the conversation downstairs. 'How stupid!' said Mrs Newberry, in a tone of confusion. 'Why, Marther Sarer, I did not tell you to take 'em to Mr Stockdale's room.'

'I thought they must be his as they was so muddy,' said Martha, humbly.

'You should have left 'em on the clotheshorse,' said the young mistress, severely; and she came upstairs with the garments on her arm, quickly passed Stockdale's room, and threw them forcibly into a closet at the end of a passage. With this the incident ended, and the house was silent again.

There would have been nothing remarkable in finding such clothes in a widow's house had they been clean; or motheaten, or creased, or mouldy from long lying by; but that they should be splashed with recent mud bothered Stockdale a good deal. When a young pastor is in the aspen stage of attachment, and open to agitation at the merest trifles, a really substantial incongruity of this complexion is a disturbing thing. However, nothing further occurred at that time; but he became watchful, and given to conjecture, and was unable to forget the circumstance.

One morning, on looking from his window, he saw Mrs Newberry herself brushing the tails of a long drab greatcoat, which, if he mistook not, was the very same garment as the one that had adorned the chair of his room. It was densely splashed up to the hollow of the back with neighbouring Nether-Moynton mud, to judge by its colour, the spots being distinctly visible to him in the sunlight. The previous day or two having been wet, the inference was irresistible that the wearer had quite recently been walking some considerable distance about the lanes and fields. Stockdale opened the window and looked out, and Mrs Newberry turned her head. Her face became slowly red; she never had looked prettier, or more incomprehensible. He waved his hand affectionately, and said good-morning; she answered with embarrassment, having ceased her occupation on the instant that she saw him, and rolled up the coat half-cleaned.

Stockdale shut the window. Some simple explanation of her proceeding was doubtless within the bounds of possibility; but he himself could not think of one; and he wished that she had placed the matter beyond conjecture by voluntarily saying something about it there and then.

But, though Lizzy had not offered an explanation at the moment, the subject was brought forward by her at the next time of their meeting. She was chatting to him concerning some other event, and remarked that it happened about the time when she was dusting some old clothes that had belonged to her poor husband.

'You keep them clean out of respect to his memory?' said Stockdale, tentatively.

'I air and dust them sometimes,' she said, with the most charming innocence in the world.

'Do dead men come out of their graves and walk in mud?' murmured the minister, in a cold sweat at the deception that she was practising.

'What did you say?' asked Lizzy.

'Nothing, nothing,' said he, mournfully. 'Mere words – a phrase that will do for my sermon next Sunday.' It was too plain that Lizzy was unaware that he had seen fresh pedestrian splashes upon the skirts of the telltale overcoat, and that she imagined him to believe it had come direct from some chest or drawer.

The aspect of the case was now considerably darker. Stockdale was so much depressed by it that he did not challenge her explanation, or threaten to go off as a missionary to benighted islanders, or reproach her in any way whatever. He simply parted from her when she had done talking, and lived on in perplexity, till by degrees his natural manner became sad and constrained.

FOUR

At the Time of the New Moon

The following Thursday was changeable, damp, and gloomy; and the night threatened to be windy and unpleasant. Stockdale had gone away to Knollsea in the morning, to be present at some commemoration service there, and on his return he was met by the attractive Lizzy in the passage. Whether influenced by the tide of cheerfulness which had attended him that day, or by the drive through the open air, or whether from a natural disposition to let bygones alone, he allowed himself to be fascinated into forgetfulness of the greatcoat incident, and upon the whole passed a pleasant evening; not so much in her society as within sound of her voice, as she sat talking in the back parlour to her mother, till the latter went to bed. Shortly after this Mrs Newberry retired, and then Stockdale prepared to go upstairs himself. But before he left the room he remained standing by the dying embers awhile, thinking long of one thing and another; and was only aroused by the flickering of his candle in the socket as it suddenly declined and went out.

Knowing that there were a tinderbox, matches, and another candle in his bedroom, he felt his way upstairs without a light. On reaching his chamber he laid his hand on every possible ledge and corner for the tinderbox, but for a long time in vain. Discovering it at length, Stockdale produced a spark, and was kindling the brimstone, when he fancied that he heard a movement in the passage. He blew harder at the lint, the match flared up, and looking by aid of the blue light through the door, which had been standing open all this time, he was surprised to see a male figure vanishing round the top of the staircase with the evident intention of escaping unobserved. The personage wore the clothes which Lizzy had been brushing, and something in the outline and gait suggested to the minister that the wearer was Lizzy herself.

But he was not sure of this; and, greatly excited, Stockdale determined to investigate the mystery, and to adopt his own way for doing it. He blew out the match without lighting the candle, went into the passage, and proceeded on tiptoe towards Lizzy's room. A faint grey square of light in the direction of the chamber-window as he approached told him that the door was open, and at once suggested that the occupant was gone. He turned and brought down his fist upon the handrail of the staircase: 'It was she; in her late husband's coat and hat!'

Somewhat relieved to find that there was no intruder in the case, yet none the less surprised, the minister crept down the stairs, softly put on his boots, overcoat, and hat, and tried the front door. It was fastened as usual: he went to the back door, found this unlocked, and emerged into the garden. The night was mild and moonless, and rain had lately been falling, though for the present it had ceased. There was a sudden dropping from the trees and bushes every now and then, as each passing wind shook their boughs. Among these sounds Stockdale heard the faint fall of feet upon the road outside, and he guessed from the step that it was Lizzy's. He followed the sound, and, helped by the circumstance of the wind blowing from the direction in which the pedestrian moved, he got nearly close to her, and kept there, without risk of being overheard. While he thus followed her up the street or lane, as it might indifferently be called, there being more hedge than houses on either side, a figure came forward to her from one of the cottage doors. Lizzy stopped; the minister stepped upon the grass and stopped also.

'Is that Mrs Newberry?' said the man who had come out, whose voice Stockdale recognised as that of one of the most devout members of his congregation.

'It is,' said Lizzy.

'I be quite ready – I've been here this quarter-hour.'

'Ah John,' said she, 'I have bad news; there is danger tonight for our venture.'

'And d'ye tell o't! I dreamed there might be.'

'Yes,' she said hurriedly; 'and you must go at once round to where the chaps are waiting, and tell them they will not be wanted till tomorrow night at the same time. I go to burn the lugger off.'

'I will,' he said; and instantly went off through a gate, Lizzy continuing her way.

On she tripped at a quickening pace till the lane turned into the turnpike road, which she crossed, and got into the track for Ringsworth. Here she ascended the hill without the least hesitation, passed the lonely hamlet of Holworth, and went down the vale on the other side. Stockdale had never taken any extensive walks in this direction, but he was aware that if she persisted in her course much longer she would draw near to the coast, which was here between two and three miles distant from Nether-Moynton; and as it had been about a quarter-past eleven o'clock when they set out, her intention seemed to be to reach the shore about midnight.

Lizzy soon ascended a small mound, which Stockdale at the same time adroitly skirted on the left; and a dull monotonous roar burst upon his ear. The hillock was about fifty yards from the top of the cliffs, and by day it apparently commanded a full view of the bay. There was light enough in the sky to show her disguised figure against it when she reached the top, where she paused, and afterwards sat down. Stockdale, not wishing on any account to alarm her at this moment, yet desirous of being near her, sank upon his hands and knees, crept a little higher up, and there stayed still.

The wind was chilly, the ground damp, and his position one in which he did not care to remain long. However, before he had decided to leave it, the young man heard voices behind him. What they signified he did not know; but, fearing that Lizzy was in danger, he was about to run forward and warn her that she might be seen, when she crept to the shelter of a little bush which maintained a precarious existence in that exposed spot; and her form was absorbed in its dark and stunted outline as if she had become part of it. She had evidently heard the men as well as he. They passed near him, talking in loud and careless tones, which could be heard above the uninterrupted washings of the sea, and which suggested that they were not engaged in any business at their own risk. This proved to be the fact: some of their words floated across to him, and caused him to forget at once the coldness of his situation.

'What's the vessel?'

'A lugger, about fifty tons.'

'From Cherbourg, I suppose?'

'Yes, 'ab'lieve.'

'But it don't all belong to Owlett?'

'Oh no. He's only got a share. There's another or two in it – a farmer and suchlike, but the names I don't know.'

The voices died away, and the heads and shoulders of the men diminished towards the cliff, and dropped out of sight.

'My darling has been tempted to buy a share by that unbeliever Owlett,' groaned the minister, his honest affection for Lizzy having quickened to its intensest point during these moments of risk to her person and name. 'That's why she's here,' he said to himself. 'Oh, it will be the ruin of her!'

His perturbation was interrupted by the sudden bursting out of a bright and increasing light from the spot where Lizzy was in hiding. A few seconds later, and before it had reached the height of a blaze, he heard her rush past him down the hollow like a stone from a sling, in the direction of home. The light now flared high and wide, and showed its position clearly. She had kindled a bough of furze and stuck it into the bush under which she had been crouching; the wind fanned the flame, which crackled fiercely, and threatened to consume the bush as well as the bough. Stockdale paused just long enough to notice thus much, and then followed rapidly the route taken by the young woman. His intention was to overtake her, and reveal himself as a friend; but run as he would he could see nothing of her. Thus he flew across the open country about Holworth, twisting his legs and ankles in unexpected fissures and descents, till, on coming to the gate between the downs and the road, he was forced to pause to get breath. There was no audible movement either in front or behind him, and he now concluded that she had not outrun him, but that, hearing him at her heels, and believing him one of the excise party, she had hidden herself somewhere on the way, and let him pass by.

He went on at a more leisurely pace towards the village. On reaching the house he found his surmise to be correct, for the gate was on the latch, and the door unfastened, just as he had left them. Stockdale closed the door behind him, and waited silently in the passage. In about ten minutes he heard the same light footstep that he had heard in going out; it paused at the gate, which opened and shut softly, and then the door-latch was lifted, and Lizzy came in.

Stockdale went forward and said at once, 'Lizzy, don't be frightened. I have been waiting up for you.'

She started, though she had recognised the voice. 'It is Mr Stockdale, isn't it?' she said.

'Yes,' he answered, becoming angry now that she was safe indoors, and not alarmed. 'And a nice game I've found you out in tonight. You are in man's clothes, and I am ashamed of you.'

Lizzy could hardly find a voice to answer this unexpected reproach.

'I am only partly in man's clothes,' she faltered, shrinking back to the wall. 'It is only his greatcoat and hat and breeches that I've got on, which is no harm, as he was my own husband; and I do it only because a cloak blows about so, and you can't use your arms. I have got my own dress under just the same – it is only tucked in! Will you go away upstairs and let me pass? I didn't want you to see me at such a time as this.'

'But I have a right to see you. How do you think there can be anything between us now?' Lizzy was silent. 'You are a smuggler,' he continued sadly.

'I have only a share in the run,' she said.

'That makes no difference. Whatever did you engage in such a trade as that for, and keep it such a secret from me all this time?'

'I don't do it always. I only do it in wintertime when 'tis new moon.'

'Well, I suppose that's because it can't be done anywhen else . . . You have regularly upset me, Lizzy.'

'I am sorry for that,' Lizzy meekly replied.

'Well now,' said he more tenderly, 'no harm is done as yet. Won't you for the sake of me give up this blamable and dangerous practice altogether?'

'I must do my best to save this run,' said she, getting rather husky in the throat. 'I don't want to give you up – you know that; but I don't want to lose my venture. I don't know what to do now! Why I have kept it so secret from you is that I was afraid you would be angry if you knew.'

'I should think so. I suppose if I had married you without finding this out you'd have gone on with it just the same?'

'I don't know. I did not think so far ahead. I only went tonight to burn the folks off, because we found that the preventive-men knew where the tubs were to be landed.'

'It is a pretty mess to be in altogether, is this,' said the distracted young minister. 'Well, what will you do now?'

Lizzy slowly murmured the particulars of their plan, the chief of which were that they meant to try their luck at some other point of the shore the next night; that three landing places were always agreed upon before the run was attempted, with the understanding that, if the vessel was 'burnt off' from the first point, which was Ringsworth, as it had been by her tonight, the crew should attempt to make the second, which was Lulwind Cove, on the second night; and if there, too, danger threatened, they should on the third night try the third place, which was behind a headland further west.

'Suppose the officers hinder them landing there too?' he said, his attention to this interesting programme displacing for a moment his concern at her share in it.

'Then we shan't try anywhere else all this dark – that's what we call the time between moon and moon – and perhaps they'll string the tubs to a stray-line, and sink 'em a little-ways from shore, and take the bearings; and then when they have a chance they'll go to creep for 'em.'

'What's that?'

'Oh, they'll go out in a boat and drag a creeper – that's a grapnel – along the bottom till it catch hold of the stray-line.'

The minister stood thinking; and there was no sound within doors but the tick of the clock on the stairs, and the quick breathing of Lizzy, partly from her walk and partly from agitation, as she stood close to the wall, not in such complete darkness but that he could discern against its whitewashed surface the greatcoat, breeches, and broad hat which covered her.

'Lizzy, all this is very wrong,' he said. 'Don't you remember the lesson of the tribute-money? "Render unto Caesar the things that are Caesar's." Surely you have heard that read times enough in your growing up.'

'He's dead,' she pouted.

'But the spirit of the text is in force just the same.'

'My father did it, and so did my grandfather, and almost everybody in Nether-Moynton lives by it, and life would be so dull if it wasn't for that, that I should not care to live at all.'

'I am nothing to live for, of course,' he replied bitterly. 'You would not think it worth while to give up this wild business and live for me alone?'

'I have never looked at it like that.'

'And you won't promise, and wait till I am ready?'

'I cannot give you my word tonight.' And, looking thoughtfully down, she gradually moved and moved away, going into the adjoining room, and closing the door between them. She remained there in the dark till he was tired of waiting, and had gone up to his own chamber.

Poor Stockdale was dreadfully depressed all the next day by the discoveries of the night before. Lizzy was unmistakably a fascinating young woman; but as a minister's wife she was hardly to be contemplated. 'If I had only stuck to father's little grocery business, instead of going in for the ministry, she would have suited me beautifully!' he said sadly, until he remembered that in that case he would never have come from his distant home to Nether-Moynton, and never have known her.

The estrangement between them was not complete, but it was sufficient to keep them out of each other's company. Once during the day he met her in the garden-path, and said, turning a reproachful eye upon her, 'Do you promise, Lizzy?' But she did not reply. The evening drew on, and he knew well enough that Lizzy would repeat her excursion at night – her half-offended manner had shown that she had not the slightest intention of altering her plans at present. He did not wish to repeat his own share of the adventure; but, act as he would, his uneasiness on her account increased with the decline of day. Supposing that an accident should befall her, he would never forgive himself for not being there to help, much as he disliked the idea of seeming to countenance such unlawful escapades.

FIVE

How They Went to Lulwind Cove

As he had expected, she left the house at the same hour at night, this time passing his door without stealth, as if she knew very well that he would be watching, and were resolved to brave his displeasure. He was quite ready, opened the door quickly, and reached the back door almost as soon as she.

'Then you will go, Lizzy?' he said as he stood on the step beside her, who now again appeared as a little man with a face altogether unsuited to his clothes.

'I must,' she said, repressed by his stern manner.

'Then I shall go too,' said he.

'And I am sure you will enjoy it!' she exclaimed, in more buoyant tones. 'Everybody does who tries it.'

'God forbid that I should,' he said. 'But I must look after you.'

They opened the wicket and went up the road

abreast of each other, but at some distance apart, scarcely a word passing between them. The evening was rather less favourable to smuggling enterprise than the last had been, the wind being lower, and the sky somewhat clear towards the north.

'It is rather lighter,' said Stockdale.

' 'Tis, unfortunately,' said she. 'But it is only from those few stars over there. The moon was new today at four o'clock, and I expected clouds. I hope we shall be able to do it this dark, for when we have to sink 'em for long it makes the stuff taste bleachy, and folks don't like it so well.'

Her course was different from that of the preceding night, branching off to the left over Lord's Barrow as soon as they had got out of the lane and crossed the highway. By the time they reached Shaldon Down, Stockdale, who had been in perplexed thought as to what he should say to her, decided that he would not attempt expostulation now, while she was excited by the adventure, but wait till it was over, and endeavour to keep her from such practices in future. It occurred to him once or twice, as they rambled on, that should they be surprised by the preventive-guard, his situation would be more awkward than hers, for it would be difficult to prove his true motive in coming to the spot; but the risk was a slight consideration beside his wish to be with her.

They now arrived at a ravine which lay on the outskirts of Shaldon, a village two miles on their way towards the point of the shore they sought. Lizzy broke the silence this time: 'I have to wait here to meet the carriers. I don't know if they have come yet. As I told you, we go to Lulwind Cove tonight, and it is two miles further than Ringsworth.'

It turned out that the men had already come; for while she spoke two or three dozen heads broke the line of the slope, and a company of them at once descended from the bushes where they had been lying in wait. These carriers were men whom Lizzy and other proprietors regularly employed to bring the tubs from the boat to a hiding-place inland. They were all young fellows of Nether-Moynton, Shaldon, and the neighbourhood, quiet and inoffensive persons, even though some held heavy sticks, who simply engaged to carry the cargo for Lizzy and her cousin Owlett, as they would have engaged in any other labour for which they were fairly well paid.

At a word from her they closed in together. 'You had better take it now,' she said to them; and handed to each a packet. It contained six shillings, their remuneration for the night's undertaking, which was paid beforehand without reference to success or failure; but, besides this, they had the privilege of selling as agents when the run was successfully made. As soon as it was done, she said to them, 'The place is the old one, Dagger's Grave, near Lulwind Cove'; the men till that moment not having been told whither they were bound, for obvious reasons. 'Mr Owlett will meet you there,' added Lizzy. 'I shall follow behind, to see that we are not watched.'

The carriers went on, and Stockdale and Mrs Newberry followed at a distance of a stone's-throw. 'What do these men do by day?' he said.

'Twelve or fourteen of them are labouring men. Some are brickmakers, some carpenters, some shoemakers, some thatchers. They are all known to me very well. Nine of 'em are of your own congregation.'

'I can't help that,' said Stockdale.

'Oh, I know you can't. I only told you. The others are more church-inclined, because they supply the pa'son with all the spirits he requires, and they don't wish to show unfriendliness to a customer.'

'How do you choose 'em?' said Stockdale.

'We choose 'em for their closeness, and because they are strong and surefooted, and able to carry a heavy load a long way without being tired.'

Stockdale sighed as she enumerated each particular, for it proved how far involved in the business a woman must be who was so well acquainted with its conditions and needs. And yet he felt more tenderly towards her at this moment than he had felt all the foregoing day. Perhaps it was that her experienced manner and bold indifference stirred his admiration in spite of himself.

'Take my arm, Lizzy,' he murmured.

'I don't want it,' she said. 'Besides, we may never be to each other again what we once have been.'

'That depends upon you,' said he, and they went on again as before.

The hired carriers paced along over Shaldon Down with as little hesitation as if it had been day, avoiding the cart-way, and leaving the village of East Shaldon on the left, so as to reach the crest of the hill at a lonely trackless place not far from the ancient earthwork called Round Pound. A quarter-hour more of brisk walking brought them within sound of the sea, to the place called Dagger's Grave, not many hundred yards from Lulwind Cove. Here they paused, and Lizzy and Stockdale came up with them, when they went on together to the verge of the cliff. One of the men now produced an iron bar, which he drove firmly into the soil a yard from the edge, and attached to it a rope that he had uncoiled from his body. They all began to descend, partly stepping, partly sliding down the incline, as the rope slipped through their hands.

'You will not go to the bottom, Lizzy?' said Stockdale anxiously.

'No. I stay here to watch,' she said. 'Mr Owlett is down there.'

The men remained quite silent when they reached the shore; and the next thing audible to the two at the top was the dip of heavy oars, and the dashing of waves against a boat's bow. In a moment the keel gently touched the shingle, and Stockdale heard the footsteps of the thirty-six carriers running forwards over the pebbles towards the point of landing.

There was a sousing in the water as of a brood of ducks plunging in, showing that the men had not been particular about keeping their legs, or even their waists, dry from the brine; but it was impossible to see what they were doing, and in a few minutes the shingle was trampled again. The iron bar sustaining the rope, on which Stockdale's hand rested, began to swerve a little, and the carriers one by one appeared climbing up the sloping cliff, dripping audibly as they came, and sustaining themselves by the guide-rope. Each man on reaching the top was seen to be carrying a pair of tubs, one on his back and one on his chest, the two being slung together by cords passing round the chine hoops, and resting on the carrier's shoulders. Some of the stronger men carried three by putting an extra one on the top behind, but the customary load was a pair, these being quite weighty enough to give their bearer the sensation of having chest and backbone in contact after a walk of four or five miles.

'Where is Mr Owlett?' said Lizzy to one of them.

'He will not come up this way,' said the carrier.

'He's to bide on shore till we be safe off.' Then, without waiting for the rest, the foremost men plunged across the down; and, when the last had ascended, Lizzy pulled up the rope, wound it round her arm, wriggled the bar from the sod, and turned to follow the carriers.

'You are very anxious about Owlett's safety,' said the minister.

'Was there ever such a man!' said Lizzy. 'Why, isn't he my cousin?'

'Yes. Well, it is a bad night's work,' said Stockdale heavily. 'But I'll carry the bar and rope for you.'

'Thank God, the tubs have got so far all right,' said she. Stockdale shook his head, and, taking the bar, walked by her side towards the downs; and the moan of the sea was heard no more.

'Is this what you meant the other day when you spoke of having business with Owlett?' the young man asked.

'This is it,' she replied. 'I never see him on any other matter.'

'A partnership of that kind with a young man is very odd.'

'It was begun by my father and his, who were brother-laws.'

Her companion could not blind himself to the fact that where tastes and pursuits were so akin as Lizzy's and Owlett's, and where risks were shared, as with them, in every undertaking, there would be a peculiar appropriateness in her answering Owlett's standing question on matrimony in the affirmative. This did not soothe Stockdale, its tendency being rather to stimulate in him an effort to make the pair as inappropriate as possible, and to win her away from this nocturnal crew to correctness of conduct and a minister's parlour in some far-removed inland county.

They had been walking near enough to the file of carriers for Stockdale to perceive that, when they got into the road to the village, they split up into two companies of unequal size, each of which made off in a direction of its own. One company, the smaller of the two, went towards the church, and by the time that Lizzy and Stockdale reached their own house these men had scaled the churchyard wall, and were proceeding noiselessly over the grass within.

'I see that Mr Owlett has arranged for one batch to be put in the church again,' observed Lizzy. 'Do you remember my taking you there the first night you came?'

'Yes, of course,' said Stockdale. 'No wonder you had permission to broach the tubs – they were his, I suppose?'

'No, they were not – they were mine; I had permission from myself. The day after that they went several miles inland in a wagon-load of manure, and sold very well.'

At this moment the group of men who had made off to the left some time before began leaping one by one from the hedge opposite Lizzy's house, and the first man, who had no tubs upon his shoulders, came forward.

'Mrs Newberry, isn't it?' he said hastily.

'Yes, Jim,' said she. 'What's the matter?'

'I find that we can't put any in Badger's Clump tonight, Lizzy,' said Owlett. 'The place is watched. We must sling the apple tree in the orchet if there's time. We can't put any more under the church lumber than I have sent on there, and my mixen hev already more in en than is safe.'

'Very well,' she said. 'Be quick about it – that's all. What can I do?'

'Nothing at all, please. Ah, it is the minister – you two that can't do anything had better get indoors and not be zeed.'

While Owlett thus conversed, in a tone so full of contraband anxiety and so free from lover's jealousy, the men who followed him had been descending one by one from the hedge; and it unfortunately happened that when the hindmost took his leap, the cord slipped which sustained his tubs: the result was that both the kegs fell into the road, one of them being stove in by the blow.

' 'Od drown it all!' said Owlett, rushing back.

'It is worth a good deal, I suppose?' said Stockdale.

'Oh no – about two guineas and half to us now,' said Lizzy, excitedly. 'It isn't that – it is the smell. It is so blazing strong before it has been lowered by water, that it smells dreadfully when spilt in the road like that! I do hope Latimer won't pass by till it is gone off.'

Owlett and one or two others picked up the burst tub and began to scrape and trample over the spot, to disperse the liquor as much as possible; and then they all entered the gate of Owlett's orchard, which adjoined Lizzy's garden on the right. Stockdale did not care to follow them, for several on recognising him had looked wonderingly at his presence, though they said nothing. Lizzy left his side and went to the bottom of the garden, looking over the hedge into the orchard, where the men could be dimly seen bustling about, and apparently hiding the tubs. All was done noiselessly, and without a light; and when it was over they dispersed in different directions, those who had taken their cargoes to the church having already gone off to their homes.

Lizzy returned to the garden-gate, over which Stockdale was still abstractedly leaning. 'It is all finished: I am going indoors now,' she said gently. 'I will leave the door ajar for you.'

'Oh no – you needn't,' said Stockdale; 'I am coming too.'

But before either of them had moved, the faint clatter of horses' hoofs broke upon the ear, and it seemed to come from the point where the track across the down joined the hard road.

'They are just too late!' cried Lizzy exultingly.

'Who?' said Stockdale.

'Latimer, the riding-officer, and some assistant of his. We had better go indoors.'

They entered the house, and Lizzy bolted the door. 'Please don't get a light, Mr Stockdale,' she said.

'Of course I will not,' said he.

'I thought you might be on the side of the king,' said Lizzy, with faintest sarcasm.

'I am,' said Stockdale. 'But, Lizzy Newberry, I love you, and you know it perfectly well; and you ought to know, if you do not, what I have suffered in my conscience on your account these last few days.'

'I guess very well,' she said hurriedly. 'Yet I don't see why. Ah, you are better than I!'

The trotting of the horses seemed to have again died away, and the pair of listeners touched each other's fingers in the cold 'Good-night' of those whom something seriously divided. They were on the landing, but before they had taken three steps apart, the tramp of the horsemen suddenly revived, almost close to the house. Lizzy turned to the staircase-window, opened the casement about an inch, and put her face close to the aperture. 'Yes, one of 'em is

Latimer,' she whispered. 'He always rides a white horse. One would think it was the last colour for a man in that line.'

Stockdale looked, and saw the white shape of the animal as it passed by; but before the riders had gone another ten yards, Latimer reined in his horse, and said something to his companion which neither Stockdale nor Lizzy could hear. Its drift was, however, soon made evident, for the other man stopped also; and sharply turning the horses' heads they cautiously retraced their steps. When they were again opposite Mrs Newberry's garden, Latimer dismounted, and the man on the dark horse did the same.

Lizzy and Stockdale, intently listening and observing the proceedings, naturally put their heads as close as possible to the slit formed by the slightly opened casement; and thus it occurred that at last their cheeks came positively into contact. They went on listening, as if they did not know of the singular incident which had happened to their faces, and the pressure of each to each rather increased than lessened with the lapse of time.

They could hear the Customs-men sniffing the air like hounds as they paced slowly along. When they reached the spot where the tub had burst, both stopped on the instant.

'Ay, ay, 'tis quite strong here,' said the second officer. 'Shall we knock at the door?'

'Well, no,' said Latimer. 'Maybe this is only a trick to put us off the scent. They wouldn't kick up this stink anywhere near their hiding-place. I have known such things before.'

'Anyhow, the things, or some of 'em, must have been brought this way,' said the other.

'Yes,' said Latimer musingly. 'Unless 'tis all done to tole us the wrong way. I have a mind that we go home for tonight without saying a word, and come the first thing in the morning with more hands. I know they have storages about here, but we can do nothing by this owl's light. We will look round the parish and see if everybody is in bed, John; and if all is quiet, we will do as I say.'

They went on, and the two inside the window could hear them passing leisurely through the whole village, the street of which curved round at the bottom and entered the turnpike-road at another junction. This way the officers followed, and the amble of their horses died quite away.

'What will you do?' said Stockdale, withdrawing from his position.

She knew that he alluded to the coming search by the officers, to divert her attention from their own tender incident by the casement, which he wished to be passed over as a thing rather dreamt of than done. 'Oh, nothing,' she replied, with as much coolness as she could command under her disappointment at his manner. 'We often have such storms as this. You would not be frightened if you knew what fools they are. Fancy riding o' horseback through the place: of course they will hear and see nobody while they make that noise; but they are always afraid to get off, in case some of our fellows should burst out upon 'em, and tie them up to the gatepost, as they have done before now. Good-night, Mr Stockdale.'

She closed the window and went to her room, where a tear fell from her eyes; and that not because of the alertness of the riding-officers.

The Great Search at Nether-Moynton

Stockdale was so excited by the events of the evening, and the dilemma that he was placed in between conscience and love, that he did not sleep, or even doze, but remained as broadly awake as at noonday. As soon as the grey light began to touch ever so faintly the whiter objects in his bedroom he arose, dressed himself, and went downstairs into the road.

The village was already astir. Several of the carriers had heard the well-known canter of Latimer's horse while they were undressing in the dark that night, and had already communicated with each other and Owlett on the subject. The only doubt seemed to be about the safety of those tubs which had been left under the church gallery-stairs, and after a short discussion at the corner of the mill, it was agreed that these should be removed before it got lighter, and hidden in the middle of a double hedge bordering the adjoining field. However, before anything could be carried into effect, the footsteps of many men were heard coming down the lane from the highway.

'Damn it, here they be,' said Owlett, who, having already drawn the hatch and started his mill for the day, stood stolidly at the mill door covered with flour, as if the interest of his whole soul was bound up in the shaking walls around him.

The two or three with whom he had been talking dispersed to their usual work, and when the Customs-officers, and the formidable body of men they had hired, reached the village cross, between the mill and

Mrs Newberry's house, the village wore the natural aspect of a place beginning its morning labours.

'Now,' said Latimer to his associates, who numbered thirteen men in all, 'what I know is that the things are somewhere in this here place. We have got the day before us, and 'tis hard if we can't light upon 'em and get 'em to Budmouth Custom-house before night. First we will try the fuel-houses, and then we'll work our way into the chimmers, and then to the ricks and stables, and so creep round. You have nothing but your noses to guide ye, mind, so use 'em today if you never did in your lives before.'

Then the search began. Owlett, during the early part, watched from his mill-window, Lizzy from the door of her house, with the greatest self-possession. A farmer down below, who also had a share in the run, rode about with one eye on his fields and the other on Latimer and his myrmidons, prepared to put them off the scent if he should be asked a question. Stockdale, who was no smuggler at all, felt more anxiety than the worst of them, and went about his studies with a heavy heart, coming frequently to the door to ask Lizzy some question or other on the consequences to her of the tubs being found.

'The consequences,' she said quietly, 'are simply that I shall lose 'em. As I have none in the house or garden, they can't touch me personally.'

'But you have some in the orchard.'

'Mr Owlett rents that of me, and he lends it to others. So it will be hard to say who put any tubs there if they should be found.'

There was never such a tremendous sniffing known as that which took place in Nether-Moynton parish and its vicinity this day. All was done methodically, and mostly on hands and knees. At different hours of the day they had different plans. From daybreak to breakfast-time the officers used their sense of smell in a direct and straightforward manner only, pausing nowhere but at such places as the tubs might be supposed to be secreted in at that very moment, pending their removal on the following night. Among the places tested and examined were: hollow trees, cupboards, culverts, potato-graves, clock-cases, hedgerows, fuel-houses, chimney-flues, faggot-ricks, bedrooms, rainwater-butts, haystacks, apple-lofts, pig-sties, coppers and ovens.

After breakfast they recommenced with renewed vigour, taking a new line; that is to say, directing their attention to clothes that might be supposed to have come in contact with the tubs in their removal from the shore; such garments being usually tainted with the spirit, owing to its oozing between the staves. They now sniffed at: smock-frocks, smiths' and shoe-makers' aprons, old shirts and waistcoats, knee-naps and hedging-gloves, coats and hats, tarpaulins, breeches and leggings, market-cloaks, scarecrows, women's shawls and gowns.

And, as soon as the midday meal was over, they pushed their search into places where the spirits might have been thrown away in alarm: horse-ponds, mixens, sinks in yards, stable-drains, wet ditches, road-scrapings and cinder-heaps, cesspools and back-door gutters.

But still these indefatigable Custom-house men discovered nothing more than the original telltale smell in the road opposite Lizzy's house, which even yet had not passed off.

'I'll tell ye what it is, men,' said Latimer, about three

o'clock in the afternoon; 'we must begin over again. Find them tubs I will.'

The men, who had been hired for the day, looked at their hands and knees, muddy with creeping on all fours so frequently, and rubbed their noses, as if they had almost had enough of it; for the quantity of bad air which had passed into each one's nostril had rendered it nearly as insensible as a flue. However, after a moment's hesitation they prepared to start anew, except three, whose power of smell had quite succumbed under the excessive wear and tear of the day.

By this time not a male villager was to be seen in the parish. Owlett was not at his mill, the farmers were not in their fields, the parson was not in his garden, the smith had left his forge and the wheelwright's shop was silent.

'Where the divil are the folk gone?' said Latimer, waking up to the fact of their absence, and looking round. 'I'll have 'em up for this! Why don't they come and help us? There's not a man about the place but the Methodist parson; and he's an old woman. I demand assistance in the king's name.'

'We must find the jineral public afore we can demand that,' said his lieutenant.

'Well, well, we shall do better without 'em,' said Latimer, who changed his moods at a moment's notice. 'But there's great cause of suspicion in this silence and this keeping out of sight, and I'll bear it in mind. Now we will go across to Owlett's orchard, and see what we can find there.'

Stockdale, who heard this discussion from the garden-gate, over which he had been leaning, was rather alarmed, and thought it a mistake of the villagers to keep so completely out of the way. He himself, like the preventives, had been wondering for the last half-hour what could have become of them. Some labourers were of necessity engaged in distant fields, but the master-workmen should have been at home; though one and all, after just showing themselves at their shops, had apparently gone off for the day. He went in to Lizzy, who sat at a back window sewing, and said, 'Lizzy, where are the men?'

Lizzy laughed. 'Where they mostly are when they're run so hard as this.' She cast her eyes to heaven. 'Up there,' she said.

Stockdale looked up. 'What – on the top of the church tower?' he asked, seeing the direction of her glance.

'Yes.'

'Well, I expect they will soon have to come down,' said he, gravely. 'I have been listening to the officers, and they are going to search the orchard over again; and then every nook in the church.'

Lizzy looked alarmed for the first time. 'Will you go and tell our folk?' she said. 'They ought to be let know.' Seeing his conscience struggling within him like a boiling pot, she added, 'No, never mind, I'll go myself.'

She went out, descended the garden, and climbed over the churchyard wall at the same time that the preventive-men were ascending the road to the orchard. Stockdale could do no less than follow her. By the time that she reached the tower-entrance he was at her side, and they entered together.

Nether-Moynton church tower was, as in many villages, without a turret, and the only way to the top was by going up to the singers' gallery, and thence ascending by a ladder to a square trap-door in the floor of the bell-loft; above which a permanent ladder was fixed, passing through the bells to a hole in the roof. When Lizzy and Stockdale reached the gallery and looked up, nothing but the trap-door and the five holes for the bell-ropes appeared. The ladder was gone.

'There's no getting up,' said Stockdale.

'Oh yes there is,' said she. 'There's an eye looking at us at this moment through a knot hole in that trap-door.'

And as she spoke the trap opened, and the dark line of the ladder was seen descending against the white-washed wall. When it touched the bottom Lizzy dragged it to its place, and said, 'If you'll go up, I'll follow.'

The young man ascended, and presently found himself among consecrated bells for the first time in his life, nonconformity having been in the Stockdale blood for some generations. He eyed them uneasily, and looked round for Lizzy. Owlett stood here, holding the top of the ladder.

'What, be you really one of us?' said the miller.

'It seems so,' said Stockdale, sadly.

'He's not,' said Lizzy, who overheard. 'He's neither for nor against us. He'll do us no harm.'

She stepped up beside them, and then they went on to the next stage, which, when they had clambered over the dusty bell-carriages, was of easy ascent, leading towards the hole through which the pale sky appeared, and into the open air. Owlett remained behind for a moment, to pull up the lower ladder.

'Keep down your heads,' said a voice, as soon as they set foot on the flat.

Stockdale here beheld all the missing parishioners,

lying on their stomachs on the tower-roof, except a few who, elevated on their hands and knees, were peeping through the embrasures of the parapet. Stockdale did the same, and saw the village lying like a map below him, over which moved the figures of the Customs-men, each foreshortened to a crab-like object, the crown of his hat forming a circular disc in the centre of him. Some of the men had turned their heads when the young preacher's figure arose among them.

'What, Mr Stockdale?' said Matt Grey, in a tone of surprise.

'I'd as lief that it hadn't been,' said Jim Clarke. 'If the pa'son should see him a trespassing here in his tower, 'twould be none the better for we, seeing how 'ado hate chapel-members. He'd never buy a tub of us again, and he's as good a customer as we have got this side o' Warm'll.'

'Where is the pa'son?' said Lizzy.

'In his house to be sure, that he may see nothing of what's going on – where all good folks ought to be, and this young man likewise.'

'Well, he has brought some news,' said Lizzy. 'They are going to search the orchard and church; can we do anything if they should find?'

'Yes,' said her cousin Owlett. 'That's what we've been talking o', and we have settled our line. Well, be dazed!'

The exclamation was caused by his perceiving that some of the searchers, having got into the orchard, and begun stooping and creeping hither and thither, were pausing in the middle, where a tree smaller than the rest was growing. They drew closer, and bent lower than ever upon the ground.

'Oh my tubs!' said Lizzy, faintly, as she peered through the parapet at them.

'They have got 'em, 'ab'lieve,' said Owlett.

The interest in the movements of the officers was so keen that not a single eye was looking in any other direction; but at that moment a shout from the church beneath them attracted the attention of the smugglers, as it did also of the party in the orchard, who sprang to their feet and went towards the churchyard wall. At the same time those of the Government men who had entered the church unperceived by the smugglers cried aloud, 'Here be some of 'em at last.'

The smugglers remained in a blank silence, uncertain whether 'some of 'em' meant tubs or men; but again peeping cautiously over the edge of the tower they learnt that tubs were the things descried; and soon these fated articles were brought one by one into the middle of the churchyard from their hiding place under the gallery-stairs.

'They are going to put 'em on Hinton's vault till they find the rest,' said Lizzy hopelessly. The Customs-men had, in fact, begun to pile up the tubs on a large stone slab which was fixed there; and when all were brought out from the tower, two or three of the men were left standing by them, the rest of the party again proceeding to the orchard.

The interest of the smugglers in the next manoeuvres of their enemies became painfully intense. Only about thirty tubs had been secreted in the lumber of the tower, but seventy were hidden in the orchard, making up all that they had brought ashore as yet, the remainder of the cargo having been tied to a sinker and dropped overboard for another night's operations. The preventives, having re-entered the orchard, acted as if they were positive that here lay hidden the rest of the tubs, which they were determined to find before nightfall. They spread themselves out round the field, and advancing on all fours as before, went anew round every apple tree in the enclosure. The young tree in the middle again led them to pause, and at length the whole company gathered there in a way which signified that a second chain of reasoning had led to the same results as the first.

When they had examined the sod hereabouts for some minutes, one of the men rose, ran to a disused part of the church where tools were kept, and returned with the sexton's pickaxe and shovel, with which they set to work.

'Are they really buried there?' said the minister, for the grass was so green and uninjured that it was difficult to believe it had been disturbed. The smugglers were too interested to reply, and presently they saw, to their chagrin, the officers stand several on each side of the tree; and stooping and applying their hands to the soil, they bodily lifted the tree and the turf around it. The apple tree now showed itself to be growing in a shallow box, with handles for lifting at each of the four sides. Under the site of the tree a square hole was revealed, and an officer went and looked down.

'It is all up now,' said Owlett quietly. 'And now all of ye get down before they notice we are here; and be ready for our next move. I had better bide here till dark, or they may take me on suspicion, as 'tis on my ground. I'll be with ye as soon as daylight begins to pink in.'

'And I?' said Lizzy.

'You please look to the linchpins and screws; then go indoors and know nothing at all. The chaps will do the rest.'

The ladder was replaced, and all but Owlett descended, the men passing off one by one at the back of the church, and vanishing on their respective errands. Lizzy walked boldly along the street, followed closely by the minister.

'You are going indoors, Mrs Newberry?' he said.

She knew from the words 'Mrs Newberry' that the division between them had widened yet another degree.

'I am not going home,' she said. 'I have a little thing to do before I go in. Martha Sarah will get your tea.'

'Oh, I don't mean on that account,' said Stockdale. 'What *can you* have to do further in this unhallowed affair?'

'Only a little,' she said.

'What is that? I'll go with you.'

'No, I shall go by myself. Will you please go indoors? I shall be there in less than an hour.'

'You are not going to run any danger, Lizzy?' said the young man, his tenderness reasserting itself.

'None whatever – worth mentioning,' answered she, and went down towards the Cross.

Stockdale entered the garden-gate, and stood behind it looking on. The preventive-men were still busy in the orchard, and at last he was tempted to enter, and watch their proceedings. When he came closer he found that the secret cellar, of whose existence he had been totally unaware, was formed by timbers placed across from side to side about a foot under the ground, and grassed over.

The officers looked up at Stockdale's fair and downy countenance, and evidently thinking him above suspicion, went on with their work again. As soon as all the tubs were taken out, they began tearing up the turf, pulling out the timbers, and breaking in the sides, till the cellar was wholly dismantled and shapeless, the apple tree lying with its roots high to the air. But the hole which had in its time held so much contraband merchandise was never completely filled up, either then or afterwards, a depression in the greensward marking the spot to this day.

SEVEN

The Walk to Warm'ell Cross; and Afterwards

As the goods had all to be carried to Budmouth that night, the next object of the Custom-house officers was to find horses and carts for the journey, and they went about the village for that purpose. Latimer strode hither and thither with a lump of chalk in his hand, marking broad arrows so vigorously on every vehicle and set of harness that he came across, that it seemed as if he would chalk broad arrows on the very hedges and roads. Stockdale, who had had enough of the scene, turned indoors thoughtful and depressed. Lizzy was already there, having come in at the back, though she had not yet taken off her bonnet. She looked tired, and her mood was not much brighter than his own. They had but little to say to each other; and the minister went away and attempted to read; but at this he could not succeed, and he shook the little bell for tea.

Lizzy herself brought in the tray, the girl having run off into the village during the afternoon, too full of excitement at the proceedings to remember her state of life. However, almost before the sad lovers had said anything to each other, Martha came in in a steaming state.

'Oh there's such a stoor, Mrs Newberry and Mr Stockdale! The king's officers can't get the carts ready nohow at all! They pulled Thomas Artnell's, and William Rogers's, and Stephen Sprake's carts into the road, and off came the wheels, and down fell the carts; and they found there was no linchpins in the arms; and then they tried Samuel Shane's wagon, and found that the screws were gone from he, and at last they looked at the dairyman's cart, and he's got none neither! They have gone now to the blacksmith's to get some made, but he's nowhere to be found!'

Stockdale looked at Lizzy, who blushed very slightly, and went out of the room followed by Martha Sarah. But before they had got through the passage there was a rap at the front door, and Stockdale recognised Latimer's voice addressing Mrs Newberry, who had turned back.

'For God's sake, Mrs Newberry, have you seen Hardman the blacksmith up this way? If we could get hold of him, we'd e'en a'most drag him by the hair of his head to his anvil, where he ought to be.'

'He's an idle man, Mr Latimer,' said Lizzy archly. 'What do you want him for?'

'Why there isn't a horse in the place that has got more than three shoes on, and some have only two. The wagon-wheels be without strakes, and there's no linchpins to the carts. What with that, and the bother about every set of harness being out of order, we shan't be off before nightfall – upon my soul we shan't. 'Tis a rough lot, Mrs Newberry, that you've got about you here; but they'll play at this game once too often, mark my words they will. There's not a man in the parish that don't deserve to be whipped.'

It happened that Hardman was at that moment a little further up the lane, smoking his pipe behind a holly bush. When Latimer had done speaking he went on in this direction, and Hardman, hearing the riding-officer's steps, found curiosity too strong for prudence. He peeped out from the bush at the very moment that Latimer's glance was on it. There was nothing left for him to do but to come forward with unconcern.

'I've been looking for you for the last hour!' said Latimer, with a glare in his eye.

'Sorry to hear that,' said Hardman. 'I've been out for a stroll, to look for more hid tubs, to deliver 'em up to Gover'ment.'

'Oh yes, Hardman, we know it,' said Latimer, with withering sarcasm. 'We know that you'll deliver 'em up to Gover'ment. We know that all the parish is helping us, and have been all day. Now you please walk along with me down to your shop, and kindly let me hire ye in the king's name.'

They went down the lane together; and presently there resounded from the smithy the ring of a hammer not very briskly swung. However, the carts and horses were got into some sort of travelling condition, but it was not until after the clock had struck six, when the muddy roads were glistening under the horizontal light of the fading day. The smuggled tubs were soon packed into the vehicles, and Latimer, with three of his assistants, drove slowly out of the village in the direction of the port of Budmouth, some considerable number of miles distant, the other men of the preventive-guard being left to watch for the remainder of the cargo, which they knew to have been sunk somewhere between Ringsworth and Lulwind Cove, and to unearth Owlett, the only person clearly implicated by the discovery of the cave.

Women and children stood at the doors as the carts, each chalked with the Government pitchfork, passed in the increasing twilight; and as they stood they looked at the confiscated property with a melancholy expression that told only too plainly the relation which they bore to the trade.

'Well, Lizzy,' said Stockdale, when the crackle of the wheels had nearly died away. 'This is a fit finish to your adventure. I am truly thankful that you have got off without suspicion, and the loss only of the liquor. Will you sit down and let me talk to you?'

'By and by,' she said. 'But I must go out now.'

'Not to that horrid shore again?' he said blankly.

'No, not there. I am only going to see the end of this day's business.'

He did not answer to this, and she moved towards the door slowly, as if waiting for him to say something more.

'You don't offer to come with me,' she added at last. 'I suppose that's because you hate me after all this?'

'Can you say it, Lizzy, when you know I only want to save you from such practices? Come with you! – of course I will, if it is only to take care of you. But why will you go out again?'

'Because I cannot rest indoors. Something is happening, and I must know what. Now, come.' And they went into the dusk together.

When they reached the turnpike-road she turned to the right, and he soon perceived that they were following the direction of the preventive-men and their load. He had given her his arm, and every now and then she suddenly pulled it back, to signify that he was to halt a moment and listen. They had walked rather quickly along the first quarter of a mile, and on the second or third time of standing still she said, 'I hear them ahead – don't you?'

'Yes,' he said; 'I hear the wheels. But what of that?'

'I only want to know if they get clear away from the neighbourhood.'

'Ah,' said he, a light breaking upon him. 'Something desperate is to be attempted! – and now I remember there was not a man about the village when we left.'

'Hark!' she murmured. The noise of the cartwheels had stopped, and given place to another sort of sound.

' 'Tis a scuffle!' said Stockdale. 'There'll be murder. Lizzy, let go my arm; I am going on. On my conscience, I must not stay here and do nothing!'

'There'll be no murder, and not even a broken head,' she said. 'Our men are thirty to four of them: no harm will be done at all.'

'Then there *is* an attack!' exclaimed Stockdale; 'and you knew it was to be. Why should you side with men who break the laws like this?'

'Why should you side with men who take from country traders what they have honestly bought wi' their own money in France?' said she firmly.

'They are not honestly bought,' said he.

'They are,' she contradicted. 'I and Mr Owlett and the others paid thirty shillings for every one of the tubs before they were put on board at Cherbourg, and if a king who is nothing to us sends his people to steal our property, we have a right to steal it back again.'

Stockdale did not stop to argue the matter, but went quickly in the direction of the noise, Lizzy keeping at his side. 'Don't you interfere, will you, dear Richard?'

she said anxiously, as they drew near. 'Don't let us go any closer: 'tis at Warm'ell Cross where they are seizing 'em. You can do no good, and you may meet with a hard blow.'

'Let us see first what is going on,' he said. But before they had got much further the noise of the cartwheels began again; and Stockdale soon found that they were coming towards him. In another minute the three carts came up, and Stockdale and Lizzy stood in the ditch to let them pass.

Instead of being conducted by four men, as had happened when they went out of the village, the horses and carts were now accompanied by a body of from twenty to thirty, all of whom, as Stockdale perceived to his astonishment, had blackened faces. Among them walked six or eight huge female figures whom, from their wide strides, Stockdale guessed to be men in disguise. As soon as the party discerned Lizzy and her companion four or five fell back, and when the carts had passed, came close to the pair.

'There is no walking up this way for the present,' said one of the gaunt women, who wore curls a foot long, dangling down the sides of her face, in the fashion of the time. Stockdale recognised this lady's voice as Owlett's.

'Why not?' said Stockdale. 'This is the public highway.'

'Now look here, youngster,' said Owlett. 'Oh, 'tis the Methodist parson! – what, and Mrs Newberry! Well, you'd better not go up that way, Lizzy. They've all run off, and folks have got their own again.'

The miller then hastened on and joined his comrades. Stockdale and Lizzy also turned back. 'I wish all this hadn't been forced upon us,' she said regretfully. 'But if those coast-men had got off with the tubs, half the people in the parish would have been in want for the next month or two.'

Stockdale was not paying much attention to her words, and he said, 'I don't think I can go back like this. Those four poor preventives may be murdered for all I know.'

'Murdered!' said Lizzy impatiently. 'We don't do murder here.'

'Well, I shall go as far as Warm'ell Cross to see,' said Stockdale decisively; and, without wishing her safe home or anything else, the minister turned back. Lizzy stood looking at him till his form was absorbed in the shades; and then, with sadness, she went in the direction of Nether-Moynton.

The road was lonely, and after nightfall at this time of the year there was often not a passer for hours. Stockdale pursued his way without hearing a sound beyond that of his own footsteps; and in due time he passed beneath the trees of the plantation which surrounded the Warm'ell Cross road. Before he had reached the point of intersection he heard voices from the thicket.

'Hoi-hoi-hoi! Help, help!'

The voices were not at all feeble or despairing, but they were unmistakably anxious. Stockdale had no weapon, and before plunging into the pitchy darkness of the plantation he pulled a stake from the hedge, to use in case of need. When he got among the trees he shouted: 'What's the matter – where are you?'

'Here,' answered the voices; and, pushing through the brambles in that direction, he came near the objects of his search.

'Why don't you come forward?' said Stockdale.

'We be tied to the trees.'

'Who are you?'

'Poor Will Latimer the Customs-officer,' said one, plaintively.

'Just come and cut these cords, there's a good man. We were afraid nobody would pass by tonight.'

Stockdale soon loosened them, upon which they stretched their limbs and stood at their ease.

'The rascals!' said Latimer, getting now into a rage, though he had seemed quite meek when Stockdale first came up. ' 'Tis the same set of fellows. I know they were Moynton chaps to a man.'

'But we can't swear to 'em,' said another. 'Not one of 'em spoke.'

'What are you going to do?' said Stockdale.

'I'd fain go back to Moynton, and have at 'em again!' said Latimer.

'So would we!' said his comrades.

'Fight till we die!' said Latimer.

'We will, we will!' said his men.

'But,' said Latimer, more frigidly, as they came out of the plantation, 'we don't *know* that these chaps with black faces were Moynton men. And proof is a hard thing.'

'So it is,' said the rest.

'And therefore we won't do nothing at all,' said Latimer, with complete dispassionateness. 'For my part, I'd sooner be them than we. The clitches of my arms are burning like fire from the cords those two strapping women tied round 'em. My opinion is, now I have had time to think o't, that you may serve your Gover'ment at too high a price. For these two nights and days I have not had an hour's rest; and, please God, here's for home-along.'

The other officers agreed heartily to this course; and, thanking Stockdale for his timely assistance, they parted from him at the Cross, taking themselves the western road, and Stockdale going back to Nether-Moynton.

During that walk the minister was lost in reverie of the most painful kind. As soon as he got into the house, and before entering his own rooms, he advanced to the door of the little back parlour in which Lizzy usually sat with her mother. He found her there alone. Stockdale went forward, and, like a man in a dream, looked down upon the table that stood between him and the young woman, who had her bonnet and cloak still on. As he did not speak, she looked up from her chair at him, with misgiving in her eye.

'Where are they gone?' he then said listlessly.

'Who? – I don't know. I have seen nothing of them since. I came straight in here.'

'If your men can manage to get off with those tubs, it will be a great profit to you, I suppose?'

'A share will be mine, a share my cousin Owlett's, a share to each of the two farmers, and a share divided amongst the men who helped us.'

'And you still think,' he went on slowly, 'that you will not give this business up?'

Lizzy rose, and put her hand upon his shoulder. 'Don't ask that,' she whispered. 'You don't know what you are asking. I must tell you, though I meant not to do it. What I make by that trade is all I have to keep my mother and myself with.'

He was astonished. 'I did not dream of such a thing,' he said. 'I would rather have scraped the roads, had I been you. What is money compared with a clear conscience?'

'My conscience is clear. I know my mother, but the king I have never seen. His dues are nothing to me. But it is a great deal to me that my mother and I should live.'

'Marry me, and promise to give it up. I will keep your mother.'

'It is good of you,' she said, moved a little. 'Let me think of it by myself. I would rather not answer now.'

She reserved her answer till the next day, and came into his room with a solemn face. 'I cannot do what you wished,' she said passionately. 'It is too much to ask. My whole life ha' been passed in this way.' Her words and manner showed that before entering she had been struggling with herself in private, and that the contention had been strong.

Stockdale turned pale, but he spoke quietly. 'Then, Lizzy, we must part. I cannot go against my principles in this matter, and I cannot make my profession a mockery. You know how I love you, and what I would do for you; but this one thing I cannot do.'

'But why should you belong to that profession?' she burst out. 'I have got this large house; why can't you marry me, and live here with us, and not be a Methodist preacher any more? I assure you, Richard, it is no harm, and I wish you could only see it as I do. We only carry it on in winter: in summer it is never done at all. It stirs up one's dull life at this time o' the year, and gives excitement, which I have got so used to now that I should hardly know how to do 'ithout it. At nights, when the wind blows, instead of being dull and stupid, and not noticing whether it do blow or not, your mind is afield, even if you are not afield yourself; and you are wondering how the chaps are getting on; and you walk up and down the room, and look out o' window, and then you go out yourself, and know your way about as well by night as by day, and have hair-breadth escapes from old Latimer and his fellows, who are too stupid ever to really frighten us, and only make us a bit nimble.'

'He frightened you a little last night, anyhow; and I would advise you to drop it before it is worse.'

She shook her head. 'No, I must go on as I have begun. I was born to it. It is in my blood, and I can't be cured. Oh, Richard, you cannot think what a hard thing you have asked, and how sharp you try me when you put me between this and my love for 'ee!'

Stockdale was leaning with his elbow on the mantel-piece, his hands over his eyes. 'We ought never to have met, Lizzy,' he said. 'It was an ill day for us! I little thought there was anything so hopeless and impossible in our engagement as this. Well, it is too late now to regret consequences in this way. I have had the happiness of seeing you and knowing you at least.'

'You dissent from Church, and I dissent from State,' she said. 'And I don't see why we are not well matched.'

He smiled sadly, while Lizzy remained looking down, her eyes beginning to overflow.

That was an unhappy evening for both of them, and the days that followed were unhappy days. Both she and he went mechanically about their employments, and his depression was marked in the village by more than one of his denomination with whom he came in contact. But Lizzy, who passed her days indoors, was unsuspected of being the cause; for it was generally understood that a quiet engagement to marry existed between her and her cousin Owlett, and had existed for some time.

One day, two years after the parting, Stockdale, now settled in a midland town, came into Nether-Moynton by carrier in the original way. Jogging along in the van that afternoon he had put questions to the driver, and the answers that he received interested the minister deeply. The result of them was that he went without the least hesitation to the door of his former lodging. It was about six o'clock in the evening, and the same time of year as when he had left; now, too, the ground was damp and glistening, the west was bright, and Lizzy's snowdrops were raising their heads in the border under the wall.

Lizzy must have caught sight of him from the window, for by the time that he reached the door she was there holding it open; and then, as if she had not sufficiently considered her act of coming out, she drew herself back, saying with some constraint, 'Mr Stockdale!'

'You knew it was,' said Stockdale, taking her hand. 'I wrote to say I should call.'

'Yes, but you did not say when,' she answered.

'I did not. I was not quite sure when my business would lead me to these parts.'

'You only came because business brought you near?'

'Well, that is the fact; but I have often thought I should like to come on purpose to see you . . . But what's all this that has happened? I told you how it would be, Lizzy, and you would not listen to me.'

'I would not,' she said sadly. 'But I had been brought up to that life; and it was second nature to me. However, it is all over now. The officers have blood-money for taking a man dead or alive, and the trade is going to nothing. We were hunted down like rats.'

'Owlett is quite gone, I hear.'

'Yes. He is in America. We had a dreadful struggle that last time, when they tried to take him. It is a perfect miracle that he lived through it; and it is a wonder that I was not killed. I was shot in the hand. It was not by aim; the shot was really meant for my cousin; but I was behind, looking on as usual, and the bullet came to me. It bled terribly, but I got home without fainting; and it healed after a time. You know how he suffered?'

'No,' said Stockdale. 'I only heard that he just escaped with his life.'

'He was shot in the back; but a rib turned the ball. He was badly hurt. We would not let him be took. The men carried him all night across the meads to Kingsbere, and hid him in a barn, dressing his wound as well as they could, till he was so far recovered as to be able to get about. Then he was caught, and tried with the others at the assizes; but they all got off. He had given up his mill for some time; and at last he went to Bristol, and took a passage to America, where he's settled.'

'What do you think of smuggling now?' said the minister, gravely.

'I own that we were wrong,' said she. 'But I have suffered for it. I am very poor now, and my mother has been dead these twelve months . . . But won't you come in, Mr Stockdale?'

Stockdale went in; and it is to be supposed that they came to an understanding; for a fortnight later there was a sale of Lizzy's furniture, and after that a wedding at a chapel in a neighbouring town.

He took her away from her old haunts to the home that he had made for himself in his native county, where she studied her duties as a minister's wife with praiseworthy assiduity. It is said that in after years she wrote an excellent tract called *Render unto Caesar; or, the Repentant Villagers*, in which her own experience was anonymously used as the introductory story. Stockdale got it printed, after making some corrections, and putting in a few powerful sentences of his own; and many hundreds of copies were distributed by the couple in the course of their married life.

April 1879

Note – The ending of this story with the marriage of Lizzy and the minister was almost *de rigueur* in an English magazine at the time of writing. But at this late date, thirty years after, it may not be amiss to give the ending that would have been preferred by the writer to the convention used above. Moreover it corresponds more closely with the true incidents of which the tale is a vague and flickering shadow. Lizzy did not, in fact, marry the minister, but – much to her credit in the author's opinion – stuck to Jim the smuggler, and emigrated with him after their marriage, an expatrial step rather forced upon him by his adventurous antecedents. They both died in Wisconsin between 1850 and 1860.

May 1912

An Imaginative Woman

When William Marchmill had finished his enquiries
for lodgings at the well-known watering-place of Solentsea in Upper Wessex, he returned to the hotel to find
his wife. She, with the children, had rambled along
the shore, and Marchmill followed in the direction
indicated by the military-looking hall-porter.

'By Jove, how far you've gone! I am quite out of
breath,' Marchmill said, rather impatiently, when he
came up with his wife, who was reading as she walked,
the three children being considerably further ahead
with the nurse.

Mrs Marchmill started out of the reverie into which
the book had thrown her. 'Yes,' she said, 'you've been
such a long time. I was tired of staying in that dreary
hotel. But I am sorry if you have wanted me, Will?'

'Well, I have had trouble to suit myself. When you
see the airy and comfortable rooms heard of, you find
they are stuffy and uncomfortable. Will you come and
see if what I've fixed on will do? There is not much
room, I am afraid; but I can light on nothing better.
The town is rather full.'

The pair left the children and nurse to continue
their ramble, and went back together.

In age well-balanced, in personal appearance fairly
matched, and in domestic requirements conformable,
in temper this couple differed, though even here they
did not often clash, he being equable, if not lymphatic,

and she decidedly nervous and sanguine. It was to their tastes and fancies, those smallest, greatest particulars, that no common denominator could be applied. Marchmill considered his wife's likes and inclinations somewhat silly; she considered his sordid and material. The husband's business was that of a gunmaker in a thriving city northwards, and his soul was in that business always; the lady was best characterised by that superannuated phrase of elegance 'a votary of the muse'. An impressionable, palpitating creature was Ella, shrinking humanely from detailed knowledge of her husband's trade whenever she reflected that everything he manufactured had for its purpose the destruction of life. She could only recover her equanimity by assuring herself that some, at least, of his weapons were sooner or later used for the extermination of horrid vermin and animals almost as cruel to their inferiors in species as human beings were to theirs.

She had never antecedently regarded this occupation of his as any objection to having him for a husband. Indeed, the necessity of getting life-leased at all cost, a cardinal virtue which all good mothers teach, kept her from thinking of it at all till she had closed with William, had passed the honeymoon, and reached the reflecting stage. Then, like a person who has stumbled upon some object in the dark, she wondered what she had got; mentally walked round it, estimated it; whether it were rare or common; contained gold, silver, or lead; were a clog or a pedestal, everything to her or nothing.

She came to some vague conclusions, and since then had kept her heart alive by pitying her proprietor's obtuseness and want of refinement, pitying herself, and letting off her delicate and ethereal emotions in imaginative occupations, daydreams, and night-sighs, which perhaps would not much have disturbed William if he had known of them.

Her figure was small, elegant, and slight in build, tripping, or rather bounding, in movement. She was dark-eyed, and had that marvellously bright and liquid sparkle in each pupil which characterises persons of Ella's cast of soul, and is too often a cause of heartache to the possessor's male friends, ultimately sometimes to herself. Her husband was a tall, long-featured man, with a brown beard; he had a pondering regard; and was, it must be added, usually kind and tolerant to her. He spoke in squarely shaped sentences, and was supremely satisfied with a condition of sublunary things which made weapons a necessity.

Husband and wife walked till they had reached the house they were in search of, which stood in a terrace facing the sea, and was fronted by a small garden of wind-proof and salt-proof evergreens, stone steps leading up to the porch. It had its number in the row, but, being rather larger than the rest, was in addition sedulously distinguished as Coburg House by its landlady, though everybody else called it 'Thirteen, New Parade'. The spot was bright and lively now; but in winter it became necessary to place sandbags against the door, and to stuff up the keyhole against the wind and rain, which had worn the paint so thin that the priming and knotting showed through.

The householder, who had been watching for the gentleman's return, met them in the passage, and showed the rooms. She informed them that she was a professional man's widow, left in needy circumstances by the rather sudden death of her husband,

Ella Marchmill, sitting down alone a few minutes later, thought with interested surprise of Robert Trewe. Her own latter history will best explain that interest. Herself the only daughter of a struggling man of letters, she had during the last year or two taken to writing poems, in an endeavour to find a congenial channel in which to let flow her painfully embayed emotions, whose former limpidity and sparkle seemed departing in the stagnation caused by the routine of a practical household and the gloom of bearing children to a commonplace father. These poems, subscribed with a masculine pseudonym, had appeared in various obscure magazines, and in two cases in rather prominent ones. In the second of the latter the page which bore her effusion at the bottom, in smallish print, bore at the top, in large print, a few verses on the same subject by this very man, Robert Trewe. Both of them had, in fact, been struck by a tragic incident reported in the daily papers, and had used it simultaneously as an inspiration, the editor remarking in a note upon the coincidence, and that the excellence of both poems prompted him to give them together.

After that event Ella, otherwise 'John Ivy', had watched with much attention the appearance anywhere in print of verse bearing the signature of Robert Trewe, who, with a man's unsusceptibility on the question of sex, had never once thought of passing himself off as a woman. To be sure, Mrs Marchmill had satisfied herself with a sort of reason for doing the contrary in her case; since nobody might believe in her inspiration if they found that the sentiments came from a pushing tradesman's wife, from the mother of three children by a matter-of-fact small-arms manufacturer.

Trewe's verse contrasted with that of the rank and file of recent minor poets in being impassioned rather than ingenious, luxuriant rather than finished. Neither *symboliste* nor *décadent*, he was a pessimist in so far as that character applies to a man who looks at the worst contingencies as well as the best in the human condition. Being little attracted by excellencies of form and rhythm apart from content, he sometimes, when feeling outran his artistic speed, perpetrated sonnets in the loosely rhymed Elizabethan fashion, which every right-minded reviewer said he ought not to have done.

With sad and hopeless envy Ella Marchmill had often and often scanned the rival poet's work, so much stronger as it always was than her own feeble lines. She had imitated him, and her inability to touch his level would send her into fits of despondency. Months passed away thus, till she observed from the publishers' list that Trewe had collected his fugitive pieces into a volume, which was duly issued, and was much or little praised according to chance, and had a sale quite sufficient to pay for the printing.

This step onward had suggested to John Ivy the idea of collecting her pieces also, or at any rate of making up a book of her rhymes by adding many in manuscript to the few that had seen the light, for she had been able to get no great number into print. A ruinous charge was made for costs of publication; a few reviews noticed her poor little volume; but nobody talked of it, nobody bought it, and it fell dead in a fortnight – if it had ever been alive.

The author's thoughts were diverted to another groove just then by the discovery that she was going to have a third child, and the collapse of her poetical rather than literary made her anxious to read the inscriptions alone; and she accordingly waited till she could do so, with a sense that a great store of emotion would be enjoyed in the act.

Perhaps because the sea was choppy outside the Island, Ella's husband found it much pleasanter to go sailing and steaming about without his wife, who was a bad sailor, than with her. He did not disdain to go thus alone on board the steamboats of the cheap-trippers, where there was dancing by moonlight, and where the couples would come suddenly down with a lurch into each other's arms; for, as he blandly told her, the company was too mixed for him to take her amid such scenes. Thus, while this thriving manufacturer got a great deal of change and sea-air out of his sojourn here, the life, external at least, of Ella was monotonous enough, and mainly consisted in passing a certain number of hours each day in bathing and walking up and down a stretch of shore. But the poetic impulse having again waxed strong, she was possessed by an inner flame which left her hardly conscious of what was proceeding around her.

She had read till she knew by heart Trewe's last little volume of verses, and spent a great deal of time in vainly attempting to rival some of them, till, in her failure, she burst into tears. The personal element in the magnetic attraction exercised by this circum-ambient, unapproachable master of hers was so much stronger than the intellectual and abstract that she could not understand it. To be sure, she was surrounded noon and night by his customary environment, which literally whispered of him to her at every moment; but he was a man she had never seen, and that all that moved her was the instinct to specialise a waiting emotion on the first fit thing that came to hand did not, of course, suggest itself to Ella.

In the natural way of passion under the too practical conditions which civilisation has devised for its fruition, her husband's love for her had not survived, except in the form of fitful friendship, any more than, or even so much as, her own for him; and, being a woman of very living ardours, that required sustenance of some sort, they were beginning to feed on this chancing material, which was, indeed, of a quality far better than chance usually offers.

One day the children had been playing hide-and-seek in a closet, whence, in their excitement, they pulled out some clothing. Mrs Hooper explained that it belonged to Mr Trewe, and hung it up in the closet again. Possessed of her fantasy, Ella went later in the afternoon, when nobody was in that part of the house, opened the closet, unhitched one of the articles, a mackintosh, and put it on, with the waterproof cap belonging to it.

'The mantle of Elijah!' she said. 'Would it might inspire me to rival him, glorious genius that he is!'

Her eyes always grew wet when she thought like that, and she turned to look at herself in the glass. *His* heart had beat inside that coat, and *his* brain had worked under that hat at levels of thought she would never reach. The consciousness of her weakness beside him made her feel quite sick. Before she had got the things off her the door opened, and her husband entered the room.

'What the devil – '

She blushed, and removed them. 'I found them in the closet here,' she said, 'and put them on in a freak. What have I else to do? You are always away!'

'Always away? Well . . . '

That evening she had a further talk with the land-lady, who might herself have nourished a half-tender regard for the poet, so ready was she to discourse ardently about him. 'You are interested in Mr Trewe, I know, ma'am,' she said; 'and he has just sent to say that he is going to call tomorrow afternoon to look up some books of his that he wants, if I'll be in, and may he select them from your room?'

'Oh yes!'

'You could very well meet Mr Trewe then, if you'd like to be in the way!'

She promised with secret delight, and went to bed musing of him.

Next morning her husband observed: 'I've been thinking of what you said, Ell: that I have gone about a good deal and left you without much to amuse you. Perhaps it's true. Today, as there's not much sea, I'll take you with me on board the yacht.'

For the first time in her experience of such an offer Ella was not glad. But she accepted it for the moment. The time for setting out drew near, and she went to get ready. She stood reflecting. The longing to see the poet she was now distinctly in love with overpowered all other considerations.

'I don't want to go,' she said to herself. 'I can't bear to be away! And I won't go.'

She told her husband that she had changed her mind about wishing to sail. He was indifferent, and went his way.

For the rest of the day the house was quiet, the children having gone out upon the sands. The blinds waved in the sunshine to the soft, steady stroke of the sea beyond the wall; and the notes of the Green

Silesian band, a troop of foreign gentlemen hired for the season, had drawn almost all the residents and promenaders away from the vicinity of Coburg House. A knock was audible at the door.

Mrs Marchmill did not hear any servant go to answer it, and she became impatient. The books were in the room where she sat; but nobody came up. She rang the bell. 'There is some person waiting at the door,' she said.

'Oh no, ma'am! He's gone long ago. I answered it,' the servant replied.

Mrs Hooper came in herself. 'So disappointing!' she said. 'Mr Trewe not coming after all!'

'But I heard him knock, I fancy?'

'No; that was somebody enquiring for lodgings who came to the wrong house. I forgot to tell you that Mr Trewe sent a note just before lunch to say I needn't get any tea for him, as he should not require the books, and wouldn't come to select them.'

Ella was miserable, and for a long time could not even re-read his mournful ballad on 'Severed Lives', so aching was her erratic little heart, and so tearful her eyes. When the children came in with wet stockings, and ran up to her to tell her of their adventures, she could not feel that she cared about them half as much as usual.

'Mrs Hooper, have you a photograph of – the gentleman who lived here?' She was getting to be curiously shy in mentioning his name.

'Why, yes. It's in the ornamental frame on the mantelpiece in your own bedroom, ma'am.'

'No; the Royal Duke and Duchess are in that.'

'Yes, so they are; but he's behind them. He belongs

rightly to that frame, which I bought on purpose; but as he went away he said: "Cover me up from those strangers that are coming, for God's sake. I don't want them staring at me, and I am sure they won't want me staring at them." So I slipped in the Duke and Duchess temporarily in front of him, as they had no frame, and Royalties are more suitable for letting furnished than a private young man. If you take 'em out you'll see him under. Lord, ma'am, he wouldn't mind if he knew it! He didn't think the next tenant would be such an attractive lady as you, or he wouldn't have thought of hiding himself, perhaps.'

'Is he handsome?' she asked timidly.

'*I* call him so. Some, perhaps, wouldn't.'

'Should I?' she asked, with eagerness.

'I think you would, though some would say he's more striking than handsome; a large-eyed thoughtful fellow, you know, with a very electric flash in his eye when he looks round quickly, such as you'd expect a poet to be who doesn't get his living by it.'

'How old is he?'

'Several years older than yourself, ma'am; about thirty-one or two, I think.'

Ella was, as a matter of fact, a few months over thirty herself; but she did not look nearly so much. Though so immature in nature, she was entering on that tract of life in which emotional women begin to suspect that last love may be stronger than first love; and she would soon, alas, enter on the still more melancholy tract when at least the vainer ones of her sex shrink from receiving a male visitor otherwise than with their backs to the window or the blinds half down. She reflected on Mrs Hooper's remark, and said no more about age.

Just then a telegram was brought up. It came from

her husband, who had gone down the Channel as far as Budmouth with his friends in the yacht, and would not be able to get back till next day.

After her light dinner Ella idled about the shore with the children till dusk, thinking of the yet uncovered photograph in her room, with a serene sense of something ecstatic to come. For, with the subtle luxuriousness of fancy in which this young woman was an adept, on learning that her husband was to be absent that night she had refrained from incontinently rushing upstairs and opening the picture-frame, preferring to reserve the inspection till she could be alone, and a more romantic tinge be imparted to the occasion by silence, candles, solemn sea and stars outside, than was afforded by the garish afternoon sunlight.

The children had been sent to bed, and Ella soon followed, though it was not yet ten o'clock. To gratify her passionate curiosity she now made her preparations, first getting rid of superfluous garments and putting on her dressing-gown, then arranging a chair in front of the table and reading several pages of Trewe's tenderest utterances. Next she fetched the portrait-frame to the light, opened the back, took out the likeness, and set it up before her.

It was a striking countenance to look upon. The poet wore a luxuriant black moustache and imperial, and a slouched hat which shaded the forehead. The large dark eyes described by the landlady showed an unlimited capacity for misery; they looked out from beneath well-shaped brows as if they were reading the universe in the microcosm of the confronter's face, and were not altogether overjoyed at what the spectacle portended.

'Oh no. I'm as tired as a dog. I've had a good feed, and I shall turn in straight off. I want to get out at six o'clock tomorrow if I can . . . I shan't disturb you by my getting up; it will be long before you are awake.' And he came forward into the room.

While her eyes followed his movements, Ella softly pushed the photograph further out of sight.

'Sure you're not ill?' he asked, bending over her.

'No, only wicked!'

'Never mind that.' And he stooped and kissed her. 'I wanted to be with you tonight.'

Next morning Marchmill was called at six o'clock; and in waking and yawning she heard him muttering to himself: 'What the deuce is this that's been crackling under me so?' Imagining her asleep he searched round him and withdrew something. Through her half-opened eyes she perceived it to be Mr Trewe.

'Well, I'm damned!' her husband exclaimed.

'What, dear?' said she.

'Oh, you are awake? Ha! ha!'

'What *do* you mean?'

'Some bloke's photograph – a friend of our landlady's, I suppose. I wonder how it came here; whisked off the mantelpiece by accident perhaps when they were making the bed.'

'I was looking at it yesterday, and it must have dropped in then.'

'Oh, he's a friend of yours? Bless his picturesque heart!'

Ella's loyalty to the object of her admiration could not endure to hear him ridiculed. 'He's a clever man!' she said, with a tremor in her gentle voice which she herself felt to be absurdly uncalled for. 'He is a rising poet – the gentleman who occupied two of these rooms before we came, though I've never seen him.'

'How do you know, if you've never seen him?'

'Mrs Hooper told me when she showed me the photograph.'

'Oh, well, I must up and be off. I shall be home rather early. Sorry I can't take you today, dear. Mind the children don't go getting drowned.'

That day Mrs Marchmill enquired if Mr Trewe were likely to call at any other time.

'Yes,' said Mrs Hooper. 'He's coming this day week to stay with a friend near here till you leave. He'll be sure to call.'

Marchmill did return quite early in the afternoon; and, opening some letters which had arrived in his absence, declared suddenly that he and his family would have to leave a week earlier than they had expected to do – in short, in three days.

'Surely we can stay a week longer?' she pleaded. 'I like it here.'

'I don't. It is getting rather slow.'

'Then you might leave me and the children!'

'How perverse you are, Ell! What's the use? And have to come to fetch you! No: we'll all return together; and we'll make out our time in North Wales or Brighton a little later on. Besides, you've three days longer yet.'

It seemed to be her doom not to meet the man for whose rival talent she had a despairing admiration, and to whose person she was now absolutely attached. Yet she determined to make a last effort; and having gathered from her landlady that Trewe was living in a lonely spot not far from the fashionable town on the Island opposite, she crossed over in the packet from the neighbouring pier the following afternoon.

What a useless journey it was! Ella knew but vaguely where the house stood, and when she fancied she had found it, and ventured to enquire of a pedestrian if he lived there, the answer returned by the man was that he did not know. And if he did live there, how could she call upon him? Some women might have the assurance to do it, but she had not. How crazy he would think her. She might have asked him to call upon her, perhaps; but she had not the courage for that, either. She lingered mournfully about the picturesque seaside eminence till it was time to return to the town and enter the steamer for recrossing, reaching home for dinner without having been greatly missed.

At the last moment, unexpectedly enough, her husband said that he should have no objection to letting her and the children stay on till the end of the week, since she wished to do so, if she felt herself able to get home without him. She concealed the pleasure this extension of time gave her; and Marchmill went off the next morning alone.

But the week passed, and Trewe did not call.

On Saturday morning the remaining members of the Marchmill family departed from the place which had been productive of so much fervour in her. The dreary, dreary train; the sun shining in moted beams upon the hot cushions; the dusty permanent way; the mean rows of wire – these things were her accompaniment: while out of the window the deep blue sea-levels disappeared from her gaze, and with them her poet's home. Heavy-hearted, she tried to read, and wept instead.

Mr Marchmill was in a thriving way of business, and he and his family lived in a large new house, which stood in rather extensive grounds a few miles outside the midland city wherein he carried on his trade. Ella's life was lonely here, as the suburban life is apt to be, particularly at certain seasons; and she had ample time to indulge her taste for lyric and elegiac composition. She had hardly got back when she encountered a piece by Robert Trewe in the new number of her favourite magazine, which must have been written almost immediately before her visit to Solentsea, for it contained the very couplet she had seen pencilled on the wallpaper by the bed, and Mrs Hooper had declared to be recent. Ella could resist no longer, but seizing a pen impulsively, wrote to him as a brother-poet, using the name of John Ivy, congratulating him in her letter on his triumphant executions in metre and rhythm of thoughts that moved his soul, as compared with her own browbeaten efforts in the same pathetic trade.

To this address there came a response in a few days, little as she had dared to hope for it – a civil and brief note, in which the young poet stated that, though he was not well acquainted with Mr Ivy's verse, he recalled the name as being one he had seen attached to some very promising pieces; that he was glad to gain Mr Ivy's acquaintance by letter, and should certainly look with much interest for his productions in the future.

There must have been something juvenile or timid in her own epistle, as one ostensibly coming from a man, she declared to herself; for Trewe quite adopted the tone of an elder and superior in this reply. But what did it matter? He had replied; he had written to her with his own hand from that very room she knew so well, for he was now back again in his quarters.

The correspondence thus begun was continued for two months or more, Ella Marchmill sending him from time to time some that she considered to be the best of her pieces, which he very kindly accepted, though he did not say he sedulously read them, nor did he send her any of his own in return. Ella would have been more hurt at this than she was if she had not known that Trewe laboured under the impression that she was one of his own sex.

Yet the situation was unsatisfactory. A flattering little voice told her that, were he only to see her, matters would be otherwise. No doubt she would have helped on this by making a frank confession of womanhood, to begin with, if something had not happened, to her delight, to render it unnecessary. A friend of her husband's, the editor of the most important newspaper in their city and county, who was dining with them one day, observed during their conversation about the poet that his (the editor's) brother the landscape-painter was a friend of Mr Trewe's, and that the two men were at that very moment in Wales together.

Ella was slightly acquainted with the editor's brother. The next morning down she sat and wrote, inviting him to stay at her house for a short time on his way back, and requesting him to bring with him, if practicable, his companion Mr Trewe, whose acquaintance she was anxious to make. The answer arrived after some few days. Her correspondent and his friend Trewe would have much satisfaction in accepting her invitation on their way southward, which would be on such and such a day in the following week.

Ella was blithe and buoyant. Her scheme had succeeded; her beloved though as yet unseen one was coming. 'Behold, he standeth behind our wall; he looketh forth at the windows, showing himself through the lattice,' she thought ecstatically. 'And, lo, the winter is past, the rain is over and gone, the flowers appear on the earth, the time of the singing of birds is come, and the voice of the turtle is heard in our land.'

But it was necessary to consider the details of lodging and feeding him. This she did most solicitously, and awaited the pregnant day and hour.

It was about five in the afternoon when she heard a ring at the door and the editor's brother's voice in the hall. Poetess as she was, or as she thought herself, she had not been too sublime that day to dress with infinite trouble in a fashionable robe of rich material, having a faint resemblance to the *chiton* of the Greeks, a style just then in vogue among ladies of an artistic and romantic turn, which had been obtained by Ella of her Bond Street dressmaker when she was last in London. Her visitor entered the drawing-room. She looked towards his rear; nobody else came through the door. Where, in the name of the God of Love, was Robert Trewe?

'Oh, I'm sorry,' said the painter, after their introductory words had been spoken. 'Trewe is a curious fellow, you know, Mrs Marchmill. He said he'd come; then he said he couldn't. He's rather dusty. We've been doing a few miles with knapsacks, you know; and he wanted to get on home.'

'He – he's not coming?'

'He's not; and he asked me to make his apologies.'

'When did you p–p–part from him?' she asked, her nether lip starting off quivering so much that it was like a *tremolo* stop opened in her speech. She longed to run away from this dreadful bore and cry her eyes out.

'Just now, in the turnpike road yonder there.'

'What! he has actually gone past my gates?'

'Yes. When we got to them – handsome gates they are, too, the finest bit of modern wrought-iron work I have seen – when we came to them we stopped, talking article may have partially conduced to the sad act, as a copy of the review in question was found on his writing-table; and he has been observed to be in a somewhat depressed state of mind since the critique appeared.

Then came the report of the inquest, at which the following letter was read, it having been addressed to a friend at a distance –

DEAR —, Before these lines reach your hands I shall be delivered from the inconveniences of seeing, hearing, and knowing more of the things around me. I will not trouble you by giving my reasons for the step I have taken, though I can assure you they were sound and logical. Perhaps had I been blessed with a mother, or a sister, or a female friend of another sort tenderly devoted to me, I might have thought it worth while to continue my present existence. I have long dreamt of such an unattainable creature, as you know; and she, this undiscoverable, elusive one, inspired my last volume; the imaginary woman alone, for, in spite of what has been said in some quarters, there is no real woman behind the title. She has continued to the last unrevealed, unmet, unwon. I think it desirable to mention this in order that no blame may attach to any real woman as having been the cause of my decease by cruel or cavalier treatment of me. Tell my landlady that I am sorry to have caused her this unpleasantness; but my occupancy of the rooms will soon be forgotten. There are ample funds in my name at the bank to pay all expenses.

R. TREWE

Ella sat for a while as if stunned, then rushed into the adjoining chamber and flung herself upon her face on the bed.

Her grief and distraction shook her to pieces; and she lay in this frenzy of sorrow for more than an hour. Broken words came every now and then from her quivering lips: 'Oh, if he had only known of me – known of me – me! . . . Oh, if I had only once met him – only once; and put my hand upon his hot forehead – kissed him – let him know how I loved him – that I would have suffered shame and scorn, would have lived and died, for him! Perhaps it would have saved his dear life! . . . But no – it was not allowed! God is a jealous God; and that happiness was not for him and me!'

All possibilities were over; the meeting was stultified. Yet it was almost visible to her in her fantasy even now, though it could never be substantiated:

> The hour which might have been, yet
> might not be,
> Which man's and woman's heart conceived
> and bore,
> Yet whereof life was barren.

She wrote to the landlady at Solentsea in the third person, in as subdued a style as she could command, enclosing a postal order for a sovereign, and informing Mrs Hooper that Mrs Marchmill had seen in the papers the sad account of the poet's death, and having been, as Mrs Hooper was aware, much interested in Mr Trewe during her stay at Coburg House, she would be obliged if Mrs Hooper could obtain a small portion of his hair before his coffin was closed down, and send it her as a memorial of him, as also the photograph that was in the frame.

By the return post a letter arrived containing what had been requested. Ella wept over the portrait and secured it in her private drawer; the lock of hair she tied with white ribbon and put in her bosom, whence she drew it and kissed it every now and then in some unobserved nook.

'What's the matter?' said her husband, looking up from his newspaper on one of these occasions. 'Crying over something? A lock of hair? Whose is it?'

'He's dead!' she murmured.

'Who?'

'I don't want to tell you, Will, just now, unless you insist!' she said, a sob hanging heavy in her voice.

'Oh, all right.'

'Do you mind my refusing? I will tell you someday.'

'It doesn't matter in the least, of course.'

He walked away whistling a few bars of no tune in particular; and when he had got down to his factory in the city the subject came into Marchmill's head again.

He, too, was aware that a suicide had taken place recently at the house they had occupied at Solentsea. Having seen the volume of poems in his wife's hand of late, and heard fragments of the landlady's conversation about Trewe when they were her tenants, he all at once said to himself, 'Why of course it's he! . . . How the devil did she get to know him? What sly animals women are!'

Then he placidly dismissed the matter, and went on with his daily affairs. By this time Ella at home had come to a determination. Mrs Hooper, in sending the hair and photograph, had informed her of the day of the funeral; and as the morning and noon wore on an overpowering wish to know where they were laying him took possession of the sympathetic woman. Caring very little now what her husband or anyone else might think of her eccentricities, she wrote Marchmill a brief note, stating that she was called away for the afternoon and evening, but would return on the following morning. This she left on his desk, and having given the same information to the servants, went out of the house on foot.

When Mr Marchmill reached home early in the afternoon the servants looked anxious. The nurse took him privately aside, and hinted that her mistress's sadness during the past few days had been such that she feared she had gone out to drown herself. Marchmill reflected. Upon the whole he thought that she had not done that. Without saying whither he was bound he also started off, telling them not to sit up for him. He drove to the railway-station, and took a ticket for Solentsea.

It was dark when he reached the place, though he had come by a fast train, and he knew that if his wife had preceded him thither it could only have been by a slower train, arriving not a great while before his own. The season at Solentsea was now past: the parade was gloomy, and the flys were few and cheap. He asked the way to the cemetery, and soon reached it. The gate was locked, but the keeper let him in, declaring, however, that there was nobody within the precincts. Although it was not late, the autumnal darkness had now become intense; and he found some difficulty in keeping to the serpentine path which led to the quarter where, as the man had told him, the one or two interments for the day had taken place. He stepped upon the grass, and, stumbling over some pegs, stooped now and then to discern if possible a figure against the sky. He could see none; but lighting on a spot where the soil was trodden, beheld a crouching object beside a newly made grave. She heard him, and sprang up.

'Ell, how silly this is!' he said indignantly. 'Running away from home—I never heard such a thing! Of course I am not jealous of this unfortunate man; but it is too ridiculous that you, a married woman with three children and a fourth coming, should go losing your head like this over a dead lover! . . . Do you know you were locked in? You might not have been able to get out all night.'

She did not answer.

'I hope it didn't go far between you and him, for your own sake.'

'Don't insult me, Will.'

'Mind, I won't have any more of this sort of thing; do you hear?'

'Very well,' she said.

He drew her arm within his own, and conducted her out of the cemetery. It was impossible to get back that night; and not wishing to be recognised in their present sorry condition he took her to a miserable little coffee-house close to the station, whence they departed early in the morning, travelling almost without speaking, under the sense that it was one of those dreary situations occurring in married life which words could not mend, and reaching their own door at noon.

The months passed, and neither of the twain ever ventured to start a conversation upon this episode. Ella seemed to be only too frequently in a sad and listless mood, which might almost have been called pining. The time was approaching when she would have to undergo the stress of childbirth for a fourth time, and that apparently did not tend to raise her spirits.

'I don't think I shall get over it this time!' she said one day.

'Pooh! what childish foreboding! Why shouldn't it be as well now as ever?'

She shook her head. 'I feel almost sure I am going to die; and I should be glad, if it were not for Nelly, and Frank, and Tiny.'

'And me?'

'You'll soon find somebody to fill my place,' she murmured, with a sad smile. 'And you'll have a perfect right to; I assure you of that.'

'Ell, you are not thinking still about that – poetical friend of yours?'

She neither admitted nor denied the charge. 'I am not going to get over my illness this time,' she reiterated. 'Something tells me I shan't.'

This view of things was rather a bad beginning, as it usually is; and, in fact, six weeks later, in the month of May, she was lying in her room, pulseless and bloodless, with hardly strength enough left to follow up one feeble breath with another, the infant for whose unnecessary life she was slowly parting with her own being fat and well. Just before her death she spoke to Marchmill softly: 'Will, I want to confess to you the entire circumstances of that – about you know what – that time we visited Solentsea. I can't tell what possessed me – how I could forget you so, my husband! But I had got into a morbid state: I thought you had been unkind; that you had neglected me; that you weren't up to my intellectual level, while he was, and far above it. I wanted a fuller appreciator, perhaps, rather than another lover – '

She could get no further then for very exhaustion; and she went off in sudden collapse a few hours later, without having said anything more to her husband on the subject of her love for the poet. William Marchmill, in truth, like most husbands of several years' standing, was little disturbed by retrospective jealousies, and had not shown the least anxiety to press her for confessions concerning a man dead and gone beyond any power of inconveniencing him more.

But when she had been buried a couple of years it chanced one day that, in turning over some forgotten papers that he wished to destroy before his second wife entered the house, he lighted on a lock of hair in an envelope, with the photograph of the deceased poet, a date being written on the back in his late wife's hand. It was that of the time they spent at Solentsea.

Marchmill looked long and musingly at the hair and portrait, for something struck him. Fetching the little boy who had been the death of his mother, now a noisy toddler, he took him on his knee, held the lock of hair against the child's head, and set up the photograph on the table behind, so that he could closely compare the features each countenance presented.

By a known but inexplicable trick of Nature there were undoubtedly strong traces of resemblance to the man Ella had never seen; the dreamy and peculiar expression of the poet's face sat, as the transmitted idea, upon the child's, and the hair was of the same hue.

'I'm damned if I didn't think so!' murmured Marchmill. 'Then she *did* play me false with that fellow at the lodgings! Let me see: the dates – the second week in August . . . the third week in May . . . Yes . . . yes . . . Get away, you poor little brat! You are nothing to me!'

1893

The First Countess of Wessex

King's-Hintock Court (said the narrator, turning over his memoranda for reference) – King's-Hintock Court is, as we know, one of the most imposing of the mansions that overlook our beautiful Blackmoor or Blakemore Vale. On the particular occasion of which I have to speak this building stood, as it had often stood before, in the perfect silence of a calm clear night, lighted only by the cold shine of the stars. The season was winter, in days long ago, the last century having run but little more than a third of its length. North, south, and west, not a casement was unfastened, not a curtain undrawn; eastward, one window on the upper floor was open, and a girl of twelve or thirteen was leaning over the sill. That she had not taken up the position for purposes of observation was apparent at a glance, for she kept her eyes covered with her hands.

The room occupied by the girl was an inner one of a suite, to be reached only by passing through a large bedchamber adjoining. From this apartment voices in altercation were audible, everything else in the building being so still. It was to avoid listening to these voices that the girl had left her little cot, thrown a cloak round her head and shoulders, and stretched into the night air.

But she could not escape the conversation, try as she would. The words reached her in all their painfulness, one sentence in masculine tones, those of her father, being repeated many times.

'I tell 'ee there shall be no such betrothal! I tell 'ee there sha'n't! A child like her!'

She knew the subject of dispute to be herself. A cool feminine voice, her mother's, replied: 'Have done with you, and be wise. He is willing to wait a good five or six years before the marriage takes place, and there's not a man in the county to compare with him.'

'It shall not be! He is over thirty. It is wickedness.'

'He is just thirty, and the best and finest man alive – a perfect match for her.'

'He is poor!'

'But his father and elder brothers are made much of at Court – none so constantly at the palace as they; and with her fortune, who knows? He may be able to get a barony.'

'I believe you are in love with en yourself!'

'How can you insult me so, Thomas! And is it not monstrous for you to talk of my wickedness when you have a like scheme in your own head? You know you have. Some bumpkin of your own choosing – some petty gentleman who lives down at that outlandish place of yours, Falls Park – one of your pot-companions' sons – '

There was an outburst of imprecation on the part of her husband in lieu of further argument. As soon as he could utter a connected sentence he said: 'You crow and you domineer, mistress, because you are heiress-general here. You are in your own house; you are on your own land. But let me tell 'ee that if I did come here to you instead of taking you to me, it was done at the dictates of convenience merely. Hell! I'm no beggar! Ha'n't I a place of my own? Ha'n't I an avenue as long as thine? Ha'n't I beeches that will more than match thy oaks? I should have lived in my own quiet house and land, contented, if you had not called me off with your airs and graces. Faith, I'll go back there; I'll not stay with thee longer! If it had not been for our Betty I should have gone long ago!'

After this there were no more words; but presently, hearing the sound of a door opening and shutting below, the girl again looked from the window. Footsteps crunched on the gravel-walk, and a shape in a drab greatcoat, easily distinguishable as her father, withdrew from the house. He moved to the left, and she watched him diminish down the long east front till he had turned the corner and vanished. He must have gone round to the stables.

She closed the window and shrank into bed, where she cried herself to sleep. This child, their only one, Betty, beloved ambitiously by her mother, and with uncalculating passionateness by her father, was frequently made wretched by such episodes as this; though she was too young to care very deeply, for her own sake, whether her mother betrothed her to the gentleman discussed or not.

The Squire had often gone out of the house in this manner, declaring that he would never return, but he had always reappeared in the morning. The present occasion, however, was different in the issue: next day she was told that her father had ridden to his estate at Falls Park early in the morning on business with his agent, and might not come back for some days.

Falls Park was over twenty miles from King's-Hintock Court, and was altogether a more modest centrepiece to a more modest possession than the latter. But as Squire Dornell came in view of it that February morning, he thought that he had been a fool ever to leave it, though

The journey back, vague and Quixotic as were his intentions, was performed with a far lighter heart than his setting forth. He would see Betty, and talk to her, come what might of his plan.

So he rode along the dead level which stretches between the hills skirting Falls Park and those bounding the town of Ivell, trotted through that borough, and out by the King's-Hintock highway, till, passing the village, he entered the mile-long drive through the park to the Court. The drive being open, without an avenue, the Squire could discern the north front and door of the Court a long way off, and was himself visible from the windows on that side; for which reason he hoped that Betty might perceive him coming, as she sometimes did on his return from an outing, and run to the door or wave her handkerchief.

But there was no sign. He inquired for his wife as soon as he set foot to earth.

'Mistress is away. She was called to London, sir.'

'And Mistress Betty?' said the Squire blankly.

'Gone likewise, sir, for a little change. Mistress has left a letter for you.'

The note explained nothing, merely stating that she had posted to London on her own affairs, and had taken the child to give her a holiday. On the flyleaf were some words from Betty herself to the same effect, evidently written in a state of high jubilation at the idea of her jaunt. Squire Dornell murmured a few expletives, and submitted to his disappointment. How long his wife meant to stay in town she did not say; but on investigation he found that the carriage had been packed with sufficient luggage for a sojourn of two or three weeks.

King's-Hintock Court was in consequence as gloomy as Falls Park had been. He had lost all zest for hunting of late, and had hardly attended a meet that season. Dornell read and re-read Betty's scrawl, and hunted up some other such notes of hers to look over, this seeming to be the only pleasure there was left for him. That they were really in London he learnt in a few days by another letter from Mrs Dornell, in which she explained that they hoped to be home in about a week, and that she had had no idea he was coming back to King's-Hintock so soon, or she would not have gone away without telling him.

Squire Dornell wondered if, in going or returning, it had been her plan to call at the Reynards' place near Melchester, through which city their journey lay. It was possible that she might do this in furtherance of her project, and the sense that his own might become the losing game was harassing.

He did not know how to dispose of himself, till it occurred to him that, to get rid of his intolerable heaviness, he would invite some friends to dinner and drown his cares in grog and wine. No sooner was the carouse decided upon than he put it in hand; those invited being mostly neighbouring landholders, all smaller men than himself, members of the hunt; also the doctor from Evershead, and the like – some of them rollicking blades whose presence his wife would not have countenanced had she been at home. 'When the cat's away – !' said the Squire.

They arrived, and there were indications in their manner that they meant to make a night of it. Baxby of Sherton Castle was late, and they waited a quarter of an hour for him, he being one of the liveliest of Dornell's friends; without whose presence no such dinner as this would be considered complete, and, it may be added, with whose presence no dinner which included both sexes could be conducted with strict propriety. He had just returned from London, and the Squire was anxious to talk to him – for no definite reason; but he had lately breathed the atmosphere in which Betty was.

At length they heard Baxby driving up to the door, whereupon the host and the rest of his guests crossed over to the dining-room. In a moment Baxby came hastily in at their heels, apologising for his lateness.

'I only came back last night, you know,' he said; 'and the truth o't is, I had as much as I could carry.' He turned to the Squire. 'Well, Dornell – so cunning Reynard has stolen your little ewe lamb? Ha, ha!'

'What?' said Squire Dornell vacantly, across the dining-table, round which they were all standing, the cold March sunlight streaming in upon his full, clean-shaven face.

'Surely th'st know what all the town knows? – you've had a letter by this time? – that Stephen Reynard has married your Betty? Yes, as I'm a living man. It was a carefully-arranged thing: they parted at once, and are not to meet for five or six years. But, Lord, you must know!'

A thud on the floor was the only reply of the Squire. They quickly turned. He had fallen down like a log behind the table, and lay motionless on the oak boards.

Those at hand hastily bent over him, and the whole group were in confusion. They found him to be quite unconscious, though puffing and panting like a black-smith's bellows. His face was livid, his veins swollen, and beads of perspiration stood upon his brow.

'What's happened to him?' said several.

'An apoplectic fit,' said the doctor from Evershead, gravely.

He was only called in at the Court for small ailments, as a rule, and felt the importance of the situation. He lifted the Squire's head, loosened his cravat and clothing, and rang for the servants, who took the Squire upstairs.

There he lay as if in a drugged sleep. The surgeon drew a basin-full of blood from him, but it was nearly six o'clock before he came to himself. The dinner was completely disorganised, and some had gone home long ago; but two or three remained.

'Bless my soul,' Baxby kept repeating, 'I didn't know things had come to this pass between Dornell and his lady! I thought the feast he was spreading today was in honour of the event, though privately kept for the present! His little maid married without his knowledge!'

As soon as the Squire recovered consciousness he gasped: ' 'Tis abduction! 'Tis a capital felony! He can be hung! Where is Baxby? I am very well now. What items have ye heard, Baxby?'

The bearer of the untoward news was extremely unwilling to agitate Dornell further, and would say little more at first. But an hour after, when the Squire had partially recovered and was sitting up, Baxby told as much as he knew, the most important particular being that Betty's mother was present at the marriage, and showed every mark of approval. 'Everything appeared to have been done so regularly that I, of course, thought you knew all about it,' he said.

'I knew no more than the underground dead that such a step was in the wind! A child not yet thirteen!

her share in the exploit. He never once believed that she had acted voluntarily. Anxious to know how she was getting on, he despatched the trusty servant Tupcombe to Evershead village, close to King's-Hintock, timing his journey so that he should reach the place under cover of dark. The emissary arrived without notice, being out of livery, and took a seat in the chimney-corner of the Sow and Acorn.

The conversation of the droppers-in was always of the nine days' wonder – the recent marriage. The smoking listener learnt that Mrs Dornell and the girl had returned to King's-Hintock for a day or two, that Reynard had set out for the Continent, and that Betty had since been packed off to school. She did not realise her position as Reynard's child-wife – so the story went – and though somewhat awestricken at first by the ceremony, she had soon recovered her spirits on finding that her freedom was in no way to be interfered with.

After that, formal messages began to pass between Dornell and his wife, the latter being now as persistently conciliating as she was formerly masterful. But her rustic, simple, blustering husband still held personally aloof. Her wish to be reconciled – to win his forgiveness for her stratagem – moreover, a genuine tenderness and desire to soothe his sorrow, which welled up in her at times, brought her at last to his door at Falls Park one day.

They had not met since that night of altercation, before her departure for London and his subsequent illness. She was shocked at the change in him. His face had become expressionless, as blank as that of a puppet, and what troubled her still more was that she found him living in one room, and indulging freely in stimulants, in absolute disobedience to the physician's order. The fact was obvious that he could no longer be allowed to live thus uncouthly.

So she sympathised, and begged his pardon, and coaxed. But though after this date there was no longer such a complete estrangement as before, they only occasionally saw each other, Dornell for the most part making Falls his headquarters still.

Three or four years passed thus. Then she came one day, with more animation in her manner, and at once moved him by the simple statement that Betty's schooling had ended; she had returned, and was grieved because he was away. She had sent a message to him in these words: 'Ask father to come home to his dear Betty.'

'Ah! Then she is very unhappy!' said Squire Dornell.

His wife was silent.

' 'Tis that accursed marriage!' continued the Squire. Still his wife would not dispute with him. 'She is outside in the carriage,' said Mrs Dornell gently.

'What – Betty?'

'Yes.'

'Why didn't you tell me?' Dornell rushed out, and there was the girl awaiting his forgiveness, for she supposed herself, no less than her mother, to be under his displeasure.

Yes, Betty had left school, and had returned to King's-Hintock. She was nearly seventeen, and had developed to quite a young woman. She looked not less a member of the household for her early marriage-contract, which she seemed, indeed, to have almost forgotten. It was like a dream to her; that clear cold March day, the London church, with its gorgeous pews, and green-baize linings, and the great organ in pretending you are struck with Phelipson, and would ha' loved him, as your old father's choice, much more than him she has forced upon 'ee.'

The simple-souled speaker fondly imagined that it was entirely in obedience to this direction that Betty's eyes stole interested glances at the frank and impulsive Phelipson that day at dinner, and he laughed grimly within himself to see how this joke of his, as he imagined it to be, was disturbing the peace of mind of the lady of the house. 'Now Sue sees what a mistake she has made!' said he.

Mrs Dornell was verily greatly alarmed, and as soon as she could speak a word with him alone she upbraided him. 'You ought not to have brought him here. Oh Thomas, how could you be so thoughtless! Lord, don't you see, dear, that what is done cannot be undone, and how all this foolery jeopardises her happiness with her husband? Until you interfered, and spoke in her hearing about this Phelipson, she was as patient and as willing as a lamb, and looked forward to Mr Reynard's return with real pleasure. Since her visit to Falls Park she has been monstrous close-mouthed and busy with her own thoughts. What mischief will you do? How will it end?'

'Own, then, that my man was best suited to her. I only brought him to convince you.'

'Yes, yes; I do admit it. But oh! do take him back again at once! Don't keep him here! I fear she is even attracted by him already.'

'Nonsense, Sue. 'Tis only a little trick to tease 'ee!'

Nevertheless her motherly eye was not so likely to be deceived as his, and if Betty were really only playing at being love-struck that day, she played at it with the perfection of a Rosalind, and would have deceived the best professors into a belief that it was no counterfeit. The Squire, having obtained his victory, was quite ready to take back the too attractive youth, and early in the afternoon they set out on their return journey.

A silent figure who rode behind them was as interested as Dornell in that day's experiment. It was the staunch Tupcombe, who, with his eyes on the Squire's and young Phelipson's backs, thought how well the latter would have suited Betty, and how greatly the former had changed for the worse during these last two or three years. He cursed his mistress as the cause of the change.

After this memorable visit to prove his point, the lives of the Dornell couple flowed on quietly enough for the space of a twelvemonth, the Squire for the most part remaining at Falls, and Betty passing and repassing between them now and then, once or twice alarming her mother by not driving home from her father's house till midnight.

The repose of King's-Hintock was broken by the arrival of a special messenger. Squire Dornell had had an access of gout so violent as to be serious. He wished to see Betty again: why had she not come for so long?

Mrs Dornell was extremely reluctant to take Betty in that direction too frequently; but the girl was so anxious to go, her interests latterly seeming to be so entirely bound up in Falls Park and its neighbourhood, that there was nothing to be done but to let her set out and accompany her.

Squire Dornell had been impatiently awaiting her arrival. They found him very ill and irritable. It had been his habit to take powerful medicines to drive away his enemy, and they had failed in their effect on this occasion.

The presence of his daughter, as usual, calmed him much, even while, as usual too, it saddened him; for he could never forget that she had disposed of herself for life in opposition to his wishes, though she had secretly assured him that she would never have consented had she been as old as she was now.

As on a former occasion, his wife wished to speak to him alone about the girl's future, the time now drawing nigh at which Reynard was expected to come and claim her. He would have done so already, but he had been put off by the earnest request of the young woman herself, which accorded with that of her parents, on the score of her youth. Reynard had deferentially submitted to their wishes in this respect, the understanding between them having been that he would not visit her before she was eighteen, except by the mutual consent of all parties. But this could not go on much longer, and there was no doubt, from the tenor of his last letter, that he would soon take possession of her whether or no.

To be out of the sound of this delicate discussion Betty was accordingly sent downstairs, and they soon saw her walking away into the shrubberies, looking very pretty in her sweeping green gown, and flapping broad-brimmed hat overhung with a feather.

On returning to the subject, Mrs Dornell found her husband's reluctance to reply in the affirmative to Reynard's letter to be as great as ever.

'She is three months short of eighteen!' he exclaimed. ' 'Tis too soon. I won't hear of it! If I have to keep him off sword in hand, he shall not have her yet.'

'But, my dear Thomas,' she expostulated, 'consider

if anything should happen to you or to me, how much better it would be that she should be settled in her home with him!'

'I say it is too soon!' he argued, the veins of his forehead beginning to swell. 'If he gets her this side o' Candlemas I'll challenge en – I'll take my oath on't! I'll be back to King's-Hintock in two or three days, and I'll not lose sight of her day or night!'

She feared to agitate him further, and gave way, assuring him, in obedience to his demand, that if Reynard should write again before he got back, to fix a time for joining Betty, she would put the letter in her husband's hands, and he should do as he chose. This was all that required discussion privately, and Mrs Dornell went to call in Betty, hoping that she had not heard her father's loud tones.

She had certainly not done so this time. Mrs Dornell followed the path along which she had seen Betty wandering, but went a considerable distance without perceiving anything of her. The Squire's wife then turned round to proceed to the other side of the house by a short cut across the grass, when, to her surprise and consternation, she beheld the object of her search sitting on the horizontal bough of a cedar, beside her being a young man, whose arm was round her waist. He moved a little, and she recognised him as young Phelipson.

Alas, then, she was right. The so-called counterfeit love was real. What Mrs Dornell called her husband at that moment, for his folly in originally throwing the young people together, it is not necessary to mention. She decided in a moment not to let the lovers know that she had seen them. She accordingly retreated, reached the front of the house by another route, and called at the top of her voice from a window, 'Betty!'

For the first time since her strategic marriage of the child, Susan Dornell doubted the wisdom of that step. Her husband had, as it were, been assisted by destiny to make his objection, originally trivial, a valid one. She saw the outlines of trouble in the future. Why had Dornell interfered? Why had he insisted upon producing his man? This, then, accounted for Betty's pleading for postponement whenever the subject of her husband's return was broached; this accounted for her attachment to Falls Park. Possibly this very meeting that she had witnessed had been arranged by letter.

Perhaps the girl's thoughts would never have strayed for a moment if her father had not filled her head with ideas of repugnance to her early union, on the ground that she had been coerced into it before she knew her own mind; and she might have rushed to meet her husband with open arms on the appointed day.

Betty at length appeared in the distance in answer to the call, and came up pale, but looking innocent of having seen a living soul. Mrs Dornell groaned in spirit at such duplicity in the child of her bosom. This was the simple creature for whose development into womanhood they had all been so tenderly waiting – a forward minx, old enough not only to have a lover, but to conceal his existence as adroitly as any woman of the world! Bitterly did the Squire's lady regret that Stephen Reynard had not been allowed to come to claim her at the time he first proposed.

The two sat beside each other almost in silence on their journey back to King's-Hintock. Such words as were spoken came mainly from Betty, and their formality indicated how much her mind and heart were occupied with other things.

Mrs Dornell was far too astute a mother to openly attack Betty on the matter. That would be only fanning flame. The indispensable course seemed to her to be that of keeping the treacherous girl under lock and key till her husband came to take her off her mother's hands. That he would disregard Dornell's opposition, and come soon, was her devout wish.

It seemed, therefore, a fortunate coincidence that on her arrival at King's-Hintock a letter from Reynard was put into Mrs Dornell's hands. It was addressed to both her and her husband, and courteously informed them that the writer had landed at Bristol, and proposed to come on to King's-Hintock in a few days, at last to meet and carry off his darling Betty, if she and her parents saw no objection.

Betty had also received a letter of the same tenor. Her mother had only to look at her face to see how the girl received the information. She was as pale as a sheet.

'You must do your best to welcome him this time, my dear Betty,' her mother said gently.

'But – but – I –'

'You are a woman now,' added her mother severely, 'and these postponements must come to an end.'

'But my father – oh, I am sure he will not allow this! I am not ready. If he could only wait a year longer – if he could only wait a few months longer! Oh, I wish – I wish my dear father were here! I will send to him instantly.' She broke off abruptly, and falling upon her mother's neck, burst into tears, saying, 'Oh my mother, have mercy upon me – I do not love this man, my husband!'

The agonised appeal went too straight to Mrs Dornell's heart for her to hear it unmoved. Yet, things when he should appear in the hall, was a plan charming in its simplicity, till her mother found, on trying the door of the girl's chamber softly, that Betty had already locked and bolted it on the inside, and had given directions to have her meals served where she was, by leaving them on a dumb-waiter outside the door.

Thereupon Mrs Dornell noiselessly sat down in her boudoir, which, as well as her bedchamber, was a passage-room to the girl's apartment, and she resolved not to vacate her post night or day till her daughter's husband should appear, to which end she too arranged to breakfast, dine, and sup on the spot. It was impossible now that Betty should escape without her knowledge, even if she had wished, there being no other door to the chamber, except one admitting to a small inner dressing-room inaccessible by any second way.

But it was plain that the young girl had no thought of escape. Her ideas ran rather in the direction of intrenchment: she was prepared to stand a siege, but scorned flight. This, at any rate, rendered her secure. As to how Reynard would contrive a meeting with her coy daughter while in such a defensive humour, that, thought her mother, must be left to his own ingenuity to discover.

Betty had looked so wild and pale at the announcement of her husband's approaching visit that Mrs Dornell, somewhat uneasy, could not leave her to herself. She peeped through the keyhole an hour later. Betty lay on the sofa, staring listlessly at the ceiling.

'You are looking ill, child,' cried her mother. 'You've not taken the air lately. Come with me for a drive.'

Betty made no objection. Soon they drove through the park towards the village, the daughter still in the strained, strung-up silence that had fallen upon her.

They left the park to return by another route, and on the open road passed a cottage.

Betty's eye fell upon the cottage-window. Within it she saw a young girl about her own age, whom she knew by sight, sitting in a chair and propped by a pillow. The girl's face was covered with scales, which glistened in the sun. She was a convalescent from smallpox – a disease whose prevalence at that period was a terror of which we at present can hardly form a conception.

An idea suddenly energised Betty's apathetic features. She glanced at her mother; Mrs Dornell had been looking in the opposite direction. Betty said that she wished to go back to the cottage for a moment to speak to a girl in whom she took an interest. Mrs Dornell appeared suspicious, but observing that the cottage had no back-door, and that Betty could not escape without being seen, she allowed the carriage to be stopped. Betty ran back and entered the cottage, emerging again in about a minute, and resuming her seat in the carriage. As they drove on she fixed her eyes upon her mother and said, 'There, I have done it now!' Her pale face was stormy, and her eyes full of waiting tears.

'What have you done?' said Mrs Dornell.

'Nanny Priddle is sick of the smallpox, and I saw her at the window, and I went in and kissed her, so that I might take it; and now I shall have it, and *he* won't be able to come near me!'

'Wicked girl!' cries her mother. 'Oh, what am I to do! What – bring a distemper on yourself, and usurp the sacred prerogative of God, because you can't palate the man you've wedded!'

The alarmed woman gave orders to drive home as

rapidly as possible, and on arriving, Betty, who was by this time also somewhat frightened at her own enormity, was put into a bath, and fumigated, and treated in every way that could be thought of to ward off the dreadful malady that in a rash moment she had tried to acquire.

There was now a double reason for isolating the rebellious daughter and wife in her own chamber, and there she accordingly remained for the rest of the day and the days that followed; till no ill results seemed likely to arise from her wilfulness.

Meanwhile the first letter from Reynard, announcing to Mrs Dornell and her husband jointly that he was coming in a few days, had sped on its way to Falls Park. It was directed under cover to Tupcombe, the confidential servant, with instructions not to put it into his master's hands till he had been refreshed by a good long sleep. Tupcombe much regretted his commission, letters sent in this way always disturbing the Squire; but guessing that it would be infinitely worse in the end to withhold the news than to reveal it, he chose his time, which was early the next morning, and delivered the missive.

The utmost effect that Mrs Dornell had anticipated from the message was a peremptory order from her husband to Reynard to hold aloof a few months longer. What the Squire really did was to declare that he would go himself and confront Reynard at Bristol, and have it out with him there by word of mouth.

'But, master,' said Tupcombe, 'you can't. You cannot get out of bed.'

'You leave the room, Tupcombe, and don't say "can't" before me! Have Jerry saddled in an hour.'

The long-tried Tupcombe thought his employer demented, so utterly helpless was his appearance just then, and he went out reluctantly. No sooner was he gone than the Squire, with great difficulty, stretched himself over to a cabinet by the bedside, unlocked it, and took out a small bottle. It contained a gout specific, against whose use he had been repeatedly warned by his regular physician, but whose warning he now cast to the winds.

He took a double dose, and waited half an hour. It seemed to produce no effect. He then poured out a treble dose, swallowed it, leant back upon his pillow, and waited. The miracle he anticipated had been worked at last. It seemed as though the second draught had not only operated with its own strength, but had kindled into power the latent forces of the first. He put away the bottle, and rang up Tupcombe.

Less than an hour later one of the housemaids, who of course was quite aware that the Squire's illness was serious, was surprised to hear a bold and decided step descending the stairs from the direction of Mr Dornell's room, accompanied by the humming of a tune. She knew that the doctor had not paid a visit that morning, and that it was too heavy to be the valet or any other manservant. Looking up, she saw Squire Dornell fully dressed, descending toward her in his drab caped riding-coat and boots, with the swinging easy movement of his prime. Her face expressed her amazement.

'What the devil beest looking at?' said the Squire. 'Did you never see a man walk out of his house before, wench?'

Resuming his humming – which was of a defiant sort – he proceeded to the library, rang the bell, asked if the horses were ready, and directed them to be brought round. Ten minutes later he rode away in the direction of Bristol, Tupcombe behind him, trembling at what these movements might portend.

They rode on through the pleasant woodlands and the monotonous straight lanes at an equal pace. The distance traversed might have been about fifteen miles when Tupcombe could perceive that the Squire was getting tired – as weary as he would have been after riding three times the distance ten years before. However, they reached Bristol without any mishap, and put up at the Squire's accustomed inn. Dornell almost immediately proceeded on foot to the inn which Reynard had given as his address, it being now about four o'clock.

Reynard had already dined – for people dined early then – and he was staying indoors. He had already received Mrs Dornell's reply to his letter; but before acting upon her advice and starting for King's-Hintock he made up his mind to wait another day, that Betty's father might at least have time to write to him if so minded. The returned traveller much desired to obtain the Squire's assent, as well as his wife's, to the proposed visit to his bride, that nothing might seem harsh or forced in his method of taking his position as one of the family. But though he anticipated some sort of objection from his father-in-law, in consequence of Mrs Dornell's warning, he was surprised at the announcement of the Squire in person.

Stephen Reynard formed the completest of possible contrasts to Dornell as they stood confronting each other in the best parlour of the Bristol tavern. The Squire, hot-tempered, gouty, impulsive, generous, reckless; the younger man, pale, tall, sedate, self-possessed – a man of the world, fully bearing out at least one couplet in his epitaph, still extant in King's-Hintock church, which places in the inventory of his good qualities

> Engaging Manners, cultivated Mind,
> Adorn'd by Letters, and in Courts refin'd.

He was at this time about five-and-thirty, though careful living and an even, unemotional temperament caused him to look much younger than his years.

Squire Dornell plunged into his errand without much ceremony or preface.

'I am your humble servant, sir,' he said. 'I have read your letter writ to my wife and myself, and considered that the best way to answer it would be to do so in person.'

'I am vastly honoured by your visit, sir,' said Mr Stephen Reynard, bowing.

'Well, what's done can't be undone,' said Dornell, 'though it was mighty early, and was no doing of mine. She's your wife; and there's an end on't. But in brief, sir, she's too young for you to claim yet; we mustn't reckon by years; we must reckon by nature. She's still a girl; 'tis onpolite of 'ee to come yet; next year will be full soon enough for you to take her to you.'

Now, courteous as Reynard could be, he was a little obstinate when his resolution had once been formed. She had been promised him by her eighteenth birthday at latest – sooner if she were in robust health. Her mother had fixed the time on her own judgement, without a word of interference on his part. He had been hanging about foreign courts till he was weary. Betty was now a woman, if she would ever be one, and there was not, in his mind, the shadow of an excuse for putting him off longer. Therefore, fortified as he was by the support of her mother, he blandly but firmly told the Squire that he had been willing to waive his rights, out of deference to her parents, to any reasonable extent, but must now, in justice to himself and her insist on maintaining them. He therefore, since she had not come to meet him, should proceed to King's-Hintock in a few days to fetch her.

This announcement, in spite of the urbanity with which it was delivered, set Dornell in a passion.

'Oh dammy, sir; you talk about rights, you do, after stealing her away, a mere child, against my will and knowledge! If we'd begged and prayed 'ee to take her, you could say no more.'

'Upon my honour, your charge is quite baseless, sir,' said his son-in-law. 'You must know by this time – or if you do not, it has been a monstrous cruel injustice to me that I should have been allowed to remain in your mind with such a stain upon my character – you must know that I used no seductiveness or temptation of any kind. Her mother assented; she assented. I took them at their word. That you was really opposed to the marriage was not known to me till afterwards.'

Dornell professed to believe not a word of it. 'You sha'n't have her till she's dree sixes full – no maid ought to be married till she's dree sixes! – and my daughter sha'n't be treated out of nater!' So he stormed on till Tupcombe, who had been alarmedly listening in the next room, entered suddenly, declaring to Reynard that his master's life was in danger if the interview were prolonged, he being subject to apoplectic strokes at these crises. Reynard immediately said that he would be the last to wish to injure Squire Dornell, and left the room, and as soon as the Squire had recovered breath and equanimity, he went out of the inn, leaning on the arm of Tupcombe.

Tupcombe was for sleeping in Bristol that night, but Dornell, whose energy seemed as invincible as it was sudden, insisted upon mounting and getting back as far as Falls Park, to continue the journey to King's-Hintock on the following day. At five they started, and took the southern road toward the Mendip Hills. The evening was dry and windy, and, excepting that the sun did not shine, strongly reminded Tupcombe of the evening of that March month, nearly five years earlier, when news had been brought to King's-Hintock Court of the child Betty's marriage in London – news which had produced upon Dornell such a marked effect for the worse ever since, and indirectly upon the household of which he was the head. Before that time the winters were lively at Falls Park, as well as at King's-Hintock, although the Squire had ceased to make it his regular residence. Hunting-guests and shooting-guests came and went, and open house was kept. Tupcombe disliked the clever courtier who had put a stop to this by taking away from the Squire the only treasure he valued.

It grew darker with their progress along the lanes, and Tupcombe discovered from Mr Dornell's manner of riding that his strength was giving way; and spurring his own horse close alongside, he asked him how he felt.

'Oh, bad; damn bad, Tupcombe! I can hardly keep my seat. I shall never be any better, I fear! Have we passed Three-Man-Gibbet yet?'

'Not yet by a long ways, sir.'

'I wish we had. I can hardly hold on.' The Squire could not repress a groan now and then, and Tupcombe knew he was in great pain. 'I wish I was know – before him. This is the day he fixed. He has not passed Falls crossroads yet. If you can do that you will be able to get Betty to come – d'ye see? – after her mother has started; she'll have a reason for not waiting for him. Bring her by the lower road – he'll go by the upper. Your business is to make 'em miss each other – d'ye see? – but that's a thing I couldn't write down.'

Five minutes after, Tupcombe was astride the horse and on his way – the way he had followed so many times since his master, a florid young countryman, had first gone wooing to King's-Hintock Court. As soon as he had crossed the hills in the immediate neighbourhood of the manor, the road lay over a plain, where it ran in long straight stretches for several miles. In the best of times, when all had been gay in the united houses, that part of the road had seemed tedious. It was gloomy in the extreme now that he pursued it, at night and alone, on such an errand.

He rode and brooded. If the Squire were to die, he, Tupcombe, would be alone in the world and friendless, for he was no favourite with Mrs Dornell; and to find himself baffled, after all, in what he had set his mind on, would probably kill the Squire. Thinking thus, Tupcombe stopped his horse every now and then, and listened for the coming husband. The time was drawing on to the moment when Reynard might be expected to pass along this very route. He had watched the road well during the afternoon, and had enquired of the tavern-keepers as he came up to each, and he was convinced that the premature descent of the stranger-husband upon his young mistress had not been made by this highway as yet.

Besides the girl's mother, Tupcombe was the only member of the household who suspected Betty's tender feelings towards young Phelipson, so unhappily generated on her return from school; and he could therefore imagine, even better than her fond father, what would be her emotions on the sudden announcement of Reynard's advent that evening at King's-Hintock Court.

So he rode and rode, desponding and hopeful by turns. He felt assured that, unless in the unfortunate event of the almost immediate arrival of her son-in-law at his own heels, Mrs Dornell would not be able to hinder Betty's departure for her father's bedside.

It was about nine o'clock that, having put twenty miles of country behind him, he turned in at the lodge-gate nearest to Ivell and King's-Hintock village, and pursued the long north drive – itself much like a turnpike road – which led thence through the park to the Court. Though there were so many trees in King's-Hintock park, few bordered the carriage road-way; he could see it stretching ahead in the pale night light like an unrolled deal shaving. Presently the irregular frontage of the house came in view, of great extent, but low, except where it rose into the outlines of a broad square tower.

As Tupcombe approached he rode aside upon the grass, to make sure, if possible, that he was the first comer, before letting his presence be known. The Court was dark and sleepy, in no respect as if a bridegroom were about to arrive.

While pausing he distinctly heard the tread of a horse upon the track behind him, and for a moment despaired of arriving in time: here, surely, was Reynard! Pulling up closer to the densest tree at hand he waited, and found he had retreated nothing too soon, for the second rider avoided the gravel also, and

She crept to the window, and heard a whisper without.

'It is I – Charley,' said the voice.

Betty's face fired with excitement. She had latterly begun to doubt her admirer's staunchness, fancying his love to be going off in mere attentions which neither committed him nor herself very deeply. She opened the window, saying in a joyous whisper, 'Oh Charley; I thought you had deserted me quite!'

He assured her he had not done that, and that he had a horse in waiting, if she would ride off with him. 'You must come quickly,' he said; 'for Reynard's on the way!'

To throw a cloak round herself was the work of a moment, and assuring herself that her door was locked against a surprise, she climbed over the window-sill and descended with him as we have seen.

Her mother meanwhile, having received Tupcombe's note, found the news of her husband's illness so serious as to displace her thoughts of the coming son-in-law, and she hastened to tell her daughter of the Squire's dangerous condition, thinking it might be desirable to take her to her father's bedside. On trying the door of the girl's room, she found it still locked. Mrs Dornell called, but there was no answer. Full of misgivings, she privately fetched the old house-steward and bade him burst open the door – an order by no means easy to execute, the joinery of the Court being massively constructed. However, the lock sprang open at last, and she entered Betty's chamber only to find the window unfastened and the bird flown.

For a moment Mrs Dornell was staggered. Then it occurred to her that Betty might have privately obtained from Tupcombe the news of her father's serious illness, and, fearing she might be kept back to meet her husband, have gone off with that obstinate and biased servitor to Falls Park. The more she thought it over the more probable did the supposition appear; and binding her own headman to secrecy as to Betty's movements, whether as she conjectured, or otherwise, Mrs Dornell herself prepared to set out.

She had no suspicion how seriously her husband's malady had been aggravated by his ride to Bristol, and thought more of Betty's affairs than of her own. That Betty's husband should arrive by some other road tonight, and find neither wife nor mother-in-law to receive him, and no explanation of their absence, was possible; but never forgetting chances, Mrs Dornell as she journeyed kept her eyes fixed upon the highway on the offside, where, before she had reached the town of Ivell, the hired coach containing Stephen Reynard flashed into the lamplight of her own carriage.

Mrs Dornell's coachman pulled up, in obedience to a direction she had given him at starting; the other coach was hailed, a few words passed, and Reynard alighted and came to Mrs Dornell's carriage-window.

'Come inside,' says she. 'I want to speak privately to you. Why are you so late?'

'One hindrance and another,' says he. 'I meant to be at the Court by eight at latest. My gratitude for your letter. I hope – '

'You must not try to see Betty yet,' said she. 'There be far other and newer reasons against your seeing her now than there were when I wrote.'

The circumstances were such that Mrs Dornell could not possibly conceal them entirely; nothing short of knowing some of the facts would prevent his blindly acting in a manner which might be fatal to the future.

Moreover, there are times when deeper intriguers than Mrs Dornell feel that they must let out a few truths, if only in self-indulgence. So she told so much of recent surprises as that Betty's heart had been attracted by another image than his, and that his insisting on visiting her now might drive the girl to desperation. 'Betty has, in fact, rushed off to her father to avoid you,' she said. 'But if you wait she will soon forget this young man, and you will have nothing to fear.'

As a woman and a mother she could go no further, and Betty's desperate attempt to infect herself the week before as a means of repelling him, together with the alarming possibility that, after all, she had not gone to her father but to her lover, was not revealed.

'Well,' sighed the diplomatist, in a tone unexpectedly quiet, 'such things have been known before. After all, she may prefer me to him someday, when she reflects how very differently I might have acted than I am going to act towards her. But I'll say no more about that now. I can have a bed at your house for tonight?'

'Tonight, certainly. And you leave tomorrow morning early?' She spoke anxiously, for on no account did she wish him to make further discoveries. 'My husband is so seriously ill,' she continued, 'that my absence and Betty's on your arrival is naturally accounted for.'

He promised to leave early, and to write to her soon. 'And when I think the time is ripe,' he said, 'I'll write to her. I may have something to tell her that will bring her to graciousness.'

It was about one o'clock in the morning when Mrs Dornell reached Falls Park. A double blow awaited her there. Betty had not arrived; her flight had been elsewhither; and her stricken mother divined with whom. She ascended to the bedside of her husband, where to her concern she found that the physician had given up all hope. The Squire was sinking, and his extreme weakness had almost changed his character, except in the particular that his old obstinacy sustained him in a refusal to see a clergyman. He shed tears at the least word, and sobbed at the sight of his wife. He asked for Betty, and it was with a heavy heart that Mrs Dornell told him that the girl had not accompanied her.

'He is not keeping her away?'

'No, no. He is going back – he is not coming to her for some time.'

'Then what is detaining her – cruel, neglectful maid!'

'No, no, Thomas; she is – She could not come.'

'How's that?'

Somehow the solemnity of these last moments of his gave him inquisitorial power, and the too cold wife could not conceal from him the flight which had taken place from King's-Hintock that night.

To her amazement, the effect upon him was electrical.

'What – Betty – a trump after all? Hurrah! She's her father's own maid! She's game! She knew he was her father's own choice! She vowed that my man should win! Well done, Bet! – haw! haw! Hurrah!'

He had raised himself in bed by starts as he spoke, and now fell back exhausted. He never uttered another word, and died before the dawn. People said there had not been such an ungenteel death in a good county family for years.

Now I will go back to the time of Betty's riding off on the pillion behind her lover. They left the park by an obscure gate to the east, and presently found themselves in the lonely and solitary length of the old Roman road now called Long-Ash Lane.

By this time they were rather alarmed at their own performance, for they were both young and inexperienced. Hence they proceeded almost in silence till they came to a mean roadside-inn which was not yet closed; when Betty, who had held on to him with much misgiving all this while, felt dreadfully unwell, and said she thought she would like to get down.

They accordingly dismounted from the jaded animal that had brought them, and were shown into a small dark parlour, where they stood side by side awkwardly, like the fugitives they were. A light was brought, and when they were left alone Betty threw off the cloak which had enveloped her. No sooner did young Phelipson see her face than he uttered an alarmed exclamation.

'Why, Lord, Lord, you are sickening for the small-pox!' he cried.

'Oh – I forgot!' faltered Betty. And then she informed him that, on hearing of her husband's approach the week before, in a desperate attempt to keep him from her side, she had tried to imbibe the infection – an act which till this moment she had supposed to have been ineffectual, imagining her feverishness to be the result of her excitement.

The effect of this discovery upon young Phelipson was overwhelming. Better-seasoned men than he would not have been proof against it, and he was only a little over her own age. 'And you've been holding on to me!' he said. 'And suppose you get worse, and we both have it, what shall we do? Won't you be a fright in a month or two, poor, poor Betty!'

In his horror he attempted to laugh, but the laugh ended in a weakly giggle. She was more woman than girl by this time, and realised his feeling.

'What – in trying to keep off him, I keep off you?' she said miserably. 'Do you hate me because I am going to be ugly and ill?'

'Oh – no, no!' he said soothingly. 'But I – I am thinking if it is quite right for us to do this. You see, dear Betty, if you was not married it would be different. You are not in honour married to him we've often said; still you are his by law, and you can't be mine whilst he's alive. And with this terrible sickness coming on, perhaps you had better let me take you back, and – climb in at the window again.'

'Is *this* your love?' said Betty reproachfully. 'Oh, if you was sickening for the plague itself, and going to be as ugly as the Ooser in the church-vestry, I wouldn't – '

'No, no, you mistake, upon my soul!'

But Betty with a swollen heart had rewrapped herself and gone out of the door. The horse was still standing there. She mounted by the help of the upping-stock, and when he had followed her she said, 'Do not come near me, Charley; but please lead the horse, so that if you've not caught anything already you'll not catch it going back. After all, what keeps off you may keep off him. Now onward.'

He did not resist her command, and back they went by the way they had come, Betty shedding bitter tears at the retribution she had already brought upon herself; for though she had reproached Phelipson, she was staunch enough not to blame him in her secret heart for showing that his love was only skin-deep. The horse was stopped in the plantation, and they walked silently to the lawn, reaching the bushes wherein the ladder still lay.

'Will you put it up for me?' she asked mournfully.

He re-erected the ladder without a word; but when she approached to ascend he said, 'Goodbye, Betty!'

'Goodbye!' said she; and involuntarily turned her face towards his. He hung back from imprinting the expected kiss: at which Betty started as if she had received a poignant wound. She moved away so suddenly that he hardly had time to follow her up the ladder to prevent her falling.

'Tell your mother to get the doctor at once!' he said anxiously.

She stepped in without looking behind; he descended, withdrew the ladder, and went away.

Alone in her chamber, Betty flung herself upon her face on the bed, and burst into shaking sobs. Yet she would not admit to herself that her lover's conduct was unreasonable; only that her rash act of the previous week had been wrong. No one had heard her enter, and she was too worn out, in body and mind, to think or care about medical aid. In an hour or so she felt yet more unwell, positively ill; and nobody coming to her at the usual bedtime, she looked towards the door. Marks of the lock having been forced were visible, and this made her chary of summoning a servant. She opened the door cautiously and sallied forth downstairs.

In the dining-parlour, as it was called, the now sick and sorry Betty was startled to see at that late hour not her mother, but a man sitting, calmly finishing his supper. There was no servant in the room. He turned, and she recognised her husband.

'Where's my mamma?' she demanded without preface.

'Gone to your father's. Is that –' He stopped, aghast.

'Yes, sir. This spotted object is your wife! I've done it because I don't want you to come near me!'

He was sixteen years her senior; old enough to be compassionate. 'My poor child, you must get to bed directly! Don't be afraid of me – I'll carry you upstairs, and send for a doctor instantly.'

'Ah, you don't know what I am!' she cried. 'I had a lover once; but now he's gone! 'Twasn't I who deserted him. He has deserted me; because I am ill he wouldn't kiss me, though I wanted him to!'

'Wouldn't he? Then he was a very poor slack-twisted sort of fellow. Betty, *I've* never kissed you since you stood beside me as my little wife, twelve years and a half old! May I kiss you now?'

Though Betty by no means desired his kisses, she had enough of the spirit of Cunigonde in Schiller's ballad to test his daring. 'If you have courage to venture, yes sir!' said she. 'But you may die for it, mind!'

He came up to her and imprinted a deliberate kiss full upon her mouth, saying, 'May many others follow!'

She shook her head, and hastily withdrew, though secretly pleased at his hardihood. The excitement had supported her for the few minutes she had passed in his presence, and she could hardly drag herself back to her room. Her husband summoned the servants, and, sending them to her assistance, went off himself for a doctor.

The next morning Reynard waited at the Court till he had learnt from the medical man that Betty's attack promised to be a very light one – or, as it was expressed, 'very fine'; and in taking his leave sent up a note to her:

of marriage, if not particularly to her ecstasy. Mrs Dornell's exaggeration of her husband's wish for delay in their living together was inconvenient, but he would not openly infringe it. He wrote tenderly to Betty, and soon announced that he had a little surprise in store for her. The secret was that the King had been graciously pleased to inform him privately, through a relation, that His Majesty was about to offer him a Barony. Would she like the title to be Ivell? Moreover, he had reason for knowing that in a few years the dignity would be raised to that of an Earl, for which creation he thought the title of Wessex would be eminently suitable, considering the position of much of their property. As Lady Ivell, therefore, and future Countess of Wessex, he should beg leave to offer her his heart a third time.

He did not add, as he might have added, how greatly the consideration of the enormous estates at King's-Hintock and elsewhere which Betty would inherit, and her children after her, had conduced to this desirable honour.

Whether the impending titles had really any effect upon Betty's regard for him I cannot state, for she was one of those close‧characters who never let their minds be known upon anything. That such honour was absolutely unexpected by her from such a quarter is, however, certain; and she could not deny that Stephen had shown her kindness, forbearance, even magnanimity; had forgiven her for an errant passion which he might with some reason have denounced, notwithstanding her cruel position as a child entrapped into marriage ere able to understand its bearings.

Her mother, in her grief and remorse for the loveless life she had led with her rough, though open-hearted, husband, made now a creed of his merest whim; and continued to insist that, out of respect to his known desire, her son-in-law should not reside with Betty till the girl's father had been dead a year at least, at which time the girl would still be under nineteen. Letters must suffice for Stephen till then.

'It is rather long for him to wait,' Betty hesitatingly said one day.

'What!' said her mother. 'From *you*? not to respect your dear dead father – '

'Of course it is quite proper,' said Betty hastily. 'I don't gainsay it. I was but thinking that – that – '

In the long slow months of the stipulated interval her mother tended and trained Betty carefully for her duties. Fully awake now to the many virtues of her dear departed one, she, among other acts of pious devotion to his memory, rebuilt the church of King's-Hintock village, and established valuable charities in all the villages of that name, as far as to Little-Hintock, several miles eastward.

In superintending these works, particularly that of the church-building, her daughter Betty was her constant companion, and the incidents of their execution were doubtless not without a soothing effect upon the young creature's heart. She had sprung from girl to woman by a sudden bound, and few would have recognised in the thoughtful face of Betty now the same person who, the year before, had seemed to have absolutely no idea whatever of responsibility, moral or other. Time passed thus till the Squire had been nearly a year in his vault; and Mrs Dornell was duly asked by letter by the patient Reynard if she were willing for him to come soon. He did not wish to take Betty away if her mother's sense of loneliness would be too great, but would willingly live at King's-Hintock awhile with them.

Before the widow had replied to this communication, she one day happened to observe Betty walking on the south terrace in the full sunlight, without hat or mantle, and was struck by her child's figure. Mrs Dornell called her in, and said suddenly: 'Have you seen your husband since the time of your poor father's death?'

'Well – yes, mamma,' says Betty, colouring.

'What – against my wishes and those of your dear father! I am shocked at your disobedience!'

'But my father said eighteen, ma'am, and you made it much longer – '

'Why, of course – out of consideration for you! When have ye seen him?'

'Well,' stammered Betty, 'in the course of his letters to me he said that I belonged to him, and if nobody knew that we met it would make no difference. And that I need not hurt your feelings by telling you.'

'Well?'

'So I went to Casterbridge that time you went to London about five months ago – '

'And met him there? When did you come back?'

'Dear mamma, it grew very late, and he said it was safer not to go back till next day, as the roads were bad; and as you were away from home – '

'I don't want to hear any more! This is your respect for your father's memory,' groaned the widow. 'When did you meet him again?'

'Oh – not for more than a fortnight.'

'A fortnight! How many times have ye seen him altogether?'

'I'm sure, mamma, I've not seen him altogether a dozen times – I mean quite alone, and not reckoning – '

'A dozen! And eighteen and a half years old barely!'

'Twice we met by accident,' pleaded Betty. 'Once at Abbot's-Cernel in the ruined chamber over the gate-house, and another time at the Red Lion, Melchester.'

'Oh thou deceitful girl!' cried Mrs Dornell. 'An *accident* took you to the Red Lion whilst I was staying at the White Hart! I remember – you came in at twelve o'clock at night and said you'd been to see the cathedral by the light o' the moon!'

'My ever-honoured mamma, so I had! I only went to the Red Lion with him afterwards.'

'Oh Betty, Betty! That my child should have deceived me even in my widowed days!'

'But, my dearest mamma, you made me marry him!' says Betty with spirit, 'and of course I've to obey him more than you now!'

Mrs Dornell sighed. 'All I have to say is, that you'd better get your husband to join you as soon as possible,' she remarked. 'To go on playing the maiden like this – I'm ashamed to see you!'

She wrote instantly to Stephen Reynard: 'I wash my hands of the whole matter as between you two; though I should advise you to *openly* join each other as soon as you can – if you wish to avoid scandal.'

He came, though not till the promised title had been granted, and he could call Betty archly 'My Lady'.

People said in after years that she and her husband were very happy. However that may be, they had a numerous family; and she became in due course first Countess of Wessex, as he had foretold.

The little white frock in which she had been married to him at the tender age of twelve was carefully preserved among the relics at King's-Hintock Court, where it may still be seen by the curious – a yellowing, pathetic testimony to the small count taken of the happiness of an innocent child in the social strategy of those days, which might have led, but providentially did not lead, to great unhappiness.

When the Earl died Betty wrote him an epitaph, in which she described him as the best of husbands, fathers, and friends, and called herself his disconsolate widow.

Such is woman; or rather (not to give offence by so sweeping an assertion), such was Betty Dornell.

Afterword

> Some well-known critics have advised me to
> reprint them, informing me that they are as
> good as anything I have ever written (however
> good that may be).
>
> Thomas Hardy, *Letters*

Thomas Hardy (1840–1928) is known primarily, of
course, as one of England's most accomplished
novelists: the creator of the fictional county of Wessex
(which incorporates parts of Dorset, Devon, Wiltshire
and Hampshire), where he based such classic
Victorian works as *The Return of the Native* (1878),
The Mayor of Casterbridge (1885) and *Tess of the
D'Urbervilles* (1891). He is also respected and admired
for his second career: that of a poet, which he took up
in earnest after the disastrous critical reception of his
last novel, *Jude the Obscure* (1894). On the other hand,
Hardy's third great contribution to literature – his
short stories – have often been, and, indeed, continue
to be, overlooked: dismissed by some critics as mere
'pot-boilers'. This is patently ridiculous. As the tales in
this collection demonstrate, they are well turned,
beautifully written and captivating works in their own
right, clear proof of their author's complete mastery of
the form. Furthermore, they are also a crucial measure
of his development as a writer – and, as shorter, more
distilled treatments of his major themes, they are able

to cast a great deal of light on Hardy's better-known works.

Wessex Tales (1888), which gathered together several stories written and published over the previous ten years, was Hardy's first collection of short stories. Apart from 'The Distracted Preacher' reprinted here, the volume contained 'The Three Strangers', 'The Withered Arm', 'Fellow-Townsmen' and 'Interlopers at the Knap'. Hardy later added another tale, 'An Imaginative Woman', but soon swapped that over into *Life's Little Ironies* (1894), in exchange for 'A Tradition of Eighteen Hundred and Four' and 'The Melancholy Hussar'. This chopping and changing of contents is instructive: the stories that eventually made it into the definitive Wessex edition of 1912 form a cohesive whole, which demonstrates great similarities with the themes and locations of Hardy's earlier novelistic writing. Like *Under the Greenwood Tree* (1872) or *Far From the Madding Crowd* (1874), the *Wessex Tales* are 'historical' narratives: they do not take place at the time when they were written, but somewhere back in the eighteen-thirties, just before their author was born. They deal with a rural, rustic, superstitious world: a world unaware of progress, not yet industrialised, and mired in century after century of tradition and folklore. The two tales here collected which form part of the definitive *Wessex Tales* both contain passages which are familiar enough from Hardy's earlier fiction: scene-setting sections which, as in *The Mayor of Casterbridge* and *The Return of the Native*, emphasise the archaeological history poking through the surface of the earth. In 'The Melancholy Hussar', we hear of 'the downs, high and breezy and green, absolutely unchanged since those eventful days'; and in 'The Distracted Preacher', Hardy writes about the hole 'which had in its time held so much contraband merchandise' leaving 'a depression in the greensward marking the spot to this day'. The way in which the past leaves its scars on the landscape is a familiar technique Hardy uses to underline the ways in which people's personal histories can never remained completely buried.

In addition to this historical similarity, many of the *Wessex Tales* take for their starting point the kind of slightly unreal (or at least, seemingly unlikely) central conceit which Hardy tended to employ in some of his earlier novels. *The Mayor of Casterbridge* (whose starting point is a drunken wife-auction) and many of his other works hinge on an unusual event or practice, often followed by an equally unusual series of co-incidences: a 'concatenation of events' as Hardy would call it. Yet, these seemingly exaggerated narrative twists in Hardy's work invariably had their roots in some kind of fact: some event or tradition which had been current in Wessex for years. In his preface to the Wessex edition of 1912, Hardy, as was his wont, makes sure to point out that these situations, like those in his novels, *are*, to some extent at least, based upon historical truth. He recalls many 'Crusted Characters' from his boyhood who would tell him tall tales of old women cured by the blood of a convict's corpse, of smuggled goods hidden beneath false apple trees, and of characters called Owlett who overpowered customs men with a 'numerous body of smugglers'. Similarly, in his introduction to *Life's Little Ironies* (where 'The Melancholy Hussar' first appeared), Hardy makes sure to let us know that 'the extract from the register of burials' used in that story 'is literal, to be read any day in the original by the curious'.

Aside from these wider similarities with Hardy's other work, thematic links and similarities of character can be drawn on a smaller scale. The heroine of 'The Distracted Preacher', for instance, has much in common with Bathsheba Everdene from *Far from the Madding Crowd*, and is a very engaging central character because of it. Lizzy, like Bathsheba, is very much her own woman: a level-headed and forward-thinking business-person, making a financial success of herself in a man's world (the fact that Lizzy dresses as a man to carry out her trade underlining this none too subtly). As with Bathsheba, these qualities of boldness and efficiency are part of her attractiveness (Hardy notes that 'her experienced manner and bold indifference stirred [Stockdale's] admiration in spite of himself'), yet beneath them lie a tenderness and a romantic predisposition. Both women eventually end up with the 'right' man for themselves, although not without having to sacrifice a great deal of personal aspiration and happiness in the process. In his notes to the Wessex edition of *Wessex Tales*, Hardy complains that the coda to 'The Distracted Preacher' (i.e., the happy ending in which Lizzy marries Stockdale) was forced on him by convention; and that he would have preferred her to marry Jim the Smuggler, 'much to her credit in the author's opinion'. However, I must confess to a secret enjoyment of the conclusion to the story: Hollywood endings are rare enough in Hardy, and, when they happen, I believe they should be appreciated!

No such happy ending wraps up 'The Melancholy Hussar'; it is, in many ways, definitively Hardy, lacking the lighter tone of 'The Distracted Preacher'. A young woman forms an attachment to an arrogant and unreliable man who is, nevertheless, her social superior. Meanwhile, she falls truly in love with a simpler man, and their romance is tragically frustrated by the reappearance of her other suitor. Various permutations of this pattern are found throughout Hardy's work: in fact, it is hard to think of any of his major novels which do not feature a stark choice between rival suitors – one the happy path, the other the tragic. This theme runs through his work from his first published novel, *Desperate Remedies* (1871), to his last book, *Jude the Obscure*. What marks out 'The Melancholy Hussar', in my personal estimation, is the style of its prose. The phrasing is lyrical and beautifully evocative, wistful and yearning; and one can see why, despite its comparative brevity, it remains one of the best regarded and most fondly remembered of Hardy's short stories.

'An Imaginative Woman' occupies a strange position in the body of Hardy's work because it was, at various times, both a *Wessex Tale* and one of *Life's Little Ironies* (coming first in both collections); and one can see why Hardy found such difficulty in categorising it. Like some of the other *Wessex Tales*, it hinges on an unlikely 'concatenation of events': a woman who is greatly enamoured of an author accidentally borrowing his lodging, falling in love with him, then dying of a broken heart when he commits suicide. However, the bleak conclusion of the tale, when Ella's husband deduces that the newborn child is not his own but that of Trewe, is rather more typical of Hardy's later period, as is the contemporary setting: these things mark the story out as more thematically linked to *Life's Little*

Ironies. Such academic definitions aside, however, 'An Imaginative Woman' is one of Hardy's most compelling narratives, providing yet another strong female protagonist and playing on themes of artistic ambition and liberation which are not so widely explored in the rest of the author's *corpus*.

Hardy's next collection, *A Group of Noble Dames* (1891), from which 'The First Countess of Wessex' is taken, was written between the first and second parts of *Tess of the D'Urbervilles* and shows certain similarities with that novel. Firstly, and most obviously, both works centre around strong female characters, many of whom are seeking social and sexual liberation from their environment. This emancipative edge caused editorial and critical trouble for both works during the process of their publication: *A Group of Noble Dames* was seriously bowdlerised for serialisation in the *Graphic*, and *Tess* (which could not find a home anywhere else) had to be similarly clipped for the same magazine. Secondly, and somewhat unusually for Hardy, both works deal strongly with the aristocracy, the 'Noble Dames' in the collection being Baronesses, Ladies and Countesses, and Tess in *Tess* being seduced by, and finally murdering, the roguish Sir Alec D'Urberville. I have to confess to a strong liking for 'The First Countess of Wessex'. The similarities to *Tess* notwithstanding, it is very different in tone from the majority of Hardy's work. It is a good old-fashioned historical romance which reminds one of some of the books of Robert Louis Stevenson: plenty of moonlit gallops on horseback, stealings away and secret assignations, loyal servants and gout-ridden old men. Like 'The Distracted Preacher', it too can boast a happy ending: this time, however, it is one which allows the heroine to reach her own decision about the right suitor and end up in a greater position of power than that in which she started.

Life's Little Ironies (1894) is, for me, the most successful of Hardy's collections. Most of the short stories contained within it (represented here by 'The Son's Veto', 'A Tragedy of Two Ambitions', 'To Please His Wife' and 'The Fiddler of the Reels') were written between 1890 and 1892 and, as such, they are clear reflections of Hardy's concerns in the final period of his prose writing: concerns which were to find their ultimate expression in *Jude the Obscure*, published in the same year. There is a marked switch from the historical to the contemporary: the stories are (mostly) modern ones which turn their back on the homespun rural antiquity of the *Wessex Tales*, and, in keeping with this, there is also a move from country to town (London being the setting for 'The Son's Veto' and 'The Fiddler of the Reels', for example). The railways have arrived, so has industrialisation and increased access to education; and these things set the scene for a new social order, and a new kind of social conflict, which is explored throughout the collection.

'The Son's Veto' and 'A Tragedy of Two Ambitions' have much in common with the themes of *Jude the Obscure*. They take as their central concern the indelibility of class: how hard it is for those brought up in a lowly rural environment to throw off their background, no matter how hard they try. As with *Jude* (a rural stonemason who tries to get into Oxford (aka Christminster), these problems seem to centre around notions of education: the child in 'The Son's Veto' goes off to Eton, and the boys in 'A Tragedy of Two Ambitions' work hard to be respectable teachers and clergymen. Yet their parentage, their genetic social background, always seems to be there to hem them in. Hardy, with the bleakness of outlook he also displays in *Jude the Obscure*, can find no happy reconciliation between these two worlds: the social leap that removes the protagonists from their rural background gives them nothing but misery, cruelty and guilt. 'To Please His Wife' is another social satire, which itself has an equally unhappy ending. It too plays on the hollowness of social ambition and the dangers of education, and hinges around a similarly accidental mismarriage to that of 'The Son's Veto'.

'The Fiddler of the Reels' is interesting in this respect, because it seems to delineate the social battlefield which is glimpsed throughout *Life's Little Ironies* in clear symbolic terms, as well as drawing together elements of Hardy's earliest and last prose writings. In many ways, the tale has a lot in common with *Under the Greenwood Tree* (1873) or some of the *Wessex Tales*. It is an 'historical' piece (set in and around 1851), and concerns a fiddle-player, Mop Ollamoor, who comes from the world of the old Mellstock Quire (who dislike him for his devilish ways) and the inns of ancient Wessex. It has the same whiff of the supernatural that tends to pervade some of Hardy's earlier works: Mop is a horse-doctor, with all of the lore and wizardry that that entails, and his fiddle-playing has something undeniably magical about it. Yet he is unapologetically an individual: and this emphasis on individuality and personal morality roots the tale firmly in Hardy's latter concerns.

Mop's Svengali-like attractiveness versus the stoic modernity of the unfortunate Ned is a clear metaphor for the tugs of the ancient and modern world.

Although Ned, as the proponent of progress and technology, offers security and some sort of solidity, he represents the facelessness and uniformity of the industrial age. Although he is well-respected as an engineer, he cannot 'play the fiddle so as to draw your soul out of your body like a spider's thread'. He is part of the faceless society of London – one man in a crowd, one of the many unknown worker ants who build the Crystal Palace – and cannot hope to compete with the highly individual Mop, whose fleeting appearance at the Great Exhibition goes a long way to shattering that palace for poor Car'line. It is a satisfying conclusion to the social conflicts we have seen in the other tales from *Life's Little Ironies* that 'The Fiddler of the Reels', with its infinitely old, infinitely rural, protagonist, shows the essential victory of paganism over progress.

Further Reading

Hardy, Florence, *The Life of Thomas Hardy*, Macmillan, 1928–30

Millgate, Michael, *Thomas Hardy: A Biography*, Oxford University Press, 1982

Little criticism has been written in the past on the short stories of Thomas Hardy, but some key works have appeared over the last quarter-century, including:

Brady, Kirsten, *The Short Stories of Thomas Hardy*, Macmillan, 1982

Gatrell, Simon, *Hardy the Creator: A Textual Biography*, Clarendon, 1992

Ray, Martin, *Thomas Hardy: A Textual Study of the Short Stories*, Ashgate, 1997

Biography

Thomas Hardy was born in 1840 in Higher Bockhampton, Dorset. He trained as an architect, and began writing in his spare time. Just before his first novel, *Desperate Remedies* (1871), was published, he married Emma Gifford. His successful and often controversial career as a novelist continued until 1895, when, sickened by the public outcry over *Jude the Obscure*, Hardy decided to turn to his first love, poetry. He became one of Britain's foremost writers of verse, and received the Order of Merit eighteen years before his death in 1928.

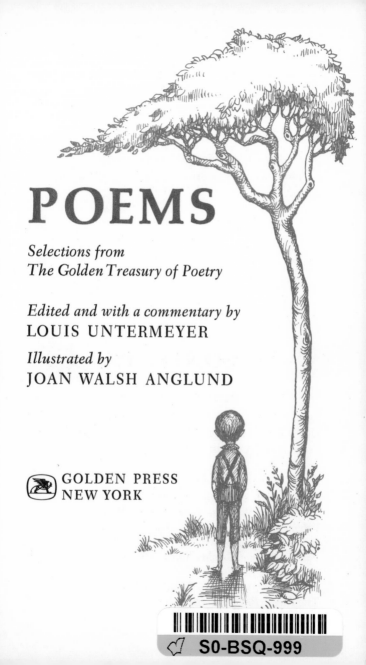

POEMS

Selections from
The Golden Treasury of Poetry

Edited and with a commentary by
LOUIS UNTERMEYER

Illustrated by
JOAN WALSH ANGLUND

GOLDEN PRESS
NEW YORK

Acknowledgments

NATHALIA CRANE for "The Janitor's Boy" and "Standards" from *The Janitor's Boy*, copyright 1924, 1952, by Nathalia Crane.

DODD, MEAD & COMPANY, INC., for "I Meant To Do My Work Today" from *The Lonely Dancer* by Richard LeGallienne, copyright 1913, 1941 by Richard LeGallienne, and reprinted by permission of Dodd, Mead & Company, Inc.

ROSALIE GRAYER for "Altar Smoke."

HARCOURT, BRACE AND WORLD, INC., for the poems by Louis Untermeyer from *Long Feud*, copyright 1959, 1962, by Louis Untermeyer and reprinted by permission of Harcourt, Brace and World, Inc.

THE HERITAGE PRESS for "The Loreley" by Louis Untermeyer, copyright 1945 by Louis Untermeyer.

MRS. HAROLD MONRO for "Milk for the Cat" by Harold Monro.

ROSALIE MOORE for "Catalog."

OXFORD UNIVERSITY PRESS for "Pied Beauty" from *Poems of Gerard Manley Hopkins*, Third Edition, edited by W. H. Gardner. Copyright 1948 by Oxford University Press, Inc. Reprinted by permission.

MISS ANNE YEATS, MR. M. B. YEATS, THE MACMILLAN COMPANY NEW YORK AND THE MACMILLAN COMPANY OF CANADA LTD. for "The Song of Wandering Aengus" from *Collected Poems of William Butler Yeats*, copyright 1906 by The Macmillan Company, renewed 1934 by William Butler Yeats.

CONTENTS

IN THE BEGINNING

GALLERY OF PEOPLE

UNFORGETTABLE STORIES

LAUGHTER HOLDING BOTH HIS SIDES

CREATURES OF EVERY KIND

GOOD THINGS IN SMALL PACKAGES

WIDE, WONDERFUL WORLD

GUIDING STARS

IN THE
BEGINNING

Here are the poems I enjoyed when I was young. Their appeal has never grown less. They continue to delight me. Some of them are serious, some of them are just funny. Some contain lessons—carefully disguised, of course—and some are simply beautiful. Most of them will help you see things as though you have never seen them before. And all of them have that magic which we call poetry.

Let us begin at the beginning...

Escape at Bedtime

The lights from the parlor and kitchen shone out
    Through the blinds and the windows and bars;
And high overhead and all moving about,
    There were thousands of millions of stars.
There ne'er were such thousands of leaves on a tree,
    Nor of people in church or the park,
As the crowds of the stars that looked down upon me,
    And that glittered and winked in the dark.

The Dog, and the Plough, and the Hunter, and all,
    And the star of the sailor, and Mars,
These shone in the sky, and the pail by the wall
    Would be half full of water and stars.
They saw me at last, and they chased me with cries,
    And they soon had me packed into bed;
But the glory kept shining and bright in my eyes,
    And the stars going round in my head.

ROBERT LOUIS STEVENSON

6

If No One Ever Marries Me

If no one ever marries me—
    And I don't see why they should,
For nurse says I'm not pretty,
    And I'm seldom very good—

If no one ever marries me
    I shan't mind very much,
I shall buy a squirrel in a cage
    And a little rabbit-hutch;

I shall have a cottage near a wood,
    And a pony all my own,
And a little lamb, quite clean and tame,
    That I can take to town.

And when I'm getting really old—
    At twenty-eight or nine—
I shall buy a little orphan-girl
    And bring her up as mine.

LAWRENCE
ALMA-TADEMA

Frog Went A-Courtin'

Mr. Froggie went a-courtin' an' he did ride;
Sword and pistol by his side.

He went to Missus Mousie's hall,
Gave a loud knock and gave a loud call.

"Pray, Missus Mousie, air you within?"
"Yes, kind sir, I set an' spin."

He tuk Miss Mousie on his knee,
An' sez, "Miss Mousie, will ya marry me?"

Miss Mousie blushed an' hung her head,
"You'll have t'ask Uncle Rat," she said.

"Not without Uncle Rat's consent
Would I marry the Pres-i-dent."

Uncle Rat jumped up an' shuck his fat side,
To think his niece would be Bill Frog's bride.

Nex' day Uncle Rat went to town,
To git his niece a weddin' gown.

Whar shall the weddin' supper be?
Way down yander in a holler tree.

First come in was a Bumble-bee,
Who danced a jig with Captain Flea.

Next came in was a Butterfly,
Sellin' butter very high.

An' when they all set down to sup,
A big gray goose come an' gobbled 'em all up.

An' this is the end of one, two, three,
The Rat an' the Mouse an' the little Froggie.

GALLERY

OF PEOPLE

Shakespeare declared, "All the world's a stage."
Here is a whole gallery of people and players on the
stage of the world. Some of them are simple, everyday people. Some, like the hag, would seldom be
seen on the streets. But, whether they have warm
blood or moonlit magic in their veins, they come
alive every time you read about them.

All the World's a Stage

All the world's a stage

And all the men and women merely players:
They have their exits and their entrances;
And one man in his time plays many parts,
His acts being seven ages. At first the infant,
Mewling and puking in the nurse's arms.
Then the whining school-boy, with his satchel
And shining morning face, creeping like snail
Unwillingly to school. And then the lover,
Sighing like furnace, with a woeful ballad
Made to his mistress' eyebrow. Then a soldier,
Full of strange oaths, and bearded like the pard,[1]
Jealous in honor, sudden and quick in quarrel,
Seeking the bubble reputation
Even in the cannon's mouth. And then the justice,
In fair round belly with good capon lined,
With eyes severe and beard of formal cut,
Full of wise saws and modern instances;
And so he plays his part. The sixth age shifts
Into the lean and slippered pantaloon,
With spectacles on nose and pouch on side,
His youthful hose, well saved, a world too wide
For his shrunk shank; and his big manly voice,
Turning again toward childish treble, pipes
And whistles in his sound. Last scene of all,
That ends this strange eventful history,
Is second childishness and mere oblivion,
Sans[2] teeth, sans eyes, sans taste, sans every thing.

WILLIAM SHAKESPEARE

[1]Pard: leopard
[2]Sans: without

I'm Nobody! Who Are You?

I'm nobody! Who are you?
Are you nobody, too?
Then there's a pair of us—don't tell!
They'd banish us, you know.

How dreary to be somebody!
How public, like a frog
To tell your name the livelong day
To an admiring bog!

EMILY DICKINSON

I Remember, I Remember

I remember, I remember
The house where I was born,
The little window where the sun
Came peeping in at morn;
He never came a wink too soon
Nor brought too long a day;
But now, I often wish the night
Had borne my breath away.

I remember, I remember
The roses, red and white,
The violets, and the lily-cups—
Those flowers made of light!

The lilacs where the robin built,
And where my brother set
The laburnum on his birthday,—
The tree is living yet!

I remember, I remember
Where I was used to swing,
And thought the air must rush as fresh
To swallows on the wing;
My spirit flew in feathers then
That is so heavy now,
The summer pools could hardly cool
The fever on my brow.

I remember, I remember
The fir-trees dark and high;
I used to think their slender tops
Were close against the sky:
It was a childish ignorance,
But now 'tis little joy
To know I'm farther off from Heaven
Than when I was a boy.

THOMAS HOOD

Jemima

There was a little girl
   who had a little curl,
Right in the middle
   of her forehead,
And when she was good,
   she was very, very good,
But when she was bad
   she was horrid.

One day she went upstairs,
   while her parents, unawares,
In the kitchen down below
   were at their meals,
And she stood upon her head,
   on her little truckle bed,
And she then began hurraying
   with her heels.

Her mother heard the noise,
   and thought it was the boys,
A-playing at a combat
   in the attic,
But when she climbed the stair
   and saw Jemima there,
She took and she did spank her
   most emphatic!

Polly

Brown eyes,
  Straight nose;
Dirt pies,
  Rumpled clothes.

Torn books,
  Spoilt toys;
Arch looks,
  Unlike a boy's.

Little rages,
  Obvious arts;
Three her age is,
  Cakes, tarts.

Falling down
  Off chairs;
Breaking crown
  Down-stairs.

Catching flies
  On the pane;
Deep sighs—
  Cause not plain.

Bribing you
  With kisses,
For a few
  Farthing blisses.

Wide-awake;
  As you hear,
"Mercy's sake,
  Quiet, dear!"

New shoes,
  New frock;
Vague views
  Of what's o'clock.

When it's time
  To go to bed;
Scorn sublime
  For what is said.

Thinks it odd;
  Smiles away;
Yet may God
  Hear her pray!

Bed-gown white;
  Kiss Dolly;
Good night!
  That's Polly.

Fast asleep,
  As you see;
Heaven keep
  My girl for me!

WILLIAM BRIGHTY RANDS

The Village Blacksmith

Under a spreading chestnut tree
  The village smithy stands;
The smith, a mighty man is he,
  With large and sinewy hands;
And the muscles of his brawny arms
  Are strong as iron bands.

His hair is crisp, and black, and long,
  His face is like the tan;
His brow is wet with honest sweat,
  He earns whate'er he can,
And looks the whole world in the face,
  For he owes not any man.

Week in, week out, from morn till night,
  You can hear his bellows blow;
You can hear him swing his heavy sledge,
  With measured beat and slow,
Like a sexton ringing the village bell,
  When the evening sun is low.

And children coming home from school
  Look in at the open door;
They love to see the flaming forge,
  And hear the bellows roar,
And catch the burning sparks that fly
  Like chaff from a threshing floor.

He goes on Sunday to the church,
    And sits among his boys;
He hears the parson pray and preach,
    He hears his daughter's voice,
Singing in the village choir,
    And it makes his heart rejoice.

It sounds to him like her mother's voice,
    Singing in Paradise!
He needs must think of her once more,
    How in the grave she lies;
And with his hard, rough hand he wipes
    A tear out of his eyes.

Toiling—rejoicing—sorrowing,
    Onward through life he goes;
Each morning sees some task begin,
    Each evening sees its close;
Something attempted, something done,
    Has earned a night's repose.

Thanks, thanks to thee, my worthy friend,
    For the lesson thou hast taught!
Thus at the flaming forge of life
    Our fortunes must be wrought;
Thus on its sounding anvil shaped
    Each burning deed and thought!

HENRY WADSWORTH LONGFELLOW

The Hag

The hag is astride,
This night for to ride—
The devil and she together;
Through thick and through thin,
Now out and then in,
Though ne'er so foul be the weather.

A thorn or a burr
She takes for a spur;
With a lash of the bramble she rides now
Through brakes and through briers,
O'er ditches and mires,
She follows the spirit that guides now.

No beast, for his food,
Dares now range the wood,
But husht in his lair he lies lurking;
While mischiefs, by these,
On land and on seas,
At noon of night are a-working.

The storm will arise,
And trouble the skies,
This night; and, more the wonder,
The ghost from the tomb
Affrighted shall come,
Called out by the clap of the thunder.

ROBERT HERRICK

UNFORGETTABLE STORIES

Since the beginning of time people have enjoyed story-poems. Their love for them has never died. All of us are as affected by ancient and modern ballads as people were in the old days when they were first sung and spoken. Such poems will last as long as there are listeners.

La Belle Dame Sans Merci

"Oh, what can ail thee, knight-at-arms,
    Alone and palely loitering?
The sedge has withered from the lake,
    And no birds sing.

"Oh, what can ail thee, knight-at-arms,
    So haggard and so woebegone?
The squirrel's granary is full,
    And the harvest's done.

"I see a lily on thy brow,
    With anguish moist and fever dew;
And on thy cheeks a fading rose
    Fast withereth, too."

I met a lady in the meads,
    Full beautiful—a faëry's child;
Her hair was long, her foot was light,
    And her eyes were wild.

I made a garland for her head,
    And bracelets too, and fragrant zone;
She looked at me as she did love,
    And made sweet moan.

I set her on my pacing steed,
    And nothing else saw, all day long.
For sidelong would she bend, and sing
    A faëry's song.

She found me roots of relish sweet,
    And honey wild, and manna dew;
And sure in language strange she said,
  "I love thee true."

She took me to her elfin grot,
    And there she wept, and sighed full sore;
And there I shut her wild, wild eyes
    With kisses four.

And there she lulled me asleep,
    And there I dreamed, ah, woe betide!
The latest dream I ever dreamt
    On the cold hill's side.

I saw pale kings, and princes, too,
    Pale warriors, death-pale were they all;
They cried, "La Belle Dame Sans Merci
    Hath thee in thrall!"

I saw their starved lips in the gloam
    With horrid warning gapèd wide—
And I awoke, and found me here,
    On the cold hill's side.

And this is why I sojourn here,
    Alone and palely loitering,
Though the sedge is withered from the lake,
    And no birds sing.

JOHN KEATS

The Outlandish Knight

An outlandish knight came out of the North
    To woo a maiden fair,
He promised to take her to the North lands,
    Her father's only heir.

"Come, fetch me some of your father's gold,
    And some of your mother's fee;
And two of the best nags out of the stable,
    Where they stand thirty and three."

She fetched him some of her father's gold
    And some of her mother's fee;
And two of the best nags out of the stable,
    Where they stood thirty and three.

She mounted her on her milk-white steed,
   He on the dapple grey;
They rode till they came unto the sea-side,
   Three hours before it was day.

"Light off, light off thy milk-white steed,
   And deliver it unto me;
Six pretty maids have I drowned here,
   And thou the seventh shall be.

"Pull off, pull off thy silken gown,
   And deliver it unto me;
Methinks it looks too rich and too gay
   To rot in the salt sea.

"Pull off, pull off thy silken stays,
   And deliver them unto me;
Methinks they are too fine and gay
   To rot in the salt sea.

"Pull off, pull off thy Holland smock,
    And deliver it unto me;
Methinks it looks too rich and gay
    To rot in the salt sea."

"If I must pull off my Holland smock,
    Pray turn thy back unto me,
For it is not fitting that such a ruffian
    A woman unclad should see."

He turned his back towards her,
    And viewed the leaves so green;
She caught him round the middle so small,
    And tumbled him into the stream.

He dropped high, and he dropped low,
    Until he came to the tide—
"Catch hold of my hand, my pretty maiden,
    And I will make you my bride."

"Lie there, lie there, you false-hearted man,
    Lie there instead of me;
Six pretty maidens have you drowned here,
    And the seventh has drowned thee."

She mounted on her milk-white steed,
    And led the dapple grey.
She rode till she came to her father's hall,
    Three hours before it was day.

The Song of Wandering Aengus

I went out to the hazel wood,
Because a fire was in my head,
And cut and peeled a hazel wand,
And hooked a berry to a thread,
And when white moths were on the wing,
And moth-like stars were flickering out,
I dropped the berry in a stream
And caught a little silver trout.

When I had laid it on the floor
I went to blow the fire a-flame,
But something rustled on the floor,
And someone called me by my name:
It had become a glimmering girl
With apple blossoms in her hair
Who called me by my name and ran
And faded through the brightening air.

Though I am old with wandering
Through hollow lands and hilly lands,
I will find out where she has gone,
And kiss her lips and take her hands;
And walk among long dappled grass,
And pluck till time and times are done,
The silver apples of the moon,
The golden apples of the sun.

WILLIAM BUTLER YEATS

The Loreley

I cannot tell why this imagined
　　Despair has fallen on me;
The ghost of an ancient legend
　　That will not let me be:

The air is cool, and twilight
　　Flows down the quiet Rhine;
A mountain alone in the high light
　　Still holds the lingering shine.

The last peak rosily gleaming
　　Reveals, enthroned in air,
A maiden, lost in dreaming,
　　Who combs her golden hair.

Combing her hair with a golden
　　Comb in her rocky bower,
She sings the tune of an olden
　　Song that has magical power.

The boatman has heard; it has bound him
　　In the throes of a strange, wild love;
Blind to the reefs that surround him,
　　He sees but the vision above.

And lo, hungry waters are springing—
　　The boat and the boatman are gone....
Then silence. And this, with her singing,
　　The Loreley has done.

HEINRICH HEINE
Translated by LOUIS UNTERMEYER

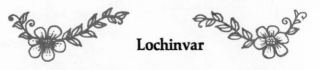

Lochinvar

Oh, young Lochinvar is come out of the West,—
Through all the wide Border his steed was the best,
And save his good broadsword he weapons had none,—
He rode all unarm'd and he rode all alone.
So faithful in love, and so dauntless in war,
There never was knight like the young Lochinvar.

He stay'd not for brake, and he stopp'd not for stone,
He swam the Eske river where ford there was none,
But ere he alighted at Netherby gate,
The bride had consented, the gallant came late;
For a laggard in love and a dastard in war
Was to wed the fair Ellen of brave Lochinvar.

So boldly he enter'd the Netherby hall,
'Mong bridesmen and kinsmen and brothers and all.
Then spoke the bride's father, his hand on his sword
(For the poor craven bridegroom said never a word),
"Oh, come ye in peace here, or come ye in war,
Or to dance at our bridal, young Lord Lochinvar?"

"I long woo'd your daughter,—my suit you denied;
Love swells like the Solway, but ebbs like its tide;
And now am I come, with this lost love of mine
To lead but one measure, drink one cup of wine.
There are maidens in Scotland more lovely, by far,
That would gladly be bride to the young Lochinvar."

The bride kissed the goblet, the knight took it up,
He quaff'd off the wine and he threw down the cup.
She look'd down to blush, and she look'd up to sigh,
With a smile on her lips and a tear in her eye.
He took her soft hand ere her mother could bar:
"Now tread we a measure," said young Lochinvar.

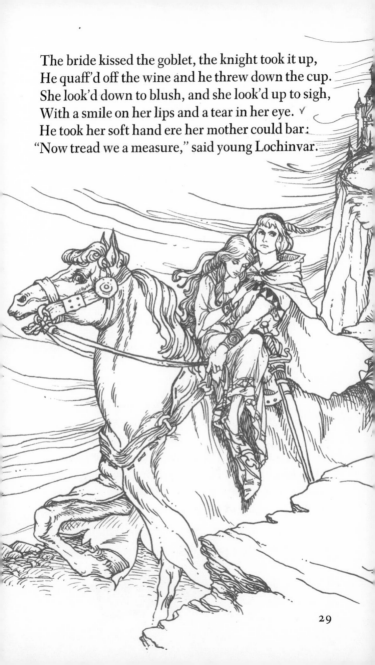

So stately his form, and so lovely her face,
That never a hall such a galliard[1] did grace,
While her mother did fret, and her father did fume,
And the bridegroom stood dangling his bonnet
and plume,
And the bridesmaids whisper'd, "'Twere better by far
To have match'd our fair cousin
with young Lochinvar."

One touch to her hand, and one word in her ear,
When they reach'd the hall-door,
and the charger stood near;
So light to the croup the fair lady he swung,
So light to the saddle before her he sprung!
"She is won! we are gone, over bank, bush, and scaur;[2]
They'll have fleet steeds that follow,"

quoth young Lochinvar.

There was mounting 'mong Graemes
of the Netherby clan;
Forsters, Fenwicks, and Musgraves,
they rode and they ran;
There was racing and chasing on Cannobie Lee,
But the lost bride of Netherby ne'er did they see.
So daring in love, and so dauntless in war,
Have ye e'er heard of gallant like young Lochinvar?

SIR WALTER SCOTT

[1]Galliard: a lively dance
[2]Scaur: a cliff

Beth Gêlert

The spearmen heard the bugle sound,
    And cheerily smiled the morn;
And many a brach, and many a hound
    Obeyed Llewellyn's horn.

And still he blew a louder blast,
    And gave a lustier cheer,
"Come, Gêlert, come, wert never last
    Llewellyn's horn to hear.

"O where does faithful Gêlert roam
    The flower of all his race;
So true, so brave—a lamb at home,
    A lion in the chase?"

In sooth, he was a peerless hound,
    The gift of royal John;
But now no Gêlert could be found,
    And all the chase rode on.

That day Llewellyn little loved
    The chase of hart and hare;
And scant and small the booty proved,
    For Gêlert was not there.

Unpleased, Llewellyn homeward hied,
    When, near the portal seat,
His truant Gêlert he espied
    Bounding his lord to greet.

But when he gained the castle door,
    Aghast the chieftain stood;
The hound all o'er was smeared with gore;
    His lips, his fangs, ran blood.

Llewellyn gazed with fierce surprise;
    Unused such looks to meet,
His favorite checked his joyful guise,
    And crouched, and licked his feet.

Onward, in haste, Llewellyn passed,
    And on went Gêlert too;
And still, where'er his eyes he cast,
    Fresh blood-gouts shocked his view.

O'erturned his infant's bed he found,
    With blood-stained covert rent;
And all around the walls and ground
    With recent blood besprent.

He called his child—no voice replied—
    He searched with terror wild;
Blood, blood he found on every side,
    But nowhere found his child.

"Hell-bound! my child's by thee devoured,"
    The frantic father cried;
And to the hilt his vengeful sword
    He plunged in Gêlert's side.

Aroused by Gêlert's dying yell,
    Some slumberer wakened nigh;
What words the parent's joy could tell
    To hear his infant's cry!

Concealed beneath a tumbled heap
    His hurried search had missed,
All glowing from his rosy sleep
    The cherub boy he kissed.

No hurt had he, nor harm, nor dread,
    But, the same couch beneath,
Lay a gaunt wolf, all torn and dead,
    Tremendous still in death.

Ah, what was then Llewellyn's pain!
    For now the truth was clear;
His gallant hound the wolf had slain
    To save Llewellyn's heir.

WILLIAM ROBERT SPENCER

Incident of the French Camp

You know, we French stormed Ratisbon.
    A mile or so away,
On a little mound, Napoleon
    Stood on our storming-day;
With neck out-thrust, you fancy how,
    Legs wide, arms locked behind,
As if to balance the prone brow
    Oppressive with its mind.

Just as perhaps he mused "My plans
    That soar, to earth may fall,
Let once my army-leader Lannes
    Waver at yonder wall"—
Out 'twixt the battery smokes there flew
    A rider, bound on bound
Full-galloping; nor bridle drew
    Until he reached the mound.

Then off there flung in smiling joy,
    And held himself erect
By just his horse's mane, a boy:
    You hardly could suspect—

(So tight he kept his lips compressed,
    Scarce any blood came through)
You looked twice ere you saw his breast
    Was all but shot in two.

"Well," cried he, "Emperor, by God's grace
    We've got you Ratisbon!
The Marshal's in the market-place,
    And you'll be there anon
To see your flag-bird flap his vans
    Where I, to heart's desire,
Perched him!" The chief's eye flashed; his plans
    Soared up again like fire.

The chief's eye flashed, but presently
    Softened itself, as sheathes
A film the mother-eagle's eye
    When her bruised eaglet breathes;
"You're wounded!" "Nay," the soldier's pride
    Touched to the quick, he said:
"I'm killed, Sire!" And, his chief beside,
    Smiling, the boy fell dead.

ROBERT BROWNING

The Janitor's Boy

Oh I'm in love with the janitor's boy,
    And the janitor's boy loves me;
He's going to hunt for a desert isle
    In our geography.

A desert isle with spicy trees
    Somewhere near Sheepshead Bay;
A right nice place, just fit for two
    Where we can live alway.

Oh I'm in love with the janitor's boy,
    He's busy as he can be;
And down in the cellar he's making a raft
    Out of an old settee.

He'll carry me off, I know that he will,
    For his hair is exceedingly red;
And the only thing that occurs to me
    Is to dutifully shiver in bed.

The day that we sail, I shall leave this brief note,
    For my parents I hate to annoy:
"I have flown away to an isle in the bay
    With the janitor's red-haired boy."

NATHALIA CRANE

LAUGHTER HOLDING BOTH HIS SIDES

Most poetry, like life, is serious and solemn. Yet even the most serious poets have relished and used comedy. The poems that follow are full of fun. They show, in the words of John Milton, "Laughter holding both his sides."

Father William

"You are old, Father William," the young man said,
  "And your hair has become very white;
And yet you incessantly stand on your head—
    Do you think, at your age, it is right?"

"In my youth," Father William replied to his son,
  "I feared it might injure the brain;
But now that I'm perfectly sure I have none,
    Why, I do it again and again."

"You are old," said the youth, "as I mentioned before,
  And have grown most uncommonly fat;
Yet you turned a back somersault in at the door—
    Pray, what is the reason of that?"

"In my youth," said the sage, as he shook his gray locks,
  "I kept all my very limbs supple
By the use of this ointment—one shilling the box—
    Allow me to sell you a couple."

"You are old," said the youth,
                "and your jaws are too weak
  For anything tougher than suet;
Yet you finished the goose,
                with the bones and the beak—
  Pray, how did you manage to do it?"

"In my youth," said his father, "I took to the law,
  And argued each case with my wife;

And the muscular strength, which it gave to my jaw,
  Has lasted the rest of my life."

"You are old," said the youth,
                    "one would hardly suppose
  That your eye was as steady as ever;
Yet you balanced an eel on the end of your nose—
  What made you so awfully clever?"

"I have answered three questions, and that is enough,"
  Said his father, "don't give yourself airs!
Do you think I can listen all day to such stuff?
  Be off, or I'll kick you down stairs!"

LEWIS CARROLL

The Common Cormorant

The common cormorant,
  or shag.
Lays eggs inside a paper bag.
The reason you will see, no doubt,
It is to keep the lightning out.
But what these unobservant birds
Have never noticed is that herds
Of wandering bears may come with buns
And steal the bags to hold the crumbs.

Poor Old Lady

Poor old lady, she swallowed a fly.
I don't know why she swallowed a fly.
Poor old lady, I think she'll die.

Poor old lady, she swallowed a spider.
It squirmed and wriggled and turned inside her.
She swallowed the spider to catch the fly.
I don't know why she swallowed a fly.
Poor old lady, I think she'll die.

Poor old lady, she swallowed a bird.
How absurd! She swallowed a bird.
She swallowed the bird to catch the spider,
She swallowed the spider to catch the fly,
I don't know why she swallowed a fly.
Poor old lady, I think she'll die.

Poor old lady, she swallowed a cat.
Think of that! She swallowed a cat.
She swallowed the cat to catch the bird.
She swallowed the bird to catch the spider,
She swallowed the spider to catch the fly,
I don't know why she swallowed a fly.
Poor old lady, I think she'll die.

Poor old lady, she swallowed a dog.
She went the whole hog when she swallowed the dog.
She swallowed the dog to catch the cat,
She swallowed the cat to catch the bird,

She swallowed the bird to catch the spider.
She swallowed the spider to catch the fly,
I don't know why she swallowed a fly.
Poor old lady, I think she'll die.

Poor old lady, she swallowed a cow.
I don't know how she swallowed the cow.
She swallowed the cow to catch the dog,
She swallowed the dog to catch the cat,
She swallowed the cat to catch the bird,
She swallowed the bird to catch the spider,
She swallowed the spider to catch the fly,
I don't know why she swallowed a fly.
Poor old lady, I think she'll die.

Poor old lady, she swallowed a horse.
She died, of course.

The Animal Fair

I went to the animal fair,
The birds and beasts were there.
The big baboon, by the light of the moon,
Was combing his auburn hair.
The monkey, he got drunk,
And sat on the elephant's trunk.
The elephant sneezed and fell on his knees,
And what became of the monk, the monk?

The Cats of Kilkenny

There were once two cats of Kilkenny,
Each thought there was one cat too many;
So they fought and they fit,
And they scratched and they bit,
Till, excepting their nails
And the tips of their tails,
Instead of two cats, there weren't any.

A Tragic Story

There lived a sage in days of yore,
And he a handsome pigtail wore;
But wondered much, and sorrowed more,
    Because it hung behind him.

He mused upon this curious case,
And swore he'd change the pigtail's place,
And have it hanging at his face,
    Not dangling there behind him.

Says he, "The mystery I've found—
I'll turn me round,"—he turned him round;
    But still it hung behind him.

Then round and round, and out and in,
All day the puzzled sage did spin;
In vain—it mattered not a pin—
    The pigtail hung behind him.

And right, and left, and round about,
And up, and down, and in, and out
He turned; but still the pigtail stout
    Hung steadily behind him.

And though his efforts never slack,
And though he twist, and twirl, and tack,
Alas! still faithful to his back,
    The pigtail hangs behind him.

WILLIAM MAKEPEACE THACKERAY

CREATURES
OF EVERY KIND

Man shares the world with creatures of every kind. Some of them serve him. Some, his favorite pets, he has learned to serve. The poet Coleridge declared, "He prayeth best who loveth best all things both great and small. For the dear God who loveth us, He made and loveth all."

44

Ballad of the Fox

A fox went out one chilly night,
And he begged of the moon to give him light
For he'd a long way to trot that night
Before he could reach his den, O.

At first he came to the farmer's fence
Where the hedge was thick and the shadows dense;
He saw the barns, and he hied him hence
All on a summer's night, O.

He took the gray goose by the sleeve.
Says he: "Madam Goose, by your gracious leave
I'll take you away, I do believe,
And carry you home to my den, O."

He seized the black duck by the neck
And swung her back across his back;
The black duck cried out: "Quack, quack, quack,"
With her legs hanging dangling a-down, O.

Then Old Mother Slipper-Slopper jumped out of bed
And out of the window she popped her head:
"John! John! the gray goose is gone,
And the fox is off to his den, O."

Then John went up to the top of the hill
And he blew a blast both loud and shrill.
Says the fox: "The music is pretty; still
I'd rather be in my den, O."

At last the fox got home to his den,
To his dear little foxes eight, nine, ten;
Says he: "You're in luck; here's a good fat duck
With her legs hanging dangling a-down, O."

He then sat down with his hungry wife
(And they did very well, with no fork and knife);
They never ate better duck in their life
In their snug little foxes' den, O.

Bob White

There's a plump little chap in a speckled coat,
And he sits on the zigzag rails remote,
Where he whistles at breezy, bracing morn,
When the buckwheat is ripe, and stacked is the corn:
    "Bob White!   Bob White!   Bob White!"

Is he hailing some comrade as blithe as he?
Now I wonder where Robert White can be!
O'er the billows of gold and amber grain
There is no one in sight—but, hark again:
    "Bob White!   Bob White!   Bob White!"

Ah! I see why he calls; in the stubble there
Hide his plump little wife and babies fair!
So contented is he, and so proud of the same,
That he wants all the world to know his name,
    "Bob White!   Bob White!   Bob White!"

GEORGE COOPER

A Night with a Wolf

High up on the lonely mountains,
    Where the wild men watched and waited;
Wolves in the forest, and bears in the bush,
    And I on my path belated.

The rain and the night together
    Came down, and the wind came after,
Bending the props of the pine-tree roof,
    And snapping many a rafter.

I crept along in the darkness,
    Stunned, and bruised, and blinded;
Crept to a fir with thick-set boughs,
    And a sheltering rock behind it.

There, from the blowing and raining,
    Crouching, I sought to hide me.
Something rustled; two green eyes shone;
    And a wolf lay down beside me!

His wet fur pressed against me;
    Each of us warmed the other;
Each of us felt, in the stormy dark,
    That beast and man were brother.

And when the falling forest
    No longer crashed in warning,
Each of us went from our hiding place
    Forth in the wild, wet morning.

BAYARD TAYLOR

The Tiger

Tiger! Tiger! burning bright
In the forests of the night,
What immortal hand or eye
Could frame thy fearful symmetry?

In what distant deeps or skies
Burnt the fire of thine eyes?
On what wings dare he aspire?
What the hand dare seize the fire?

And what shoulder, and what art,
Could twist the sinews of thy heart?
And when thy heart began to beat,
What dread hand? and what dread feet?

What the hammer? what the chain?
In what furnace was thy brain?
What the anvil? what dread grasp
Dare its deadly terrors clasp?

When the stars threw down their spears
And watered heaven with their tears,
Did he smile his work to see?
Did he who made the Lamb make thee?

Tiger! Tiger! burning bright
In the forests of the night,
What immortal hand or eye
Dare frame thy fearful symmetry?

William Blake

Dog at Night

At first he stirs uneasily in sleep
And, since the moon does not run off, unfolds
Protesting paws. Grumbling that he must keep
Both eyes awake, he whimpers; then he scolds
And, rising to his feet, demands to know
The stranger's business. You who break the dark
With insolent light, who are you? Where do you go?
But nothing answers his indignant bark.
The moon ignores him, walking on as though
Dogs never were. Stiffened to fury now,
His small hairs stand upright, his howls come fast,
And terrible to hear is the bow-wow
That tears the night. Stirred by this bugle-blast,
The farmer's bitch grows active; without pause
Summons her mastiff and the hound that lies
Three fields away to rally to the cause.
And the next county wakes. And miles beyond
Throats tear themselves and brassy lungs respond
With threats, entreaties, bellowings and cries,
Chasing the white intruder down the skies.

LOUIS UNTERMEYER

The Hummingbird

A route of evanescence
With a revolving wheel;
A resonance of emerald,
A rush of cochineal;
And every blossom on the bush
Adjusts its tumbled head—
The mail from Tunis, probably,
An easy morning's ride.

EMILY DICKINSON

The Caterpillar

Brown and furry
Caterpillar in a hurry;
Take your walk
To the shady leaf or stalk.

May no toad spy you,
May the little birds pass by you;
Spin and die,
To live again a butterfly.

CHRISTINA GEORGINA ROSSETTI

Young Lambs

The spring is coming by a many signs;
The trays are up, the hedges broken down
That fenced the haystack, and the remnant shines
Like some old antique fragment weathered brown.
And where suns peep, in every sheltered place,
The little early buttercups unfold
A glittering star or two—till many trace
The edges of the blackthorn clumps in gold.
And then a little lamb bolts up behind
The hill, and wags his tail to meet the yoe;[1]
And then another, sheltered from the wind,
Lies all his length as dead—and lets me go
Close by, and never stirs, but basking lies,
With legs stretched out as though he could not rise.

[1]yoe: ewe

JOHN CLARE

The Kitten Playing
with the Falling Leaves

See the kitten on the wall
Sporting with the leaves that fall!
Withered leaves, one, two, and three,
From the lofty elder-tree.
Through the calm and frosty air
Of this morning bright and fair
Eddying round and round they sink
Softly, slowly.—One might think,
From the motions that are made,
Every little leaf conveyed
Some small fairy, hither tending,
To this lower world descending.
—But the kitten how she starts!
Crouches, stretches, paws, and darts:
First at one, and then its fellow,
Just as light, and just as yellow:
There are many now—now one—
Now they stop and there are none.
What intentness of desire
In her up-turned eye of fire!
With a tiger-leap half way,
Now she meets the coming prey.
Lets it go at last, and then
Has it in her power again.

WILLIAM WORDSWORTH

The Dachshund

Because I waddle when I walk,
Should this give rise to silly talk
That I'm ungainly? What's ungainly?
I'm really rather graceful—mainly.
The experts have been known to state
That there's a twinkle in our gait.
One said, "They have a clumsy grace,"
Which after all is no disgrace.

My funny features may abound:
Short legs, long body, low-to-ground,
But I'm about the perfect pal
For man or woman, boy or gal.
I'm gentle, very playful, kind,
I housebreak fast 'cause I'm refined,
I'm smart but never sly or foxy—
No, do not underrate the dachsie!

EDWARD ANTHONY

53

The Crocodile

How doth the little crocodile
    Improve his shining tail,
And pour the waters of the Nile
    On every golden scale!

How cheerfully he seems to grin,
    How neatly spreads his claws,
And welcomes little fishes in,
    With gently smiling jaws!

LEWIS CARROLL

Minnows

Swarms of minnows show their little heads,
Staying their wavy bodies 'gainst the streams,
To taste the luxury of sunny beams
Tempered with coolness. How they ever wrestle
With their own sweet delight, and ever nestle
Their silver bellies on the pebbly sand.
If you but scantily hold out the hand,
That very instant not one will remain;
But turn your eye, and they are there again.
The ripples seem right glad to reach those cresses,
And cool themselves among the em'rald tresses;
The while they cool themselves, they freshness give,
And moisture, that the bowery green may live.

JOHN KEATS

The Mountain and the Squirrel

The mountain
   and the squirrel
Had a quarrel;
And the former
   called the latter "Little Prig."
Bun replied,
"You are doubtless very big;
But all sorts of things and weather
Must be taken in together,
To make up a year
And a sphere.
And I think it no disgrace
To occupy my place.
If I'm not so large as you,
You are not so small as I,
And not half so spry,
I'll not deny you make
A very pretty squirrel track;
Talents differ; all is well and wisely put;
If I cannot carry forests on my back,
Neither can you crack a nut."

RALPH WALDO EMERSON

Catalog

Cats sleep fat and walk thin.
Cats, when they sleep, slump;
When they wake, pull in—
And where the plump's been
There's skin.
Cats walk thin.

Cats wait in a lump,
Jump in a streak.
Cats, when they jump, are sleek
As a grape slipping its skin—
They have technique.
Oh, cats don't creak.
They sneak.

Cats sleep fat.
They spread comfort beneath them
Like a good mat,
As if they picked the place
And then sat.
You walk around one
As if he were the City Hall
After that.

If male,
A cat is apt to sing upon a major scale:
This concert is for everybody, this
Is wholesale.
For a baton, he wields a tail.

(He is also found,
When happy, to resound
With an enclosed and private sound.)

A cat condenses.
He pulls in his tail to go under bridges,
And himself to go under fences.
Cats fit
In any size box or kit;
And if a large pumpkin grew under one,
He could arch over it.

When everyone else is just ready to go out,
The cat is just ready to come in.
He's not where he's been.
Cats sleep fat and walk thin.

ROSALIE MOORE

Oriole

How falls it, oriole, thou hast come to fly
In tropic splendor through our Northern sky?
At some glad moment was it nature's choice
To dower a scrap of sunset with a voice?
Or did some orange tulip, flaked with black,
In some forgotten garden, ages back,
Yearning toward Heaven until its wish was heard,
Desire unspeakably to be a bird?

EDGAR FAWCETT

The Squirrel

The squirrel, flippant, pert, and full of play,
Drawn from his refuge in some lonely elm
That age or injury hath hollowed deep,
Where, on his bed of wool and matted leaves,
He has out-slept the winter, ventures forth
To frisk awhile, and bask in the warm sun:
He sees me, and at once, swift as a bird,
Ascends the neighboring beech:

                  there whisks his brush,
And perks his ears, and stamps, and cries aloud,
With all the prettiness of feigned alarm,
And anger insignificantly fierce.

WILLIAM COWPER

The Skylark

The earth was green, the sky was blue:
　　I saw and heard one sunny morn
A skylark hang between the two,
　　A singing speck above the corn;

A stage below, in gay accord,
　　White butterflies danced on the wing,
And still the singing skylark soared,
　　And silent sank, and soared to sing.

The cornfield stretched a tender green
　　To right and left beside my walks;
I knew he had a nest unseen
　　Somewhere among the million stalks.

And as I paused to hear his song,
　　While swift the sunny moments slid,
Perhaps his mate sat listening long,
　　And listened longer than I did.

CHRISTINA GEORGINA ROSSETTI

Milk for the Cat

When the tea is brought at five o'clock,
And all the neat curtains are drawn with care,
The little black cat with bright green eyes
Is suddenly purring there.

At first she pretends, having nothing to do,
She has come in merely to blink by the grate,
But, though tea may be late or the milk may be sour,
She is never late.

And presently her agate eyes
Take a soft large milky haze,
And her independent casual glance
Becomes a stiff hard gaze.

Then she stamps her claws or lifts her ears
Or twists her tail and begins to stir,
Till suddenly all her little body becomes
One breathing trembling purr.

The children eat and wriggle and laugh;
The two old ladies stroke their silk:
But the cat is grown small and thin with desire,
Transformed to a creeping lust for milk.

The white saucer like some full moon descends
At last from the clouds of the table above;
She sighs and dreams and thrills and glows,
Transfigured with love.

She nestles over the shining rim,
Buries her chin in the creamy sea;
Her tail hangs loose; each drowsy paw
Is doubled under each bending knee.

A long dim ecstasy holds her life;
Her world is an infinite shapeless white,
Till her tongue has curled the last holy drop,
Then she sinks back into the night.

Draws and dips her body to heap
Her sleepy nerves in the great arm-chair,
Lies defeated and buried deep
Three or four hours unconscious there.

HAROLD MONRO

GOOD THINGS IN SMALL PACKAGES

Short poems are often the most pointed ones. Tightly packed, they can be found everywhere, in proverbs, in epitaphs on tombstones, as well as in works of literature. Some are hundreds of years old. They are frequently twisted, often edged with humor, and always easy to remember.

Swan Song

Swans sing before they die—'twere no bad thing
Should certain persons die before they sing.

SAMUEL TAYLOR COLERIDGE

Dust to Dust

After such years of dissension and strife,
Some wonder that Peter should weep for his wife;
But his tears on her grave are nothing surprising—
He's laying her dust, for fear of its rising.

THOMAS HOOD

Boston

Here's to good old Boston,
    The home of the bean and the cod,
Where the Lowells talk only to Cabots,
    And the Cabots talk only to God.

JOHN COLLINS BOSSIDY

Here Lies...

Here lie I, Martin Eldinbrodde,
Ha' mercy on my soul, Lord God,
As I would do, were I Lord God,
An' Thou wert Martin Eldinbrodde.

✳   ✳   ✳

On a Doctor Named Isaac Letsome

When people's ill, they come to I;
   I physics, bleeds, and sweats 'em.
Sometimes they live, sometimes they die;
   What's that to I? I. Letsome.

✳   ✳   ✳

On Skugg

Here Skugg lies snug
As a bug in a rug.

BENJAMIN FRANKLIN

On a Dentist

Stranger, approach this spot with gravity:
John Brown is filling his last cavity.

✳   ✳   ✳

On a Thieving Locksmith

A thieving locksmith died of late
And soon arrived at heaven's gate.
He stood outside and would not knock
Because he meant to pick the lock.

✳   ✳   ✳

The Optimist

The optimist fell ten stories.
    At each window bar
He shouted to his friends:
    "All right so far."

WIDE, WONDERFUL WORLD

The world is full of marvels. We are struck by the small as well as the great things in nature. The American poet, Walt Whitman, said, "A leaf of grass is no less than the journeywork of the stars, and the narrowest hinge in my hand puts to scorn all machinery." Whether we behold a whole sky blazing with sunset or a single daisy shining like a star, we are moved with wonder.

66

I Meant To Do My Work Today

I meant to do my work today—
But a brown bird sang in the apple tree,
And a butterfly flitted across the field,
And all the leaves were calling me.

And the wind went sighing over the land
Tossing the grasses to and fro,
And a rainbow held out its shining hand—
So what could I do but laugh and go?

RICHARD LeGALLIENNE

The Daffodils

I wandered lonely as a cloud
That floats on high o'er vales and hills,
When all at once I saw a crowd,
A host of golden daffodils,
Beside the lake, beneath the trees
Fluttering and dancing in the breeze.

Continuous as the stars that shine
And twinkle on the milky way,
They stretched in never-ending line
Along the margin of a bay:
Ten thousand saw I at a glance
Tossing their heads in sprightly dance.

The waves beside them danced, but they
Out-did the sparkling waves in glee:
A poet could not but be gay
In such a jocund company!
I gazed—and gazed—but little thought
What wealth the show to me had brought:

For oft, when on my couch I lie
In vacant or in pensive mood,
They flash upon that inward eye
Which is the bliss of solitude;
And then my heart with pleasure fills,
And dances with the daffodils.

WILLIAM WORDSWORTH

Sunrise

The lean coyote, prowler of the night,
Slips to his rocky fastnesses.
Jack-rabbits noiselessly shuttle among the sage-brush,
And, from the castellated cliffs,
Rock-ravens launch their proud black sails
   upon the day.
The wild horses troop back to their pastures.

The poplar-trees watch beside the irrigation-ditches.
Orioles, whose nests sway in the cottonwood trees
   by the ditchside, begin to twitter.
All shy things, breathless, watch
The thin white skirts of dawn,
The dancer of the sky,
Who trips daintily down the mountain-side
Emptying her crystal chalice ....
And a red-bird, dipped in sunrise,
   cracks from a poplar's top
His exultant whip above a silver world.

CHARLES ERSKINE SCOTT WOOD

69

Precious Stones

An emerald is as green as grass;
    A ruby red as blood;
A sapphire shines as blue as heaven;
    A flint lies in the mud.

A diamond is a brilliant stone,
    To catch the world's desire;
An opal holds a fiery spark;
    But a flint holds fire.

CHRISTINA GEORGINA ROSSETTI

Pied Beauty

Glory be to God for dappled things—
    For skies of couple-color as a brinded cow;
      For rose-moles all in stipple upon trout
        that swim;
Fresh-firecoal chestnut-falls; finches' wings;
    Landscaped plotted and pieced—fold, fallow,
      and plow;
      And all trades, their gear and tackle and trim.

All things counter, original, spare, strange;
    Whatever is fickle, freckled (who knows how?)
        With swift, slow; sweet, sour; adazzle, dim;
He fathers-forth whose beauty is past change:
    Praise Him.

GERARD MANLEY HOPKINS

Coal Fire

And once, in some swamp-forest, these
Were trees.
Before the first fox thought to run,
These dead black chips were one
Green net to hold the sun.
Each leaf in turn was taught the right
Way to drink light;
The twigs were made to learn
How to catch flame and yet not burn;
Branch and then bough began to eat
Their diet of heat.
And so for years, six million years, or higher,
They held that fire.

And here, out of the splinters that remain,
The fire is loose again.
See how its hundred hands reach here and there,
Finger the air;
Then, growing bolder, twisting free,
It fastens on the remnants of the tree
And, one by one,
Consumes them; mounts beyond them; leaps; is done;
And goes back to the sun.

LOUIS UNTERMEYER

Altar Smoke

Somewhere inside of me
There must have always been
A tenderness
For the little, lived-with things
A man crowds upon his worn fistful of earth.
Somewhere inside of me
There must have always been
A love
Made to fill the square aggressiveness of new-cut
    hedges,
And feed the pursed green mouths of baby leaves;
A love made to understand
The way grass cuddles up to porch steps leaned
    upon by time,
And why dandelions nudge the stones
    along the walk;
A love for garden hose curled sleeping
    in the noon hush,
Coolness trickling lazily from its open mouth,
For shingles starched and saucy in white paint,
And an old rake rusty with dreams of tangled grass
    and butterflies.
A love
For candle flames, like pointed blossoms
    on their ghostly stems,
And frost-forests breathing wonder
    on the parlor windows.
Somewhere inside of me
There must have always been

An altar of hewn stones
Upon which my love
   casts these—
Burnt offerings—
To make a sweet savor
Unto my soul.

Give me the strength, my God,
To scatter my fires and tumble
   the altar stones in confusion;
Give me the strength
   to raise my eyes,
So that hard and sharp
   across my heart
Like shadow cut
   on mountain rock,
Will fall the agony
   of sunset—
So that I can see
The laughter of clouds spun
   into the blue web of infinity.
So that my soul can
   reach out
And melt in the sweep
   of forever
Above all these.

ROSALIE GRAYER

Travel

I should like to rise and go
Where the golden apples grow;—
Where below another sky
Parrot islands anchored lie,
And, watched by cockatoos and goats,
Lonely Crusoes building boats;—
Where in sunshine reaching out
Eastern cities, miles about,

Are with mosque and minaret
Among sandy gardens set,
And rich goods from near and far
Hang for sale in the bazaar;—
Where the Great Wall round China goes,
And on one side the desert blows,
And with bell and voice and drum,
Cities on the other hum;—
Where are forest, hot as fire,
Wide as England, tall as a spire,
Full of apes and cocoa-nuts
And the Negro hunters' huts ...
Where among the desert sands
Some deserted city stands,
All its children, sweep and prince,
Grown to manhood ages since,

Not a foot in street or house,
Not a stir of child or mouse,
And when kindly falls the night,
In all the town no spark of light.
There I'll come when I'm a man
With a camel caravan;
Light a fire in the gloom
Of some dusty dining-room;
See the pictures on the walls,
Heroes, fights, and festivals;
And in a corner find the toys
Of the old Egyptian boys.

ROBERT LOUIS STEVENSON

Out in the Fields with God

The little cares that fretted me,
    I lost them yesterday,
Among the fields above the sea,
    Among the winds at play,
Among the lowing of the herds,
    The rustling of the trees,
Among the singing of the birds,
    The humming of the bees.

The foolish fears of what might pass
    I cast them all away
Among the clover-scented grass
    Among the new-mown hay,
Among the hushing of the corn
    Where drowsy poppies nod,
Where ill thoughts die and good are born—
    Out in the fields with God.

GUIDING STARS

A poem can be not only a flash of inspiration but a guiding star. No matter how often such a poem is repeated it vibrates with life; it remains something which can help shape a present pattern or change a future.

He Who Knows

He who knows not, and knows not that he knows not,
      is a fool. Shun him;
He who knows not, and knows that he knows not,
      is a child. Teach him.
He who knows, and knows not that he knows,
      is asleep. Wake him.
He who knows, and knows that he knows,
      is wise. Follow him.

From the Persian

To See a World

To see a world in a grain of sand
And a heaven in a wild flower,
Hold Infinity in the palm of your hand
And Eternity in an hour.

WILLIAM BLAKE

Four Things

Four things a man must learn to do
If he would make his record true:
To think without confusion clearly;
To love his fellow-men sincerely;
To act from honest motives purely;
To trust in God and Heaven securely.

HENRY VAN DYKE

*　*　*

For Every Evil

For every evil under the sun
There is a remedy or there is none.
If there is one, seek till you find it;
If there be none, never mind it.

*　*　*

Standards

You cannot choose your battlefields,
    The Gods do that for you.
But you can plant your standard
    Where a standard never flew.

NATHALIA CRANE

Prayer for Miracle

O God, no more Thy miracle withhold;
To us in tents give palaces of gold;
And while we stumble among things that are,
Give us the solace of a guiding star.

ANNA WICKHAM

No Enemies

You have no enemies, you say?
Alas, my friend, the boast is poor.
He who has mingled in the fray
Of duty, that the brave endure,
Must have made foes. If you have none,
Small is the work that you have done.
You've hit no traitor on the hip,
You've dashed no cup from perjured lip,
You've never turned the wrong to right,
You've been a coward in the fight.

CHARLES MACKAY

BCDEF